CALL OF THE LOON

K.SINKO

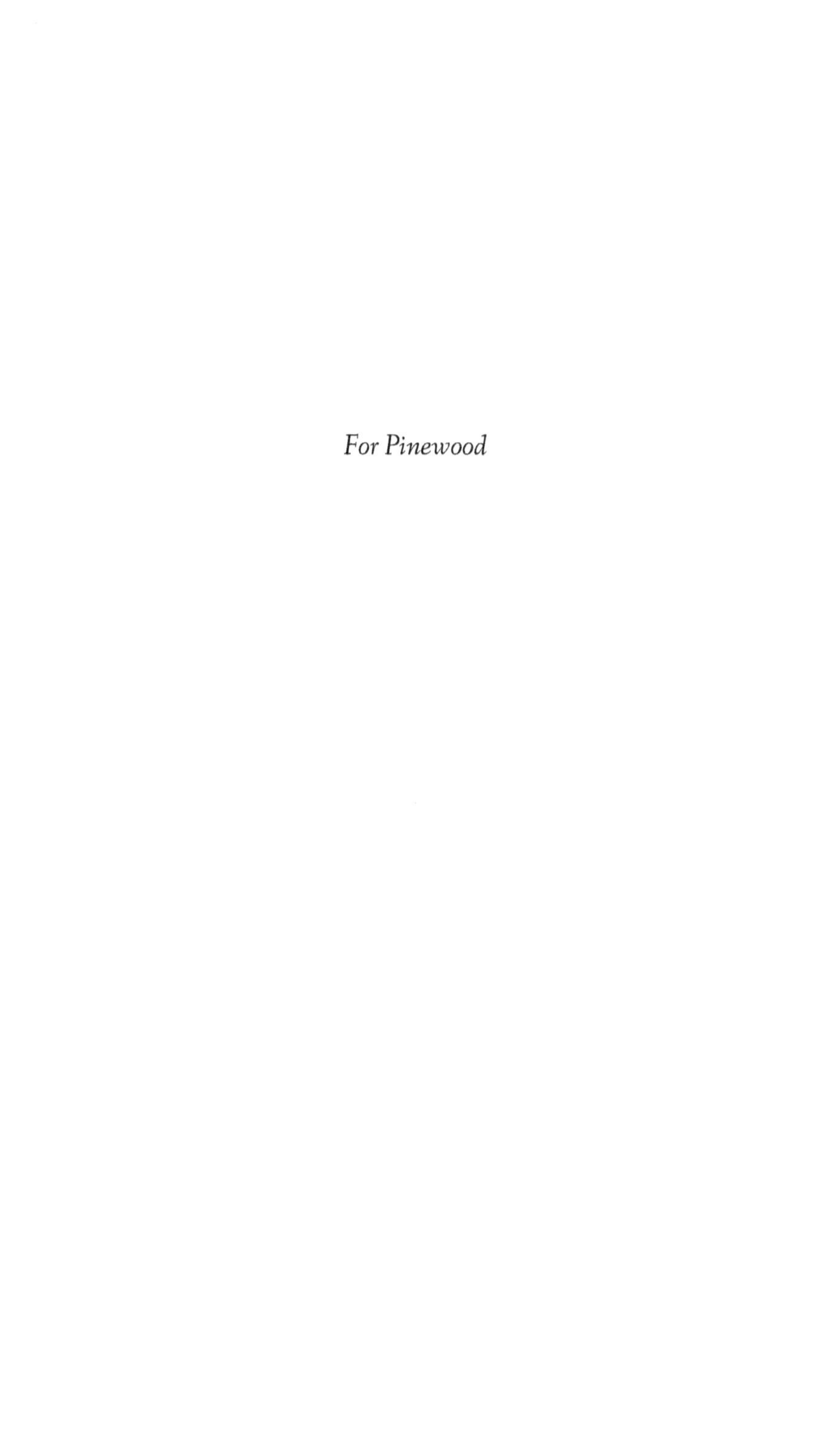

For Pinewood

Chapter 1

Tea

WHEN TEA WAS ACCEPTED into the Kellstadt Graduate School of Business, she didn't foresee spending her graduation on the hardwood floor of her empty apartment in Chicago. She also didn't expect there to be a global pandemic. No one did.

She cursed herself for not waiting one more day for that couch pickup. After she sold off the last of her furniture—"sold" being a loose term, seeing as she gave away her belongings for free on Facebook Marketplace to anyone brave enough to pick them up during a pandemic—she realized that she had nowhere to sleep, or even to sit, as she watched the dean give his commencement speech at a podium in an empty classroom, under flickering fluorescent lights on Zoom. A bed of her thickest blankets laid out in the middle of the floor was certainly not ideal, but none of her situation was ideal either. Like the rest of the world, she had to learn how to roll with it when the world went into lockdown in March.

But now, sitting on the oak floor, wearing her old cap

and gown from her undergrad graduation two years earlier, Tea concluded that she was very much done rolling with it.

Times are tough, graduates. We know that the road ahead will not be an easy one. You are entering a market that is uncertain. Will we ever sit in an office again? Will we always have to wear our masks? Is this officially our new normal?

She sighed. "This is depressing."

Mom leaned forward, her face filling Tea's phone screen that was propped up by a plastic DePaul University cup next to her laptop, and blew on the plastic party blower that was dangling from her lips.

Tea sighed again.

Mom removed the party blower, pinching it between her fingers like it was a cigarette. "Cheer up, my cute little cup of Tea. You graduated business school! Not everyone can say that."

"But what's the point if I can't even find a job?" she grumbled. "A fancy degree means literally nothing if you don't have experience."

"You have a lifetime ahead of you to get experience. Just because your internship was canceled this spring doesn't mean there aren't other opportunities down the road."

It was the same pep talk she was used to, but in a different shade of blue. The two of them had engaged in similar versions of the same conversation for months now. When Tea received the email that the internship program at Bank of America would be put on hold for the foreseeable future, she hyperventilated and called her mom. She sat in her apartment, alone ever since her roommates left to "ride this thing out" in the suburbs with their parents and never returned, and ugly cried. Dribbles-of-snot-running-down-her-nose,   using-her-forearm-because-she-was-too-distraught-to-grab-tissues kind of ugly crying. Her mom was patient and warm as she listened despite her clear exhaustion—she'd just finished a grueling nineteen-hour shift at the hospital. Thirty minutes after that phone call, Tea had been bulldozed by guilt. There she was, crying over a silly little internship, while her mother spent every possible minute she could muster at Saint Peter's in New Brunswick, working as hard as she could to prevent people from *dying*.

But Mom liked to give her these pep talks, and Tea liked hearing her voice. Seven hundred and ninety miles felt too far, and that distance was only going to grow wider this summer.

Tea pulled at a loose string on her robe as she mumbled, "And a summer spent at Silver Falls is going to get me closer to those opportunities?" She tried to tone down the bitterness in her voice, but it was getting harder with each passing day. Especially since she hadn't hugged her mom since Christmas.

"I don't think anyone is going to question why you have a gap of undeclared time off on your résumé after graduation," Mom replied. "I think a lot of résumés are going to look that way after all of this."

Tea hugged her legs close to her chest, resting a cheek on her knees, her wavy red hair cascading down her legs. "Yeah. I just hate not knowing what comes next."

"None of us do," Mom answered quietly.

The two of them watched the rest of the ceremony in silence, listening as the dean of the business school rattled off all of the names of the MBA students. When he reached Theresa Richards, Mom blew hard on the party blower. Enough to make Tea smile.

When the ceremony ended, she closed her laptop,

eyeing the apartment she'd called home for the past two years. "It feels weird to have my entire life packed up in one car," she admitted. "None of this seems real."

"I'm still impressed you were able to get rid of everything," Mom quipped. "Think of it this way, you could go anywhere after this. *Anywhere*."

"The only place I want to be is home with you."

Mom let out a heavy sigh in response. "You know it wouldn't be safe. I'm in and out of the hospital all the time—"

"I really wouldn't mind," Tea interrupted. "I'm willing to take the chance."

"Your grandparents are really...*really* excited to see you."

"And I'm excited to see them, but—"

"Go to Minnesota and have a *normal* summer. Maybe by this fall we'll have a vaccine and everything will settle down. You can come back to New Jersey and find a job in the city like you wanted, and life will feel a little more normal again."

Tea exhaled, a piece of her hair falling across her face. "Do you really think things could be over by then?"

Mom was silent for a beat too long. It made her stomach curl.

"I don't know what to think," she finally answered. "But we'll figure it out, okay? We take this one day at a time."

"Okay," Tea said, more of a reassurance for her mother than herself. Because right now, with all her belongings stuffed into her back seat and no life plan to count on, Tea certainly did not feel okay.

AFTER SHE HUNG UP, Tea did one last scan of the apartment. When she first made the move, it didn't take long to conclude that Chicago would not be forever. Two years of study, then she would head back home to New Jersey. To her mom. To the little life they created after everything fell apart. The idea of leaving Mom alone out there left tight knots in her stomach.

She stopped in the kitchen, pressing her hands into the cool counter, and took a deep breath. *One day at a time,* she reminded herself. *We take this one day at a time.*

Her roommates had collected all of their things weeks earlier, informing Tea that they would be giving up the lease in July. Tea expected as much; they were nice, but their interactions were always cordial, business-like. She'd been the third last-minute roommate they found on Craigslist, someone to pay for the tiny room with the sliding door next to the kitchen. She didn't care. She was there to get her degree and get out. Her room was merely a place for her to fit a cheap twin bed so she could sleep. It wasn't the kind of space she planned on inviting a guy into. With everything she and Mom had been through over the last eight years, inviting men into her bedroom was a *very* rare occurrence.

Her phone pinged on the counter.

NAN

Let us know when you're on the road!

Panic trickled up her neck. She rubbed the back of it as she closed out of her texts and opened up Google Maps, typing in the address for Wild Pines Resort. She expected traffic getting out of the city, but her itinerary was still the same. Eight hours and forty-seven minutes of traffic-free roads. No rush hour or construction or any other holdup that typically occurred during a drive up to the lake. Everyone was at home, still hunkered down, maybe out enjoying some of the warm June sunshine at a respectable social distance of six feet.

She curled her hands into fists as she stared at her destination on the tiny screen.

Silver Falls, Minnesota.

It used to be her favorite place in the whole world. She could still taste her palpable excitement when she thought about climbing into a fully packed SUV on the last day of school. Kayaks and paddleboards strapped to the hood as the three of them endured the twenty plus–hour road trip up to Minnesota.

But when three suddenly became two, summers at the lake no longer had that same air of shiny hope. They lingered as haunted memories, reminders of everything good she'd had and quickly lost. When Gareth Richards died, Tea and her mom never went back.

Instead of spending summers paddleboarding in the lake or eating Nan's spinach artichoke dip, Mom downsized their house in Morristown to a smaller apartment in New Brunswick. Tea attended Rutgers close by, and the two spent their summers in between semesters traveling into Manhattan. They saw every Broadway show, ate greasy slices of pizza, and enjoyed lazy afternoons reading under the shade of the great American elms in Central Park. Those summers in the city were vastly different from any other summer Tea could remember, and she was thankful for it. Thankful to create new memories and not have to face her old ones.

Until this summer. Until she had nowhere else to go.

Mom was the one who suggested it at first. *A summer in Silver Falls wouldn't be so bad*, she'd explained. Timidly, like she was approaching a bear in hibernation and contemplating poking it awake. *Think about it. Open air, lots of space, Nan's casseroles, fishing with Pop. Sailing. You used to love sailing.*

I only loved it because of who I was with, Tea had snipped back. She knew she was being cruel with the way she was digging it in. But maybe being cruel would make Mom change her mind. Make her concede, and finally tell her she could go back home to Jersey.

But she never did, and now she was looking at a nine-hour road trip—with nothing but her three bulging suitcases and a snake plant to keep her alert.

The time on her phone said 10:13. Thankfully an early graduation ceremony meant an early start on the road, and a chance to catch her first Minnesota sunset in over eight years.

The last time she saw the sun set over the lake, she was with all of her friends—the ones she hadn't spoken to since everything happened with her father. Riley. Quentin. Deanna. Austin.

Archer.

She picked up her phone and tapped out a message, not letting the onslaught of familiar nerves convince her to recalibrate the destination on her phone and drive back east.

She shrugged off her graduation gown, shoved it in her tote bag, and walked out the front door. As she hopped into her 2005 Chevy Classic and turned the ignition, giving the dashboard a love tap when the old thing revved to life, she did her best not to think about the last time she saw Archer Vincent.

Chapter 2

Archer

THE SCREECH and slam of the screen door at the front of his cabin woke Archer from his drool-covered desk. He bolted upright, a pencil clattering on his desk from where it was stuck to his forehead.

"Ouch," he mumbled. He rubbed his eyes as he looked toward the door, surprised to find someone standing inside his cabin. Panicked, he snatched the cloth mask on his desk and fastened it to his face, tucking the elastics behind his ears.

"No need for that, it's me," said a familiar gravelly voice.

Archer relaxed his shoulders but kept the mask on. "You can never be too careful. Apparently the Bramble twins were running around town yesterday without them on."

"And yet, that didn't stop you from stealing my last pale ale out of the fridge last night."

He hesitated, then sighed, removing the mask from his face. His father was right. If his dad got COVID-19, there was no way he wouldn't have also contracted it at this point. He hadn't bothered trying to set any social distancing rules with his family, even though he'd been doing his best to maintain those rules for the rest of Wild Pines. Not like anyone listened to him, though.

Archer removed the mask, tossing it back on his desk.

Astor Vincent took a few tentative steps into the cabin, a place that he used to call his. Archer hadn't changed it much since his father passed down his role as resort manager. Mostly because he hadn't had time to yet; a global pandemic got in the way. The Silver Falls Lake Association was adamant about their sanitation guidelines for all of the resorts surrounding the lake, and he was doing his best to keep their seven cabins in line. An impossible task for Midwesterners, who believed social distancing and "Midwest nice" couldn't possibly coexist. At least they heeded his rule of keeping resort activities outdoors.

Astor walked over to Archer's wall of haphazard sticky notes. It was a chaotic system, but it worked for him. Every time a task came up that needed actioning, he wrote it on a sticky note and smacked it on the wall. When the task was completed, he ripped it down.

There were currently thirty-four sticky notes plastered to the wall, rustling lightly from the north wind that blew in through the screen door. North wind meant a chillier day on the lake and stronger breezes. Perfect for sailing. Not that Archer even bothered to hop in his sailboat; there simply wasn't the time.

Astor retrieved his glasses from his front breast pocket, holding them close to his face as he leaned in to read a note. "'Send a reminder for the owners' meeting,'" he read out loud. He scanned the next one. "'Submit fees to the lake association.'" He stood up straight, his glasses falling to his side as he stared at Archer with wide eyes. "You haven't done that yet?"

Archer stood and rounded the desk. "Getting to it, Dad. Not the highest on my list of priorities."

"And what is, exactly?"

Archer crossed his arms, then flinched. The new storm cloud tattoo next to his right elbow was still tender. "Keeping people from dying?"

Astor rolled his eyes. "People aren't going to die."

"The five-hundred thousand people who already did would beg to differ."

His father sighed. "You sure you don't need me to help? I don't mind hopping back into things. Your first summer managing wasn't supposed to involve a pandemic."

Archer felt his chest tighten. *Breathe.* He reminded himself that if he could manage shaking fifty craft cocktails an hour at the most coveted bar in Minneapolis six nights a week, he could handle managing seven cabins in the middle of the woods.

Wild Pines was one of many resorts sprinkled across northern Minnesota, each a small collection of fishing cabins that eventually transformed into vacation homes. While most of the cabins were available to renters for weeks at a time, some of the owners opted out, choosing to stay in their cabins all summer long. The manager position at the resort had been in the Vincent family for generations, so for every summer of his existence, Archer spent the days between May and September in Cabin A, the small manager's cabin at the left corner of the resort, with six other cabins lined up next to it, all connected by a shared lawn and beach that overlooked the lake. He slept on the bottom bunk in the smaller second bedroom, his brother Austin at the top, but he didn't mind—especially when the window above his bed was a direct view of a certain bedroom window next door.

Even though the Richards opted out of renting their cabin, Archer hadn't seen anyone in that upstairs bedroom window for eight years. Not that he had seen much of Wild Pines since that fateful summer, except for a week or two if he could get the time off from Hermes Lounge, usually around the Fourth of July.

Then the world locked down. Weeks into the pandemic, his father called and told him he bought Cabin F from Quentin's parents. The message was clear: It was time for Archer to step up...five years earlier than planned.

Now, Cabin A was his—as well as the position of running this place. It didn't pay nearly as much as Hermes, but cocktail lounges were certainly not open during the pandemic...and he needed the cash. Managing Wild Pines was beyond exhausting, but the last thing he wanted was his father to think he couldn't handle the job he watched him easily manage for twenty-six years of Archer's life.

"Dad, seriously, I got this." He placed his hands on the other man's shoulders. "You trusted me to take over this place. Let me do it, please."

"Promise you'll ask for help if you need it?"

No. But he smiled and nodded, knowing that arguing with his father any further would be useless. Astor wanted reassurance. And Archer wanted to prove that even if he was his father's second choice, he was still a good one.

Astor dipped his chin, his face twisted with guilt. "One more thing."

He dropped his hands. "Who else went to town? Tell them they have to quarantine."

"No, no, not that." His father sighed. "We have one more person joining us this summer."

"No, not allowed." Archer swung his arms in front of

him, like a referee at a Vikings football game. *No touch-down.* "We're closed for the summer."

"I think we need to make an exception, Arch. She has nowhere to go."

He glared. "Who?"

Astor shifted on his feet, shoving his hands in the pockets of his jeans. "Someone you know."

"And that would be...?"

"Someone you used to be friends with," he amended. "Or maybe you still are, I don't know. You never talk about her anymore. But her internship was canceled and she has nowhere else to go this summer. Her grandparents are really looking forward to seeing her."

Archer's chest tightened again, but this time, he didn't give himself a moment to breathe. "Who is it, Dad?"

His father's eyes went soft, the creases of his mouth dipping into a frown. "Tea."

Tea.

Archer rolled his jaw and fixed his gaze out the back screen door, to the rough waters and the gray skies. Rough and wild, the perfect day to be out on the water. She would agree.

"When's she getting here?" he asked, the curt, cold nature of his words a poor reflection of the way he was spiraling on the inside.

"Tonight."

"Did she quarantine?"

"For two weeks, alone in her apartment in Chicago."

Archer wondered if his use of *alone* was on purpose. Making a point that she was with no one else.

He turned away from his father and strode back to his desk, plopping down in his chair. "We'll see about that. Tell her to get tested before she arrives."

"Archer…"

"Or she's not allowed in."

Astor sighed. "Are you going to come over for dinner tonight? Your mother's making tater tot hotdish."

Absolutely not. "I'll let you know," he grumbled, tapping the trackpad on his laptop, hoping it was enough of a sign to be left alone.

After a heavy sigh near the door, it was.

Archer leaned his elbows on his desk, then winced at the pressure. He grumbled, placing his forehead back down on the desk, allowing himself another ten minutes of blissful oblivion before he returned to work.

ARCHER WAS TOO preoccupied with adding a chain to the dumpsters to notice the matriarch of Wild Pines approaching him. It didn't give him enough time to hide.

"Archer, dearest!"

He groaned to himself, then plastered on the best smile he could as he turned around, stepping back to meet the required social distance. "Hi, Sandy, how are you today?"

Sandy Vanderberg had been a resident of Wild Pines for longer than he'd even existed. She was the first to buy Cabin C before anyone else in the resort, and refused to make any renovations on it except for necessary updates like heating, air conditioning, and plumbing. Her relic of an oven took twice as long to cook anything, and she let everyone know how miserable it made her. Even though she refused to replace it because it was "still in good condition" and "what's the point in replacing something that works?" Her husband Joel tuned her out during these rants, but his hearing miraculously improved whenever Wayne Richards called over the lawn asking him to go fishing.

Her nickname started out as a joke during their annual Fourth of July party almost a decade ago, when Austin got a little too drunk and proclaimed Sandy as the resort's "matriarch." Sandy didn't even pretend to hate it. She liked the attention, especially when it came from Archer's older brother. He was the charming, charismatic one, and everyone preferred him.

Her brows knitted together, nose squinted in disgust. "What are you doing over here near the dumpster?"

"I'm trying to bear-proof it," Archer said.

"*Bear* proof?! Are there bears?"

"There have been some reports of bears in the area, yes. Have you not been getting the emails from the Silver Falls Lake Association?"

"I never touch my computer. It scares me."

"Okay, well, you might need to do so before the owners' meeting—"

"About that."

He sighed. He knew what was coming. They'd had the same argument at least three times now.

"Is it really necessary to have it outside? My cabin is perfectly clean and spacious..."

Her cabin might be clean, but *spacious* was certainly not the word to describe Cabin C. Not when the other five residential cabins were three times the size, with open-plan kitchens and living rooms.

He cleared his throat, preparing to handle this delicately. Even if he understood all of the risks behind having a meeting inside a building, he couldn't expect everyone to understand. Especially someone who refused to even touch a computer.

"I know that your cabin is clean and very cozy. In any other circumstance, it would be the perfect spot for our meeting."

Sandy perked up at those words, looking satisfied at the way he was subtly complimenting her home.

"But we don't want the chance of getting others sick. We have residents going to the grocery stores and shops in town, and we decided as a community that it is safer to do everything outside this year to minimize our risk."

She huffed. "I don't get it."

Archer was used to this conversation. A lot of people in the Midwest didn't seem to understand. To them, COVID-19 was another bad cold, something you could catch then move on from. The number of casualties didn't seem to scare them in the same ways it scared him. And yet, he'd been taught to treat his elders with respect. Even if it wasn't always possible to see eye-to-eye.

"I'm sorry, Sandy," he said, crouching slightly so he could meet her eyes. "I promise next year if all of this is over, you can host the meeting."

She cocked a brow. "But we always draw from a hat."

"And your name was drawn last. Seems only fair that we carry it over a year, yes?"

Her face relaxed as she nodded. "Yes, good. Thank you, dearest."

Archer nodded and waved her off, turning back to the dumpster and the impossible task of trying to snake the heavy-duty chain around it. He then imagined Sandy trying to remove the chain in the morning to throw out her trash after breakfast, and realized maybe a chain wasn't the best idea. He groaned, dropping his face in his hands.

The popping sound of tires against gravel interrupted his sense of apparent doom. Archer eyed all of the cars parked in lots behind each cabin, making a note of who had left to go to town. But all of the cars were accounted for, which could only mean one thing.

Hands sticky from his task and once again no time to hide, Archer ducked behind the dumpster.

A beat-up Chevy crawled past the shaded entrance into the resort, then parked behind Cabin B. Archer felt his face go hot as the car turned off, and a woman stepped out of the car, her white Reeboks kicking up a cloud of dust.

She looked exactly as he remembered. A grown-up version of the girl he hadn't been able to stop thinking about for years, ever since they were kids. Long legs, slim curves, creamy white arms covered in freckles, fiery red hair. A small button nose and striking sky-blue eyes.

He didn't dare move as he watched her pull several massive suitcases and a snake plant from the back of her car. Instead, he knelt there, his pulse hammering loudly in his ears, wondering how in the world he was going to survive a summer with an even more gorgeous version of his dream girl staying in the cabin next door to him.

The very same dream girl who shattered his heart.

Chapter 3

Tea

Everything about Cabin B was exactly as Tea left it, like the memory of this place was frozen in time, waiting for her return. The chipped green paint on the awning covering the patio. The carved wooden bees nailed to the pine tree by front door. The cherry-red bird feeder dangling outside the kitchen window, giving Nan the perfect shot for eyeing hummingbirds and blue jays while she formed casseroles and baked treats.

Tea dragged her luggage up the back porch, then stood staring at the rickety screen door. Knocking felt impossible. Knocking meant inviting pain back into her heart. Pain from memories of summers in a place she tried to erase from her thoughts. Baking with Nan. Night games of Capture the Flag, followed by staying up far too late around the bonfire. Her father wrangling her out of bed for an early morning sail. She wondered how this place could possibly hold the same kind of magic when everything about it had irrevocably changed.

She took a deep breath, expecting the scent of dried

pine on the dirt driveway behind her, but was met instead by the smell of freshly baked ginger snap cookies.

Maybe some magic still exists. The scent of her favorite treats—ones she hadn't devoured in almost a decade—finally propelled her to knock on the door.

"MY ANGEL! Get in here."

Tea smiled at the sound of Nan's voice as she stepped into the cabin, the screen door snicking shut behind her. Before she could scan the inside of the house, she was clobbered by a hug.

"Oh, I'm so happy you are finally here," she said.

Tea's muscles tensed at the hug. She hadn't been hugged like this in months, and the contact had her hesitating. How strange it felt to be touched. Strange, and yet so wonderful.

She melted into the embrace, burying her nose in the crook of Nan's neck, even though she had to crouch down to do it. She inherited those tall Richards genes, just like Pop and Dad. When she kept growing and growing in high school, dating proved difficult. No one wanted to take the tall girl to prom, she learned. So the night was spent with her girlfriends, thinking about what it would be like to be swept up and kissed by a handsome guy in a tux. There was only one who could sweep her up like that, but she didn't have the courage to ask him when he was nine hundred miles away...or if his feelings were even reciprocated.

She'd learn the truth three months later.

Nan pulled back from the hug, squeezing Tea's forearms as she craned her neck to accommodate for the six inches that separated them. Nan still wore the same clothes as always; loose jean capris, a soft *Life is Good* T-shirt, her LL Bean fleece despite the warm night air. But it was hard to ignore the subtle differences, too. The way her face had thinned and the skin at her cheeks drooped. The extra crinkles around her mouth and her bright blue eyes. Her hair was completely gray instead of salt and pepper, and cropped much shorter. But her toenails were painted that same shade of hot pink, and around her neck was the small gold heart-shaped locket her father bought for his parents' twentieth wedding anniversary.

Tea reached out to wipe the tears from Nan's cheeks with the pad of her thumb, and returned the sentiment with a watery smile.

"You look *good* my girl, so strong," Nan said. "I've missed you so."

"I know," she whispered back. "I'm sorry it took me so long."

Nan sniffled and shook her head. "No need to apologize. I understand."

She swallowed, not feeling convinced by her grandmother's ability to brush off her prolonged absence. But this wasn't the moment to air her grievances. This was the time for ginger snap cookies.

Tea followed Nan farther into the cabin and into her grandmother's domain: the kitchen. No matter what time of day it was, she always had something going on in the kitchen. Fresh baked cookies were almost a daily specialty. She loved hosting "cocktail hour" with whatever dip she'd made that day, like jalapeño popper or spinach artichoke or fresh salsa—always served with margaritas or white wine. And of course supper, which was an overdone affair, despite the fact that Tea and her dad would insist that burgers on the grill were more than enough. Nan never accepted that kind of lazy cooking; casseroles in nine-by-thirteens were more her style.

Tea eyed the cookies on the counter, already cooling on

a metal rack. She slid right back into her old bar stool at the counter like she never left. Hers was at the center, where she could prop her feet up on the stool on her right and face the lake.

Like everything else at Wild Pines—the trees that stretched taller the more she drove north, the cabin, the ginger snaps—the lake was also as she remembered. She gazed out the bay window, amazed at how so much of her life could change in eight years, yet somehow ten minutes at Silver Falls was enough to ground her. It was equal parts nostalgic...and unnerving.

Nan opened the fridge. "Did you eat?"

"I stopped by the drive-thru at Dairy Queen and grabbed some fries."

Nan turned and frowned, her hand still on the door. "That's all you ate?"

She shrugged. "Haven't been very hungry."

Nan shook her head and reached into the fridge. "Well, gal dang, that won't do," she grumbled.

Tea watched as she pulled out four different Cool Whip containers, and then a large red Tupperware. She shook her head, amused by Nan's continued insistence on keeping those flimsy containers because they were "good quality" and it was "wasteful to throw them out."

"Seriously, Nan—"

"Hush," she snipped. "Go to the back fridge and grab a bottle of that Sauvignon Blanc your mother insisted I buy you and pour yourself a glass." She flipped the lid off the red Tupperware and began forking slices of ham onto a plate. "Actually, pour two glasses."

Tea slid off the stool. "Mom made you grab my favorite wine?"

"There are six bottles back there."

Tea coughed a laugh, imagining what Nan looked like carting six bottles out of Sip & Pine, the local liquor store. She made her way around the counter to the back hall, reaching out to grab a cookie on the rack on her way, but Nan slapped her hand.

"Dinner first."

Tea smiled. *Yep, nothing's changed there.* "Yes ma'am."

Minutes later, after Tea poured two glasses of wine and Nan microwaved a heaping plate of ham, cherry sauce, mashed potatoes, green bean casserole, and a toasted roll slathered with butter and honey, the two sat down at the table to watch the sunset.

"Where's Pop?" Tea asked, slicing into her ham. Dollops of sauce spilled over the plate and onto the table as she maneuvered her knife and fork. There was no way she was going to finish all of it.

Nan gestured toward the lake. "Where do you think?"

Tea smirked. "Fishing at sunset? I thought he only liked to go first thing in the morning or late at night."

"Yes, well, I told him with his poor eyesight that he's no longer allowed to fish in the dark. I think he goes out at all hours of the day now in protest."

Tea smiled to herself. It wasn't hard to imagine. Every year, at the start of summer, Nan and Pop make the six-hour drive from their farm in northern Iowa and he wouldn't waste a second before reaching into the back of their Subaru for his fishing pole.

She chewed slowly as they sat side by side, watching the sun make its descent across the lake. That was the magic of a Minnesota summer up north: The sun was in no rush to set, like it protested the end of another peaceful day. The Richards understood all too well.

She watched as teenagers congregated under the flagpole at the center of the lawn. Two of the boys took off sprinting down the dock and jumped into the lake. The girls squealed with laughter, then jogged after them.

"They're not wearing masks," Tea said.

Nan nodded. "No one does around here."

Tea's eyes went wide as she looked at her grandmother. "Excuse me?"

Nan held up her arms. "Okay, hear me out."

She bit her tongue, wanting desperately to snap back at her grandmother about how Mom was on the front lines every single day, and that her sacrifice was not worth "hearing someone out." But she learned long ago that talking back was not the Midwest way.

"The Wild Pines owners made the decision not to let anyone rent cabins this year," Nan started.

Tea nodded. That made sense. Why would any family risk traveling somewhere new for vacation and expose themselves?

"Because of this, we as a community made the decision that we are going to be a...oh, what did he call it..."

Her brow furrowed. "He?"

Nan snapped her fingers and pointed at her. "A social bubble, that's it. We're one large bubble."

"Again, who's *he*?"

"The rule is that we can all hang out outside but not in each other's cabins, and we have to wear masks if we go into town," Nan continued. "Anyone who feels sick has to get tested at the drive-thru clinic in Ashland, and then quarantine for two weeks if they're positive."

Tea couldn't decide if Nan was oblivious to her question, or simply ignoring it. She decided to drop it. "And newcomers?"

"They're not allowed."

She froze. "So...me?"

"You were an exception."

That didn't fuel Tea with a single ounce of confidence, but before she could press her grandmother for more details, a firm knock sounded at the door.

"Come on in!" Nan called through the screen.

"Nope, please meet me outside."

Tea's stomach swooped at the sound of that voice.

"Oh, right, I always forget." She stood up. "I'm so used to inviting people in."

Tea didn't move an inch as she listened to the pad of Nan's bare feet carry her to the door at the back of the cabin. She sat in frozen silence, unable to make out the mumbling conversation that was happening down the hall.

She was back a moment later. "Honey bun, do you have proof of your negative COVID test?"

She looked up at her grandmother, her face feeling hot, and hoped Nan couldn't tell. "Um..."

"You took a test, right? I told you to..."

"Yes, yes, sorry." She walked over to her purse at the counter and grabbed the slip of paper, handing it to Nan.

Before she could slot back to her seat and quietly melt into the floor of the cabin, Nan snatched her hand and pulled her down the hall. She tried wriggling out of her grasp, but was pleasantly shocked at how firm her grip was. Shocked, and terrified.

"No, Nan, please—"

Her pleading was cut short as they reached the door.

He was much taller than she remembered.

And *covered* in tattoos.

The length of his arms, his lean legs, a few crawling up the side of his neck.

Archer Vincent was a walking piece of art.

Tea sucked in a breath, holding it as Nan reached through the gap and handed Archer the paper. He took a step back and unfolded it. The mask on his face twitched as he worked his jaw, reading the sheet in his hand.

She tried to examine all of the new features on the boy she once knew. His hair was shorter, but she couldn't tell how much with the flat-brim on his head. His wardrobe had undergone a serious upgrade, from baseball jerseys to soft, plain cotton T-shirts and smart navy board shorts that showed off his lean thighs—and a sea of tattoos. She couldn't see his eyes, not with the way he was avoiding hers.

He nodded and folded up the sheet, handing it back to Nan. "All set."

Before either of them could say anything, Archer spun around and jogged down the porch steps, then made his way toward Cabin A.

"I must have forgotten to tell you..." Nan started. "Archer is now the Wild Pines's manager. He's been the one making all of these rules."

Tea was unconvinced that her grandmother "forgot" to tell her, but she kept her mouth shut, watching as he swung open the door to what was presumably now *his* cabin, and escaped inside.

She'd had a feeling she might run into him this summer; maybe in passing if he visited his parents. But she had no idea that she would be dealing with him *all* summer. She wondered if it was possible to go an entire three months avoiding Archer completely.

Chapter 4

Archer

"ARCHER, *please* give me something to do, I'm begging you."

"Six feet, Rhonda."

Rhonda mumbled an apology and stepped out of the fishing cabin, still holding the door, likely waiting for Archer to step outside. But he was determined to finish cleaning up the inside of it after a still-yet-to-be-identified resident gutted their fish and didn't bother cleaning up yesterday, leaving the place smelling as lovely as the last four times it happened. Joel Vanderberg was the one to find it—again—and he had no qualms about knocking on Archer's door early in the morning, reminding him that it was *his* job to clean it up, and *his* job to catch the culprit.

It was the first topic of discussion for the owners' meeting in three weeks.

"Archer," Rhonda continued, still holding the door. Still not leaving. "Can you get your head out of your ass and please put me to work?"

"My head is *not* in my ass," he grumbled, scrubbing the

counter raw. The tiny shack was definitely going to need a fresh coat of seal if this kept happening.

"Oh really? A certain resident at Cabin B hasn't made you all moody?"

"Low blow."

"I'll keep dishing them out until you give me a job."

He swore under his breath, then slapped the rag on the counter and stepped out of the shack. "Why the insistence on helping me today? You were adamant about *not* moving when I asked for your help cleaning the fire pit four nights ago. And we both know the real culprit behind all of those melted plastic chocolate wrappers."

Rhonda lifted her cap and scratched her head. "Come on, Arch. My kids insisted it wasn't them, and if I went and cleaned them up knowing it absolutely *was*, it would have sent a message."

"So you sent me to do it?"

She looked ashamed. "Would it make you feel better if I called both of my sons little assholes?"

He forced himself not to smirk. "Maybe."

She sighed. "Steph wants me to work out with her. I love my wife, Archer, I do. But I would really rather not."

"And your solution is chores?"

"Sounds better than lifting fifteen pounders."

Lifting weights sounded a lot more fun than trying to attack his sticky-note wall of hell, but touching a piece of gym equipment was a pipe dream for Archer at this point. The occasional run and his nightly pushup routine was the only exercise he could manage with his chaotic schedule. Or lack of schedule, since he was still struggling to figure out his routine beyond his morning pour-over coffee.

"Fine. I haven't had the chance to mow the lawn yet, so

you can do that." He reached into his pocket and tossed her the keys to the mower.

She shuffled backward and saluted him. "Brilliant, on it."

He harrumphed as he watched her walk away, jealous that he couldn't sit down on a mower for an hour. It was supposed to be his easiest job of the day. "You owe me one of your IPAs!" he shouted.

She turned back to face him and grinned. "When Moody Archer is done making an appearance, Fun Archer can join me on my porch anytime!"

He flicked her off, which had her cackling all the way to the shed.

Archer rubbed his eyes, exhausted. Rhonda had a point; he *was* acting moody. He didn't even act that way when Janelle broke up with him, despite how gutted he'd felt. Bartending at Hermes Lounge was enough of a motivation to get out of bed. Rattling off cocktail combinations at the speed of light calmed his thoughts. Margarita. Half ounce lime juice, half ounce agave, one ounce orange liquor, one and half tequila. Negroni. One ounce Campari, one ounce sweet vermouth, one ounce gin. Cocktail measurements were the only numbers that made sense to him. If only taxes and spreadsheets could be that easy.

He closed his eyes and took a deep breath, pushing those feelings of anger down into his belly, imagining them shrinking into a ball, smaller and smaller and smaller. When it was the size of a wild blueberry, he imagined reaching out and squishing it, then throwing the skin away.

When he blinked his eyes open, he was welcomed by a vision of Tea in the distance, wearing a blue-and-white-striped one-piece that dipped low on her back. She was at the small strip of beach by the lake, opening up a beach chair, a faded ball cap on her head covering her face.

He grumbled as he threw open the door of the shack, storming back inside. *So much for that.*

THE DAY MOVED by at an excruciatingly slow pace. Or maybe it was the sun, which now refused to set until nine-thirty p.m. More sunlight meant more opportunities to get things done, and fewer opportunities to call it a day and steal a beer from his parents' fridge.

But his to-do list never seemed to get smaller, so he kept going.

Archer was finally weed-whacking the lawn, cutting his way around the flagpole, when the Bramble twins approached him, shaggy blond curls piled atop their heads.

"Six feet," he said instinctively.

"Come on, man, we're outside," said Danny.

"How was going downtown this weekend? Wear masks?"

Chris's cheeks turned pink as he looked down at his feet and took a big step back. Danny crossed his arms.

Archer sighed. "What's up guys?"

Danny held his hands up in prayer. "Arch, *please* can you—"

"No."

"—convince the owners to let us have jet skis?"

The Silver Falls Lake Association was made up of five different resorts, and out of all five, Wild Pines was the only one that didn't allow jet skis on the premises. It was the hottest topic of contention between the younger and older generations in their seven cabins; particularly with Sandy Vanderberg, who threw around her "matriarch" status like she was the president of the United States. Despite having the same debate every single year at the owners' meeting, her argument was always the same, and it always won.

"They're too loud going in and out of the docks, and they cause way too many injuries." Then her face would soften as she eyed everyone in the circle. "Plus, they scare our loons."

Archer knew the last bit of her argument wasn't based in fact, given that the jet skis zipping out of the other four resorts on the lake were likely already scaring the loons. Yet for some reason, it was enough to swing the vote. Loons were sacred in Minnesota, and the owners of Wild Pines had it in their heads that the birds preferred nesting on "quiet" properties. Even though the Bramble twins and the rest of their teenage gang were up late every night screaming around the bonfire.

He sighed, frowning at Chris and Danny. This would be his first time attending an owners' meeting as the manager. It also meant for the first time he would actually get a say on what they would be voting on. He'd listened in on meetings in the past, eavesdropping through cracked bedroom doors with *his* teenage gang when his parents hosted the meeting in their cabin. He remembered pressing his ear close to the door, knees knocking against Tea who sat right beside him. His hand brushing against her thigh, and the way her breath hitched when he quickly pulled away.

The one time he sat in the circle, he was allowed to observe but not talk—part of his summer of "learning what the manager does" with Austin, even though his brother was way more interested in making out with Riley Farrington than doing what his father asked. As a result of his protest, Archer silently followed in his father's footsteps, deducing that the job of Wild Pines Resort Manager would fall on his shoulders. Even though he wasn't sure he even wanted it. Could he really spend his summers managing the grounds? Mowing lawns, weed wacking, fixing old fishing cabins, cleaning the docks, keeping everything up to code for the Silver Falls Lake Association? At least the cabins were closed up during the off season, when northern Minnesota was frosted over and the lakes were frozen solid, the entire place in hibernation waiting for the spring to come. Yet that would mean giving up his entire summer of working at the cocktail lounge—making far more of a paycheck, even before the onslaught of tips he would get on a usual night. That's if Hermes Lounge would even let him come back.

Danny kept his hands steepled under his chin, while Chris looked at him like he was their last hope. And he had no one to blame for that but himself. Last summer, when he was six beers in with Austin during their annual visit, they'd found the boys sulking by the bonfire, sad that the owners voted no on jet skis *again*. Austin confessed that it was "really fucking dumb of them," and Archer, against his better judgement, had agreed.

And now the twins thought Archer was a person on their side...on the inside.

He let out another heavy sigh. "Guys, this is my first year as the manager, I don't want to rock the boat—"

Danny fell to his knees. Chris laughed, then also held up his hands in prayer.

"*Pleaseeee*, oh wise one. We *need* you," Danny whined.

Archer eyed the fire pit in the distance, an idea springing to mind. "How about this..."

Danny jumped up with bright eyes, blond curls bouncing. The kid looked like a hopeful golden retriever ready for a treat.

He crossed his arms. "Your moms might deny who leaves the candy wrappers in the bonfire every night, but I'm not stupid."

"Wasn't us," Danny denied at the same Chris said, "We're sorry."

Archer smirked. "It takes me over an hour to clean that damn pit every day because of you, so if you leave the fire pit spotless every night...and I mean *spotless—*"

"Done," Danny said with a salute, in almost the same way his mother did earlier.

"We'll clean them up," Chris added.

"Not just the wrappers," Archer continued. "I want that fire pit to look as clean as when I do it, maybe even *better*. If you can do that...well, I can't *guarantee* that we'll have jet skis, but I'll mention them during the meeting."

Mention was a lot safer than a promise of any kind. And it wasn't like they could avoid the topic, historically speaking.

Danny thrust his hand out in front of him. "You have a deal."

Archer shook it, then laughed as the boys chased one another back to their cabin, howling at their success. They ran up to the rest of their gang: Kelsey, Liam, Ashley, and Michaela. They shared the news and they all cheered. Archer watched closely as Chris eyed Ashley, the two of them blushing at one another as Chris bumped her shoulder with his.

His mind drifted to summers spent here, long days playing lawn games, tubing behind his father's boat, sailing early in the morning, or swimming late at night. Riley was always meant for Austin, despite the two of them never wanting anything "serious." Quentin had a thing for Deanna, but she'd been clueless, and he was distraught when her parents sold Cabin G after that last summer before college.

And then there was him and Tea.

As if his wandering thoughts made her magically appear, Archer heard the screen door of Cabin B open and close. Tea was in blue pajama pants and a soft grey sweatshirt, a frosty bottle of white wine in one hand and a glass in another. A small book was tucked underneath her arm.

His eyes gravitated to her as she wandered over to the fire pit. She curled up in an Adirondack chair, poured herself a glass of wine, and flipped open her book.

It was the same nightly routine he'd watched her commit to summer after summer from the windows of Cabin A. Comfortable clothes as she waited for dinner, book by the lake, her cup of tea now replaced with a glass of wine. He used to run outside and distract her from those moments, convince her to play another round of corn hole or go water skiing. She never minded his distraction. She never said no.

He didn't take note of how long he stood there, staring at her from a distance, but at some point she finally looked up. He couldn't see her piercing blue eyes from this distance, but he could *feel* them. Those same eyes he would catch from their cabin windows. The eyes that'd blinked up at him the night everything went to shit.

"Archer, sweetie!"

He jumped at his mother's voice and whipped around to face her. "Yes?"

Larissa Vincent crossed her arms, the sleeves of her faded yellow Silver Falls hoodie bunched at her elbows. "What, no 'hi, Mom, how are you, Mom?'"

"Hi, Mom. How are you, Mom?"

She perked up. "Fantastic. Even better if you'd actually join us tonight at the dinner table."

He leaned down to pick up the power tool near his feet. "Probably not tonight. I still have three hours of sunlight to utilize."

Her frown was louder than any words she could have spoken in response.

Archer gestured toward the lawn. "This place isn't going to weed-whack itself."

"Archer Vincent, if you don't sit down at my table tonight and eat a slice of lasagna, I'm going to weed-whack that sorry little—"

"*Mom*, Jesus."

"You don't need to bring the Lord into this."

"Yeah, well, *the Lord* understood serving others, and that's kind of what I'm doing here."

"He also said to respect thine mother and father."

"Did he? Or was that God?"

"They're the same, smart-ass."

"Jesus would not like that language, mother."

She placed her hands on her hips. "He would also hate for you not to spend time with your family."

He hung his head. There was no winning with Larissa Vincent. Archer knew long ago that his mother would fight him until she got her way. Austin had that same exact gene. He loved them, but it also made them infuriating to deal with.

It wasn't that Archer didn't want a slice of his mother's lasagna—he found himself daydreaming about it a little too regularly. It was sitting at a table with his father and talking shop about the resort he dreaded. So far, Archer had successfully convinced him that he had everything under control. He didn't want to admit the truth; that he found it all overwhelming, that he was constantly drowning in to-do's. He couldn't hire their usual help to clean or maintain the facilities, given everything going on in the world. Which meant that emptying the dumpsters and cleaning the fishing shack and weed-whacking the lawn fell on his shoulders, along with filling out tax forms and understanding insurance policies and a myriad of other tasks he fell behind on daily.

"Not tonight," he answered softly. "Soon, though. I promise."

Her shoulders sagged. Then she squared them and pointed at his nose. "Don't you dare sneak in for a beer later, or I'll wrangle you into staying for dessert. You've been warned."

"Noted."

She squinted her eyes, then turned to leave.

He exhaled a long breath, then slowly turned back to that Adirondack chair in the distance.

It was empty.

Chapter 5

Tea

To: <Undisclosed recipients>

From: The Silver Falls Lake Association
   (silverfalls@minnesota.org)

Silver Falls residents!

We hope this email finds you all in good health during these trying times, and that you're enjoying the fresh air, blue skies, and north winds. We see all of those sailboats out there!

We have very exciting news to share. As you know, our lakes have been the residence of many loons over the years, both on Silver Lake and Silverstone Lagoon. But this year our mates have decided to nest and make a little family of their own.

Say hello to Pebble! (Picture attached.) He's our new resident baby loon. We spotted him riding on his mother's back in the creek between the lake and lagoon. We assume it's close to where the family's nest is, but we haven't spotted it yet, so we can't be sure.

Please keep in mind that baby loons are unable to fly for the first couple of weeks, and they stay close to their parents until about three months after birth. We ask that you please be mindful of Pebble and keep a watchful eye as you take your boats or jet skis out this summer.

The Silver Falls Lake Association is a proud member of the Ten Thousand Lake Loon Committee, dedicated to protecting and preserving our natural wildlife. We would love if a member of each resort would join our efforts this summer. If you are interested, feel free to email us at **silverfalls@minnesota.org.**

Just like our resorts, we want Silver Lake and Silverstone Lagoon to be a safe haven for many loon families in the future.

Stay safe out there, and keep an eye out for Pebble!

SFLA

SHE WAS SITTING by the lake in her dream, a steaming cup of her favorite tea by her side in the Adirondack chair, looking out at the lake, the water still. Her father popped into her vision and began pulling on her feet, telling her to get changed so they could get out for one last water ski before dinner. "We don't get nights like these often, Tea bear."

She ran to the cabin and got changed into her suit, but when she returned her father was gone. The lake was still smooth as glass, but Dad was nowhere to be found. Her mug of tea was replaced with a glass of white wine.

Revved-up boat engines and slapping screen doors startled her awake. Nan was downstairs using her "whispering" voice, but it was still loud enough to rouse Tea from her dream. She pressed the heels of her palms into her eyes, wishing for a way to see her father again, while simultaneously regretting dreaming him up in the first place. In the months following his death, Tea saw him every night: Dad telling her to get in the boat for a water ski or a sail, but always disappearing before she could join him. She knew these dreams technically should be labeled nightmares, because they haunted her every morning when she opened her eyes, but calling it so didn't feel right, especially when it gave her the opportunity to see her father again. He always looked his healthiest in her mind, no sagging gray skin or thinned-out hair. His cheeks were pink and full, red curls sticking up in every direction, and his laugh rambunctious as ever when he snuck up on her in that chair. It was how she wanted to remember her father, even if the dreams had left her feeling confused and angry and alone when she woke up.

She hadn't had felt that way in years. Yet being back in this place brought on a tsunami of memories, and a resurgence of that very same dream.

She thought of how Archer had watched her from afar last night, her skin burning hot knowing that his eyes finally landed on her, knowing that he couldn't ignore her any longer.

She wondered if he was still mad at her. A confrontation was unavoidable if they would both be spending the entire summer in Silver Falls, but it didn't have to happen quite yet. So she'd picked up her glass and escaped inside before he finished talking to his mom.

The screen door slapped downstairs again, followed by another angry whisper from Nan. This time Tea could make out what she was saying.

"Wayne, for pete's sake, stop slapping that door," Nan hissed. "You're gonna wake our girl."

"Oh she's probably already up," Pop responded in his usual deep timbre, unashamed of how loud he was being.

"It's only eight o'clock."

A cabinet door opened and shut, followed by a *ting* as someone pressed down the toaster. "Eight o'clock? It's practically midday. I've already had my coffee and listened to MPR." The fridge opened, then closed. "Would be nice if I could go fishing without so many damn boats out there."

"*Wayne.*"

They went back and forth like that, but Tea tuned it out as she slipped out of her bed and tucked herself into her robe. She tied her hair up into a ponytail as she made her way downstairs.

Pop smiled at her, his teeth smudged with a slathering of butter and jam, a half-eaten piece of toast on a plate in front of him. Crumbs lined his beard, some escaping onto the counter. He was already dressed for fishing; long-sleeve compression shirt, jeans, and the same ratty Silver Falls hat he wore all year round, bleached from a decade or two out on the water.

"See, there's our girl," he said. He wiped his beard as made his way around the counter. "I told you she was awake."

Nan rolled her eyes. "Does she *look* like she's been awake?"

Pop ignored her as he wrapped his arms around Tea,

planting a kiss on her cheek and leaving behind a dollop of jam. He laughed and wiped it off with his shirtsleeve.

Tea smiled. "Morning, Pop. Still got some coffee, or is it too late?"

"Of course we have coffee, it's still the morning," he responded.

Nan pinched the bridge of her nose.

"Kelly, Wayne, Tea! What are you doing? You gotta get out there!"

The three of them turned in unison to find Rhonda on their deck, peering through the screen door.

Pop frowned. "Now why would I do that? The lake is covered in boats right now."

"Of course they are," Rhonda replied. "They're all looking for Pebble."

Nan scrunched her nose. "Pebble?"

"The baby loon? Did you guys not read the email?"

"On my computer? Oh, I don't touch that thing," Nan responded.

"They're looking for a rock?" Pop added.

Tea opened the cabinet and grabbed the mug with a giant painted squirrel, then reached for the coffee pot. "Nan, Pop, do one of you have your email on your phone?"

"On our phones?" Nan squeaked.

Pop snapped his fingers. "Yes. Archer installed it for me last summer."

Of course he did. "Can you grab it, please?"

Tea kept her attention on her grandfather as he walked to the coffee table to retrieve his phone, ignoring the way Rhonda was pointedly looking at her after Pop's casual mention of Archer.

Pop swiped it open and handed it to her. His home screen was a mess, littered with colorful games and news apps. Yet it wasn't hard to find his Mail app after a few swipes. It was the only one that had a red bubble showing over nineteen thousand notifications.

"Christ," she mumbled to herself, tapping it open. Thankfully the one from Silver Falls was the third email from the top, followed by senior exercise tips from the American Heart Association and a 70 percent off sale on drill bit sets from Tractor Supply.

She cleared her throat, then read the entire thing out loud to them, everything from the new loon baby to the boat warnings. Nan's face glowed brighter and brighter with every word. By the end of it, she was slathering her arms with sunscreen. Rhonda was already gone, jogging over to her boat where Steph and the twins waited for her, suited up and ready to go.

"Wayne, grab the cooler and pack some water," Nan started. "Tea, go get changed."

Tea frowned. "Don't you think going out there with the boats will scare them away? Isn't this exactly what the association warned you not to do?"

Pop returned from the back with a cooler and began stuffing it with cans of seltzer and Coca-Cola, followed by sticks of string cheese and beef jerky.

"The email said to be *mindful*," Nan said. "One of us is bound to find the family nest out there."

"Has anyone found a loon nest on the lake before?" Tea countered.

Pop swung the door open, holding it as Nan adjusted the strings on her sun hat. She turned to Tea. "You coming?"

Tea pointed at the mug in her hand, then at her robe. She then watched her grandparents take off in a giddy canter, headed for Pop's fishing boat.

She stepped out of the cabin and onto the damp grass barefoot, sipped her coffee, and smiled as they disappeared down the lake. She padded across the lawn and eyed the countless boats zipping around, frantic residents hoping they would be the first to find Pebble and the family of loons.

She slowed when she glimpsed Sandy Vanderberg sitting in a beach chair by the water's edge, a scowl fixed on her face.

Tea stepped up to her, the sand sticking to her wet feet. There was a second chair beside her, but at enough of a distance that Tea felt comfortable enough to ask if she could join her.

Sandy perked up. "Of course, my dear. Sit, sit."

She dipped her chin and took a seat. The sun was already beaming down on them, making her sweat in her bathrobe, which she forgot was still wrapped around her body. She went to take it off then stopped, remembering that she only wore underwear. She never slept with pajamas, especially in the cabin that didn't have any air conditioning. She tightened her robe.

"Your grandmother must be so happy that you're here," Sandy started. "She wouldn't stop talking about it for weeks after your mother called."

Tea swallowed the lump in her throat. She didn't want to sound ungrateful that her grandmother was taking her in for the summer, but she was still feeling unsettled about leaving Mom alone in New Jersey. And the return of her dreams certainly wasn't helping.

"I'm excited to be here with them," she replied. "It's been a long time."

"How long has it been now?" Sandy asked.

"Eight years," she answered, so low she wondered if the

other woman heard her.

Sandy hummed. "That is a long time, dear. I'm so sorry for your loss. Gareth was such a light to all of us. Always knew how to make us laugh."

Tea white-knuckled the handle of her mug. "Yeah. He was good at that."

A figure in the distance caught Sandy's attention. She raised her arm. "Yoo-hoo, Archer!"

Tea's stomach curled. She took a sip of her coffee, which tasted far too acidic now that her throat threatened to puke up bile. Plus, sipping on a hot coffee was not pleasant as she baked inside her bathrobe, even with the light breeze off the lake. She pulled the robe even tighter, keeping her eyes out on Pop's boat as Archer's tall frame entered her periphery.

"Good morning, Sandy," Archer said.

She could feel his gaze on her. She sipped her coffee.

"Archer, dearest, what is the meaning of all of this?" Sandy asked him, throwing her arm out wide.

He scratched his head. Tea couldn't help but eye the tattoos on his right arm as his bicep flexed. A black bear, a pine tree, a coiled snake . There were *so* many of them.

He must have noticed her staring, because he dropped his arm and tucked them both behind him. "Apparently there's a baby loon on the lake."

"A *baby loon?*"

"Yes, didn't you read the email?"

Sandy scrunched her nose. "I hate my computer."

Tea furrowed her brow. "Why does no one ever touch a computer around here?"

"Because apparently they are the work of Satan," Archer quipped.

Tea lifted her cup in front of her mouth, trying not to laugh. Archer raised a brow at her in what could have been comprehended as a teasing manner. But his expression shifted right back into something cool, calm, and closed off.

Sandy rolled her eyes, not taking Archer's shit. "If there's really a baby loon out there, then how could you allow all of those boats out there? It's creating a disturbance."

He flashed Sandy a gleaming, charming smile, and though it had been eight years since Tea had seen Archer Vincent, she knew him enough to know that smile was his fake one. His "Minnesota Nice" one.

"Sandy, you know we're within the window that people are allowed to take their boats out on the lake. It is their right to do so. I don't oversee that."

Sandy harrumphed. "We're going to scare them away."

"Will they leave the lake?" Tea asked.

Sandy and Archer both looked at her like she'd grown a third head.

She sunk deeper into her chair. "Sorry," she mumbled.

"Of course they'll—"

"They won't leave," Archer cut in, his chocolate-brown eyes finally acknowledging her for more than a second.

Her face flushed and sweat trickled down her back. She was boiling inside her robe, and Archer was actually looking at her like she did, in fact, exist.

This was not how she'd envisioned her morning going.

"What do you mean they won't leave? Look at these boats!" Sandy exclaimed, clearly distraught.

Archer crossed his arms in front of him, forgetting that he was trying to hide them from Tea. "Once loons claim territory on a lake, they won't leave. It's not in their nature."

He was staring at her again. He was no longer smiling; his gaze was fierce, like she was simply another problem at the resort that he needed to handle.

She wiped the sweat on her brow and averted her eyes, hoping he would walk away first so she could escape into the cabin.

"Oh, well, that's good then," Sandy replied, oblivious to the tension. "Did you find out how to bear-proof the dumpsters?"

Tea's brows shot skyward. "*Bears?*"

Archer's gaze lingered on Tea for longer than a beat. "Don't worry, I'm handling it."

She squirmed in her chair, her mind beginning to spiral. No masks? Bears? *Archer?* Was Silver Falls really the place she should be all summer? New Jersey had its risks, sure, but it sounded safer to Tea than being by the lake.

Archer coughed, then flashed Sandy one last Minnesota Nice smile. "Excuse me, I have things to do."

They watched him walk away and Tea counted to five in her head before she exhaled and leaned back against the chair.

"How are you not baking in that robe?" Sandy asked. "It's a million degrees out here."

"No kidding," Tea grumbled. She stood up on wobbly legs. "I'm going to put on my suit."

Chapter 6

Archer

EVERYONE ACROSS SILVER FALLS lost their minds looking for the loons, but at least it left the resort relatively quiet so Archer could finally get shit done. By five o'clock, he was pulling eight sticky notes off his wall, a small weight easing off his chest with each rip. Until the last sticky note peeled a good chunk of paint along with it. He cursed, grabbing the yellow square pad, and scribbled *Paint this depressing cabin* before slapping it on.

He stepped back and shoved his hands in the back pockets of his jeans, eyeing the remaining sticky notes, wondering what he should tackle first thing in the morning. Tax forms? That sounded way too complicated. Wild Pines email newsletter? Also sounded like hell. Finally bear-proof the dumpster? After numerous attempts with different materials like chains and rope and clamps, he couldn't nail down something that would work well enough for the resi-dents *and* keep the bears out. The metal chain was the only secure option for bears, and he was feeling ready to settle on getting up every morning and removing the chain himself. He knew Sandy and Joel were usually up sometime around six, so that would mean getting up before them every morning, which made him want to scream. But at least everyone would be safe.

He sighed, watching out his window as residents returned from their excursions, sunburnt and laughing as they docked their boats. Archer snatched his flat brim and placed it backward on his head, then exited his cabin, deciding for the first time to call it a day before the sun went down.

He made it down to the docks as Jorge Cortez pulled his boat in. Ashley and Michaela jumped out, tossing their life jackets back in.

"Oh, *come on*," Jorge exclaimed. He stood and watched his girls jog toward the lawn where the Bramble twins and the Jansen siblings waited for them. "Girls, *girls!*"

Archer reached Jorge's boat, biting his cheek as the man grumbled curses under his breath. He began emptying things out that were looking damp: his soft cooler bag. Sweatshirts. Fishing poles. Ropes. Goggles. A first aid kit. He lifted the life jackets, now dripping wet, and cursed again.

"Need a hand?" Archer asked.

Jorge tossed the jackets onto the dock and looked up at Archer. "Hey man, yeah, no. I'm okay."

He eyed Jorge's boat, which definitely did not look okay. The bottom of it was covered in a layer of water, and his sneakers were soaked through.

"Got a leak?" Archer asked.

He sighed and stepped out of his boat. "I think so. And who knows when—or *if*—I'll be able to get it fixed with everything going on."

He frowned, then pointed to the remote dangling above

the canopy. "Lift it up all the way, let's take a look underneath."

Jorge didn't object as he reached for the remote and pressed the lift arrow until the boat was completely out of the water. The two of them ducked down and inspected the boat. Archer found it instantly; a small crack along the hull.

"There," he said. "No need to take it in, that's an easy patch job."

"Man, you don't have to do that," he said. "You've already got enough on your plate. I can—"

"Seriously, Jorge, it's fine. I can get this done in less than an hour."

"All right, well, not now, yeah? You seem like you're done for the day."

Archer hummed. "I guess. Not sure what to do with myself though."

"A Pisco sour, perhaps?"

He perked up. Archer hadn't shaken up a cocktail since arriving at Wild Pines in May, and he was itching to mix something. "You have stuff to make Pisco sours?"

"I'm Chilean, is that even a question?"

"Real lime juice, right?"

"You offend me."

He laughed. "Fair, I'm sorry. That sounds great."

Archer helped Jorge grab his soggy items off the dock, then the two of them made their way to Cabin G, where the two slung them over the patio to dry in the sun.

Jorge looked over at the group of teenagers. Ashley and Chris were sitting at a picnic table, heads turned to one another, cheeks flushed as they spoke. Chris's hand was on the bench, close enough to brush against Ashley's leg.

He cursed. "I don't know about that boy."

Archer couldn't help his smile. "At least it's Chris and not Danny."

Jorge frowned. "That should make me feel better?"

He shrugged. "I don't know, Chris seems like more of the innocent type, and he's incapable of lying unlike his brother. Good kid."

Jorge lifted a brow. "Yeah?"

"Come on, Jorge, you know the Brambles. They're good people."

Jorge shook his head. "I don't though. Lily is usually the one here with the girls. I used to only come for a week or two at most, and I was always working."

Archer pressed his lips together. Jorge was furloughed in April from his job at the Minnesota Conservation Lab. Archaeology research wasn't seen as a necessity during a global pandemic, even though everything that was happening would certainly go down in history. Jorge mentioned they had some savings, but Archer could tell he was stressed about what was to come—and if selling Cabin G would be in their future.

It was one of the reasons he was delaying asking cabin owners for their Silver Falls Lake Association fees. Everyone was struggling in their own way, and the last thing Archer wanted to do was cause more turmoil.

The screen door down at Cabin B inched open. Jorge was still watching his oldest in her clumsy attempts at flirting, but Archer's eyes were locked on the figure now making her way to the Adirondack chairs by the fire pit. Bottle of wine and glass in hand, book tucked underneath her arm.

"Jorge!" Lily called from inside their cabin. "I think I did something wrong to the mole, it's starting to burn."

"Shit." Jorge turned to Archer. "Give me a few minutes to help Lily, then I'll grab the cocktail stuff—"

"Actually..." Archer blinked, eyes still on the woman taking a seat. "I haven't, um, checked the fire pit yet today. Need to make sure it's clean."

"That should take, what? Four seconds?"

He turned to Jorge. "Rain check, okay?"

Jorge peeked around Archer's shoulder. He saw the shift in Jorge's face.

"Sounds good, man," Jorge replied. "My rain checks are only good for a week though."

Archer smiled and nodded as Jorge stepped into Cabin G, then took a deep breath and tilted his head to the sky. Was he really going to do this?

Yes, he thought. *No more hiding. You have a whole summer with her. It's been eight years, for shit's sake. Get over it.*

He felt his flat brim lift from his head and fall behind him. He snatched it quickly, scratching his head before placing the hat back on and turning toward the fire pit. She wasn't paying attention to him. She was too engrossed in whatever she was reading.

He shook his hands, cracked his neck, then put one foot in front of the other.

Tea didn't notice his approach as she scanned the pages of her book. He squinted to get a look at the title.

The Loon Song: Understanding the Mysteries of North America's Favorite Bird

He took a step closer to spy the cover art and a twig snapped underneath his foot.

Tea looked up, then her eyes widened. She shut the book and tucked her legs to her chest, like she was trying to get out of his way. "Sorry, need me to leave?"

"...Leave?"

"Yeah, am I in the way of your cleaning?"

"Oh." He eyed the fire pit, realizing that *was* technically his excuse for coming over here. "Um, no, yeah, I need to make sure everything looks good."

"Sure, yeah, okay."

Archer took his time examining the area. Once he concluded that it was indeed spotless (and silently cursed the Bramble twins for actually keeping their promise), he looked back at Tea. She had her face in her knees, her arms tight around her legs.

He smirked. "Uh, you good over there?"

"I don't have a mask," she said, her voice muffled from the fabric of her pants. "And you're closer than six feet, so—"

"Tea, we're outside."

She stiffened at his use of her name. It was the first time he'd said it to her in a long time. The first time he actually acknowledged that she was here.

He didn't want to think about it too hard, so he continued talking. "These scientists say it's safe to be outside without masks. Plus, numbers are down—" He paused, realizing what he was doing. Was he really defending himself for being closer to her? He spent the majority of his days making sure everyone else at Wild Pines kept their six feet from him. Yet, now...

"Numbers might be down, but we don't have a vaccine."

Finally, someone here gets it. "Yeah, I know. But I think we will soon."

She lifted her face, enough to reveal her sky-blue eyes, but her mouth was still covered by her knees. "You think?"

He shrugged. "I mean, hey, I'm not an expert. But they're saying that a vaccine has gone through preclinical testing and they might start trials soon."

"You sound like my mom."

His chest warmed at the thought of Molly. "How is she?"

"Too busy saving the world to have me home." Tea shook her head and stuffed her face back in her knees. "Sorry, forget I said that."

His chest fell. "You wish you weren't here?"

"I didn't say that."

"But you implied it."

She looked back up at him. "Why? Do *you* wish I weren't here?"

He pinched his brow. "Hey, I didn't say that either."

"But...do you?"

Archer shook his head, then slumped down into the chair next to her. It was a good four feet from hers, and if he leaned back, they were still at a respectable distance. He eyed her. She was watching him with rapt intensity. She'd handed him the moment that could make or break their entire summer, and if he was being honest with himself, he did not want to deal with this unpleasantness between them for a second longer.

"No, Tea. I'm glad you're here. It's good to see you again."

She lifted all of her face, including her pale pink lips. Now that he was much closer to her, with no screen doors or matriarchs between them, he could make out the four freckles that were still dotted across her top lip. His gut twisted at the sight of them.

You just told her you're glad she's here. Get it together.

"Yeah?" she answered with that familiar soft, timid voice. Like she had to make sure he was being serious with her. It was...*so* Tea. She was the gentle and calming one, the perfect contrast to the rest of their group that used to be loud and rambunctious. But when it was only the two of them, he settled into her gentleness like a warm blanket, and it soothed him.

He nodded and leaned back into his chair. They remained quiet for a long moment, watching as boats made their way back to their docks, finishing up their attempts at finding the loons.

She broke the silence. "Apparently no one found them," she started. "Which I kind of figured would happen. They don't like noise."

He lifted a mocking brow. "Learn that from your book over there?"

She smiled, teeth and all, and it felt like a gut punch. He tapped his fingers against the chair's armrest to calm himself.

"Maybe." She lifted the book in her hands. "It says here that loons are easily disturbed, but especially so when they are nesting with new families. Sometimes they get so scared they'll abandon their nests, eggs and all. Luckily the baby was already born, but there's no way the family would have been found today."

"Looks like someone is invested."

She closed the book. "It's keeping my mind preoccupied."

"You bored?"

She groaned. "Don't tell Nan, it would crush her. But yes. I really wish I had an internship or...*something*. I feel like I'm wasting my time this summer."

"You'll have plenty of time to work, trust me," he grumbled.

"Says the guy who actually has a job."

"Why, you want it?"

She frowned. "You don't?"

He chuckled to himself, mostly in disbelief at where this conversation was ending up...and how easy it was to share how he truly felt to Tea. Archer was ready to pour it all out, just like the old days. But he knew it wasn't safe to do that with her now. He needed to set boundaries. Protect himself from making his same mistakes.

He shrugged, attempting nonchalance. "Still getting used to it, I guess."

Her frown deepened. He knew she wasn't buying it, but he wasn't going to hand it to her.

He crossed his ankle over his leg and rubbed his coffee cherry tattoo. "As soon as I can figure out this dumpster, I'll be a happy man."

She nodded, waiting for him to continue, but he remained silent. The two of them sat there as the sun slowly set. A catamaran glided past them, heading north.

Archer flicked his gaze in her direction. Her eyes were wet as she watched the sailboat. He didn't say anything as she wiped them clean and looked away from him.

He wasn't the only one hiding.

"Hey," he whispered. "I'm—"

"*Don't.*"

He clamped his mouth shut.

"Everyone says the same empty words," she continued. "I don't need it from you too."

Chapter 7

Tea

Archer pursed his lips as he stared back at her.

Tea wasn't sure if she'd completely soured whatever was happening between the two of them, but she couldn't sit here and listen to *him*, of all people, repeat the words she hated hearing. *I'm sorry for your loss. He deserved better. He was gone too soon. He loved you very much.*

She knew all of those phrases came with good intentions. No one ever knew what else to say. But after suffering through them over and over and *over*, those good intentions lost all meaning to her. She never felt like she had the right words to offer back, and she was tired of having to hop into her grief every time someone felt the need to apologize. So very, very tired.

She waited for Archer to close himself off again. To leave.

Instead, his mouth softened and he nodded once. "All right."

She eyed him, watching as he tapped his fingers against the wood, his forearms flexing with each tap.

"So..." she started, hugging her legs.

Archer lifted his brow, his eyes wide with curiosity.

"Decided to ink your entire body, huh?"

He grinned and grabbed his hat, twisting the flat brim forward so he could lean his head back against the chair. He closed his eyes. "You could say I have grown an...obsession."

"Yeah, understatement."

His grin smoothed into a content smile. She took advantage of his closed eyes and raked her gaze across his body, finally allowing herself a moment to properly look at his ink. A bass guitar. A pirate ship. A walleye dangling from a pole. Every piece, from the small moon at his thumb to the massive snake wrapped around his arm, was beautifully done.

"Which was your first one?"

She watched his smile fade. He cleared his throat but didn't respond.

"Oh," she whispered, wrapping herself tight. She abhorred the way she was feeling. She couldn't handle it. She needed to say something.

"Arch—"

"*Don't.*"

It was her turn to snap her mouth shut.

Archer sat up straight, then brushed his hands down his thighs, his eyes on the patch of grass a foot in front of them. "If you don't mind, I would like to leave the past in the past and...move on."

She *did* mind. Very much. Tea spent the last few days doing everything she could to avoid talking to Archer, but now that she was, she wanted everything out in the open. She wanted to apologize for that night eight years ago, for all of the nasty things she said but did not mean.

Except he'd listened to her when she told him not to pry about her father, so it was only fair—as they attempted to mend their friendship back together—that she also did the same.

"Sure," she replied. "The past is in the past."

He nodded, closing his eyes as he tapped the tips of his fingers.

She needed *something* to say to break the tension, but she just stared at him. Went back to scanning his body. When she got to some kind of berry plant tattoo on his left ankle, she registered that he was wearing tennis shoes.

"Why are you wearing sneakers right now?

His grin returned. She exhaled with relief.

"I mean, you're kind of breaking lake etiquette," she continued. "Isn't it a rule here that you *always* have to be barefoot?"

"Try stepping on a bee three times in a single season, then come talk to me about lake etiquette."

She flinched. "Ouch. Damn clovers."

He grumbled. "Damn clovers. I need to sprinkle a solution across the lawn and kill them, but it's not my highest priority."

He lifted his hat, finally giving her a clear shot of his hair. It was shorter, but it was still wavy and midnight-black. He had a full head of it, unlike his brother Austin who skipped his balding phase and completely shaved his head. She'd seen the Instagram photos of Riley shaving off Austin's hair with an electric razor three summers earlier. Archer wasn't in any of the shots.

He tilted his head at her, eyes expectant. Eyes that were aware she was staring.

She shook out of it. "What *is* your highest priority?"

"Probably the dumpster."

She frowned. "You still haven't figured that out yet?"

He rubbed his temples. "By all means, if you have a

solution that will keep the bears out *and* make it easy for anyone to remove early in the morning, I'm all ears."

She chewed on the inside of her cheek, thinking through different possibilities.

Archer sighed at her lack of an answer, then pointed to her half empty bottle of Sauvignon Blanc. "Wanna share some of that?"

"I don't have anything for you to drink out of, and it's probably not safe for you to drink from the bottle—"

He bolted upright. "I'll grab a glass. Be right back."

He returned minutes later with an empty mason jar in one hand and two bags of Old Dutch chips in the other. He placed his glass down then held up the two bags. "Ketchup, or Barbecue?"

"Ketchup, duh."

He tossed her the unopened bag. "Some things never change."

"Yoo-hoo, Archer!"

"*No, no, no,*" he mumbled, then turned with a flourish, that Minnesota Nice smile from earlier painted on his face. "Sandy, hi!"

Tea opened her bag of chips and dug in, taking a large sip of her wine as she watched Archer play nice with Sandy. They were talking about the owners' meeting in a few weeks, and despite Archer's pleasant demeanor, Tea could tell that he was not thrilled to be talking about where they were hosting the meeting *again*.

Sandy lifted her arm toward her cabin, her gaze fixed on her porch. Archer looked above Sandy's grayish-blonde ponytail—he towered over her by a foot—and rolled his eyes at Tea. Tea grinned, then made a show of pouring more wine into her glass and taking a big gulp.

He shook his head. *You suck*, he mouthed.

She shrugged and took another long sip.

After he successfully calmed Sandy down and somehow had her walking away with a smile, Archer grabbed for the empty jar.

"Archer!"

"Jesus, what is in the air?" he grumbled to her. Then he stood up straight. "Mom, hi!"

Larissa Vincent walked up to her son with a stern face and crossed her arms. "Are you joining us tonight?"

Tea felt her throat close up, her palms go clammy. *Does she know? Is she mad at what I did to her son?*

Archer held his hand out to his jar and unopened bag of chips. "I have dinner."

"That's not a meal." Larissa eyed the chips, the jar, and finally the person who was keeping Archer company. "Ope, Tea! Darling, it's so good to see you. I would have stopped over sooner, but you know...the pandemic and all that."

She swallowed. "You too, Mrs. Vincent."

Larissa glared at her. "That is not my name." She playfully slapped her son's shoulder. "Maybe if Archer actually filled us in on *anything* about you the past eight years we wouldn't be so formal! He hasn't told us a thing."

Archer flinched at her words.

Her shoulders relaxed. *She thought we were talking. She thought we were still friends.* She rolled her eyes, making a show of it. "It's good to see you too, Mom."

"Much better," Larissa replied with a twinkle in her eye as she turned back to her son. "I made meatloaf tonight, and I was going to put it on the grill."

Archer tossed his head back and moaned. The sound... did something to her.

She poured more wine down her throat.

Archer snapped up straight and pointed at her. "You're hogging."

Tea pressed her lips together and released a satisfied *smack*. "You're taking forever."

Larissa watched the two of them with obvious glee. "It's so good to see the two of you hanging out."

Archer's shoulders sagged. "Well, we're currently not hanging out because *you're here—*"

Larissa pressed a finger into her son's chest and pushed hard, a strand of hair slipping from her ponytail. She blew it out of her face and gritted, "Archer Vincent, if you do not join us for dinner tonight, I will come into your cabin with a sledgehammer and annihilate that pathetic wall of yours—"

He lifted his hands up. "Okay, okay, I got it. Don't take it out on my sticky notes."

She huffed, then clasped her hands behind her back and grinned. "See you in thirty minutes."

Archer let out a strained sigh as he watched his mother make her way back to her cabin. His hands curled into fists, then he unfurled them and repeated the motion. Finally, he turned around to face her.

Tea held up her empty wine bottle with a triumphant smile. "Whoops."

SHE FACED the front door outside Cabin A the following morning, telling herself that it was *no big deal*. After he cursed at her for finishing up her bottle the night before, she went to grab another, but when she returned he was being summoned by Steph Bramble to fix their storage unit's roller door. By the time he finished, he had to report to dinner.

"We'll...talk," he'd said, snatching his unopened bag of chips and empty jar.

"Sure, yeah."

He frowned. "That didn't sound too convincing."

"Archer, I'm not going anywhere for another three months. We are bound to *talk*."

"Maybe sail?"

She squinted her eyes and looked away from him. "Don't push your luck."

He hadn't. He'd simply said good night and left her to watch the sunset alone.

So when she'd woken up jittery and anxious, her fingers itching to *do something*, she snatched her laptop, searched the Internet, then rushed over to Archer's cabin before she could change her mind.

She knocked.

"One minute!" he shouted from the back of his cabin.

She peered through the screen door, scanning the inside of Archer's domain. Mahogany handmade desk and chair covered in papers. Checkered tan and white wool three-seater couch with a rip down the center cushion, a home-made crocheted blanket slung over the top and a throw pillow with *Up North* stitched on the front. The carpet looked stained and old, and paint chipped at the top close to the ceiling. The Wild Pines manager cabin had certainly seen better days.

Archer approached from the back of his cabin, hair wet and already in his work clothes for the day. He didn't open the door, letting the screen act as their protection.

He titled his head, a confused expression on his face. "You actually get up at this hour?"

She scowled at him. "Har, har."

"Back in the day you would sleep in until, what? Ten? Eleven?"

"Unless you or Dad were dragging me out of bed." She didn't mention why. He already knew.

He shot her a mischievous grin. "Ah, the good old days. I miss the screaming."

"You're weird."

"No, *you're* weird for being on my porch at eight in the morning. What are you doing here?"

Tea lifted the four bungee cords she held in her hand. "I had an idea."

Thirty minutes later, they stared at two remarkably secure dumpsters, held tightly by her cords.

"How did you think of it?" Archer asked her. He circled the dumpsters—*again*—giving the cords a flick to make sure they were still taut. He rattled them as well, seeing if the tops would flip open. Nothing.

Tea shrugged. "The university of YouTube."

"I love that school. There are so many great academic minds on there."

She crossed her arms. "I'm kind of shocked you didn't try looking it up yourself. It took me, like, ten minutes to find a solution."

"Hey there, smart-ass. I barely have time to even watch television these days."

She loosened her arms. "Fair point."

He unhooked the cords with ease. "I need to make sure to come out here each night and secure them."

"Do it quickly before you go to bed." She pointed to his cabin next to them. "You're literally right there."

He nodded, shoving his hands in the back pockets of his jeans. "Coffee?"

"Oh, it's okay," she replied, pointing to her cabin. "Pop's already got his second pot going."

"Yeah, no, that won't do." He made his way toward his cabin, motioning for her to follow. "I've got something better."

"Um, all right."

She followed until he stepped inside of his cabin, then she froze.

The screen door cracked open, then a hand popped out, holding a disposable mask. "For you, my lady."

She relaxed, slipping the springy elastics around her ears. "Thanks."

Tea took a tentative step into the cabin. Archer also wore a mask as he placed different coffee contraptions onto his kitchen counter. A Chemex. A scale. A hand grinder. Filters. A bag of Ethiopian coffee beans.

"Fancy," she said, watching as he measured out the beans on his scale.

He shrugged. "It's the only luxury I have time for these days."

"Are you really that busy?"

Archer glanced up and pointed to the wall behind her. She turned around, then sucked in a shocked breath.

The entire wall was covered in yellow sticky notes.

She stepped closer to read them, realizing each note was a task he needed to complete for Wild Pines.

"'Paint this depressing cabin,'" she read aloud. She scanned the walls, the spots of peeled paint hard to ignore now that she stood inside. She kept reading. "'Send June newsletter. Submit lake association fees. Fill out tax forms.'"

"Those will be the death of me," he grumbled.

"What, the sticky notes? Or the tax forms?"

"Yes."

The smell of freshly brewed coffee wafted from behind her. She turned, stepping close enough to get a glimpse of Archer in action while still keeping her distance.

His arms were relaxed as he worked, moving the kettle slowly over the fresh grounds in the Chemex, the coffee blooming on top and smelling like heaven on earth. She couldn't see his full face, but his eyes told the whole story. They were shining.

She was thankful she wore a mask that hid the ridiculous smile on her face as she watched her former friend. Or...current friend.

"Coffee, tattoos..." she said. "Any other hobbies I should know about?"

"Cocktails."

She lifted her brow. "Cocktails?"

He nodded. "I bartended in college, and found that I loved it a lot more than what I was studying in school. So I switched my major to hospitality and got a flair-master mixology certification."

"Dang. You can actually have a career mixing drinks?"

"Definitely." He removed the filter from the Chemex, then grabbed two Silver Falls mugs out of the cupboard behind him. "Although the pandemic certainly put a wrench in my plans. The cocktail lounge I worked at closed for the time being, and I have no idea if they're planning to open back up."

"At least you have this," she replied.

His jaw ticked as he poured the coffee. "Yeah. I guess."

Tea took the mug that he slid in her direction. His face remained tight and closed off. She felt the need to pry. She wanted to know how he really felt running Wild Pines after all of these years. But she also knew that she lost privileges to Archer and his feelings a long time ago. She would have to earn them back.

She wrapped a hand around the warm ceramic and pushed her mask down to take a sip. She closed her eyes and groaned, the taste of the coffee rich and nutty with a hint of chocolate and orange peel.

"That good, huh?"

She blinked her eyes open, blushing. "Sorry."

Archer also pushed down his mask to take a sip, but he held his mug close to his lips, grinning at her. "Don't be. I love watching someone enjoy a drink I made."

She slipped her mask back on, her face feeling hot. She blamed the coffee.

She turned to the wall of sticky notes, scanning the ones she read before. *Fill out tax forms. Submit lake association fees.*

"You know," she started. "I could fill out tax forms."

Archer walked around the counter to stand next to her. He placed his coffee on the small oval kitchen table beside him, then crossed his arms in front of his chest. Tea did her best to keep her eyes on his face and *not* the seven tattoos dotted across his bicep. His eyes remained stern as he stared at his sticky notes.

"I studied business, and I'm pretty good with numbers—"

"I know," he interrupted. "And I remember."

She pursed her lips. "Seriously, Archer. Let me help."

"I would not subject you to such hell."

"Why not? Please, I am *so bored*."

"You have a summer of literally nothing before you. Why would you want to work?" He reached for his coffee and stepped away from her, removing his mask to take a sip. "Plus, I can't pay you."

"I'll work for free."

He held a palm out to her, like he was trying to make a point. "Don't you have a master's degree? I'm pretty sure they tell you to *never* work for free."

Tea knew he was right, but now that the seed was planted in her head, she couldn't ignore it. She wanted to work. She *needed* to work. She needed something to get her out of bed before ten a.m.

She crossed her arms and sank into a hip, tapping her foot. "How about instead of payment, we make a deal."

He cocked a brow. "What kind of deal?"

She pointed to her mug. "Free coffee every day."

"That sounds like an awful deal."

"And I can put on my résumé that I worked as an assistant manager for the resort."

She watched a smirk peel from the corner of his mouth. "Clever."

"I hate the idea of finishing up this summer without gaining any experience."

"Tea, there's a *pandemic—*"

She swiped her arm in front of her, cutting him off. "Don't care. I want to be doing something. I need to get my mind off of...*life.*"

He sighed, looking like he wanted to dig into what she meant by that, but he didn't, and she was grateful for it. "You sure this is what you want?"

"Absolutely." She pointed to the laptop on the coffee table. "Now grab that and meet me outside where we can drink coffee without masks and I can take a look at your spreadsheets."

"*What* spreadsheets?"

She sucked in a breath. "*Archer.*"

He grinned. "Kidding. Let's go."

Chapter 8

Archer

AFTER NOT TALKING for eight years and ignoring each other outright during her first week at Wild Pines, Archer was surprised how easy it was to fall into a routine with Tea. He wondered at first if he made a mistake agreeing to let her work for him this summer. But when she tackled his spreadsheets and filled out those pesky task forms that first morning all before it was time for lunch, he stopped questioning it. Tea was good at what she did—which wasn't a surprise to him at all. Watching her speedily spit out numbers and organize finances reminded him of those summers in their high school years, when she would fill out thick books full of impossible equations preparing for all of the advanced college courses she signed up for. He would call her a nerd, she would laugh, then he would drag her down the lawn to go sailing.

If only it were that easy to get her in a boat now. Tea didn't have any desire to go near the water, except for dipping her toes in as she sat on the dock or stood on the beach. He wanted to push, but he knew it wasn't his place. Things were...fragile. Like a delicate vase that broke into dozens of pieces, glued carefully together but left with jagged scars. He knew saying something would be the equivalent of throwing that vase across the room.

So he made her coffee, as promised. He would fill his Chemex every morning, pour the hot coffee in a carafe, and place it on his kitchen table with a fresh mug. She would come over with a plate of whatever Kelly baked in Cabin B that morning—blueberry muffins, French breakfast puffs, sticky pecan rolls—and force Archer to eat one before he left her to settle in at his table with her laptop for the day. Caffeinated and buzzed on whatever sugary creation Tea bullied him into eating, he left her to handle the outdoor tasks. He pulled pesky weeds that lined the beach. He power washed the docks until they gleamed. He even had time to spray the lawn and kill the clovers that attracted too many bees. The flowers dotted across the lawn did make the resort seem quaint, but the bees that congregated around them made it hard for people to walk safely around bare-foot. And *everyone* walked around barefoot here.

That fourth day when he returned for lunch, frustrated by whoever didn't clean up after themselves in the fishing cabin *again*, he walked in on Tea examining his wall of sticky notes. Or, what *was* his wall of sticky notes.

Instead of a haphazard collection of tasks on his wall, she organized the squares into categories, each sticky note lined up vertically under a column of tasks. Outdoor repairs. Cleaning. Administrative to-do's. Silver Falls Lake Association. Community building. She even had a column for personal goals, like painting the cabin and replacing the ripped up old couch. As impressed as he was with the organization of it all, he couldn't help imagine what this wall would look like when the resort opened up fully. Would the number of sticky notes double when there were tasks to do for renters to visit, like cleaning the cabins and arranging boat and pontoon rentals? Would the organized system go back to complete chaos without Tea helping him keep things in line?

Archer watched her pull another note from the administrative tasks, one of the only columns that had less than three sticky notes under it.

He whistled. "Damn, Richards. You don't mess around."

Tea sipped her steaming coffee, still fresh from the carafe he made her. "What did you finish up?"

"Cleared the pine tree sap on the roof of the storage unit, and replaced the batteries for all the lift remotes. I even had time to fix Jorge's boat."

She pulled three sticky notes off the wall and crinkled them in her hand.

"Oh, and the fishing cabin, but that's usually not on there." He grumbled to himself as he made his way to his kitchen, snatching his bag of Wonder bread, then opening the fridge.

She squinted at him. "And why's that?"

He shrugged. "It's practically a daily occurrence. Someone is gutting fish and not cleaning the cabin."

She rolled her eyes. Archer watched as she grabbed the pad of sticky notes and scribbled something down. She smacked it on the wall, then pointed to it. "These are talking points that need to be addressed for the owners' meeting. We'll keep adding to it, then put together the agenda on July first and email it out to everyone so they know what needs to be discussed."

"Email it out? Doesn't that seem excessive?"

"Not if we want to get everything accomplished. Those meetings aren't exactly known for being productive."

"True that." He slathered yellow mustard onto his bread, then opened his package of bologna, not meeting her eyes as he said, "Make sure you add jet skis on there."

"Already done."

His head whipped in her direction. "How did you—?"

"It used to be on the agenda every year. I assumed."

Archer smiled, thankful his mask was covering his face. She was always ten steps ahead of everyone, capable and strong and reliable. And a tad bit stubborn. Or...more than a tad bit. It was one of the many reasons why he'd fallen for her in the first place. Not like that was the case now though.

He removed his mask to take a bite of his sandwich. "Want lunch?"

"What lunch are you offering?"

"Um, a sandwich?" he said with a mouth full of food.

She sighed. "What else do you have?"

"A jar of blackberry jam and a frozen pizza."

"Seriously? That's it?"

He shrugged. "I eat whatever I can steal from my mom's fridge when she's not in her cabin."

Tea sighed, then grabbed her tote bag on the table. "Okay, let's go."

"Go...where?"

"The grocery store? I'm not spending my summer in what you call a 'depressing cabin' with nothing to eat."

"You don't think this place is depressing?"

She didn't say anything as she slipped on her hat and made her way to his back door.

"Wait...you want to go into town? Like, right now?"

She nodded. "Right now."

"But, there's still daylight and there's so much to do—"

"Archer, I finished six of those administrative tasks in a single morning. Grab your keys and get your ass to your truck." She didn't even wait for him to respond as she whipped open the door and stepped out.

He coughed a laugh, then shoved the rest of his sandwich into his mouth and followed, jogging after her as he reached for his car keys in the pocket of his shorts. He caught up to her right before she reached for the handle leading to his passenger seat, and pressed a hand to the door to stop her.

Her forehead creased. "What's wrong?"

"Are you sure about this? We'll have to sit in my car at a much closer distance than six feet."

"We'll keep our masks on, and open the windows."

"Okay, but then we have to step into a *grocery store*, likely with people who aren't wearing masks."

"And so that means we can't buy food and eat?" She rolled her eyes. "I'll make a list as you drive so we can be quick."

He shook his head. "Still as stubborn as ever."

"Did you expect anything less?"

"You're right, my mistake. I forgot who I'm working with."

"Exactly. Now move."

He hesitated, then stepped away, opening the car door for her. "After you."

"Spring mix, goat cheese, balsamic vinaigrette, pecans, apples..." Tea scanned her list as she read it off. "Think you could grill some chicken for our salads?"

"You're really going to make me eat *salad*?"

"My salads then. You can keep eating sad bologna

sandwiches."

"Hey, I *like* sad bologna sandwiches."

She scribbled down more items on her list. "Oh, I know. You have for years."

Archer tightened his grip on the steering wheel. Having Tea back in his life again felt equal parts easy and incredibly complicated. Being her friend was never hard, the two of them fell back into their usual rhythms quickly. She would frown and stare at him seriously while he made jokes until she cracked a smile that made his day.

Then she went and said things like *that*, things that reminded him how deeply she knew him and how royally fucked up it was between them, and his stomach churned. He asked himself dozens of times if befriending her again was a bad idea...until he realized how helpful it was to have her working for him, and how easy it was to do his job with an extra set of hands. The past three nights he was able to finish up work while the sun still remained above the horizon, giving him enough time to bother Jorge for Pisco sours. Twice.

He wound his way through the curving streets, heading into downtown Silver Falls. Tall pine trees blanketed the sides of the road, with promising peeks of the shining blue lake in between shaded trunks. He glanced over at Tea, noticing the way her brow furrowed as she made her list, a small crease folding at the center of her forehead. Seeing it was like déjà vu—a regular occurrence for Archer these days.

His stomach churned again as he fixed his eyes back on the road.

"You could at least make them more exciting," Tea continued, oblivious to Archer's tense shoulders and his death grip on the steering wheel. "Maybe add in some vegetables or cheese and toast it on the griddle?"

He shook his head quickly. *Focus.* He relaxed his hands. "I'll grill chicken."

She didn't answer him. When they hit a red light he turned to face her, realizing that stern look with the crease in her forehead had zeroed in on him.

"That was way too easy," she finally answered. "You never back down from a fight."

He shrugged, looking back at the road. "Maybe you don't know me as well as you think."

It was a low blow, and he knew it. Her silence was telling enough as the light turned green and he made the turn onto Main Street.

She turned back to the checklist. "Yeah, maybe I don't if you're willing to *eat salad.*"

"I didn't say that!" He huffed. "We'll grill enough chicken so I can upgrade my sandwiches. Or make quesadillas."

He didn't need to look at her to know that she was smirking underneath that mask. He may not be eating salads, but they both knew she'd won.

Archer pulled into the busy parking lot of Hector's Food Mart. Shoppers grabbed carts and made their way into the store. Some of them wore masks. Some of them didn't.

He grimaced as he cut the ignition. "You sure you're up for this?"

"We have to eat, Arch."

Arch. His stomach clenched.

She handed him a slip of paper. "Here's your list, I've got a different one so we can move quickly."

"Okay, but—"

Tea hopped out of his truck. "Loser has to buy dinner!"

"Wait, *what?!*"

She was already gone, jogging toward the store. She turned back at him, her long red waves moving with the wind, and she flipped him off.

Heat flared in his chest. He jumped out of the truck. "Oh you are so *done!*"

She picked up her pace. He ran after her, but her long legs were too quick. When he got to the automatic sliding door, the rush of cool air chilling his skin, he couldn't find her at all.

He unwrinkled the list in his fist and read his items. *Chicken thighs. Olive oil. Italian seasoning. Canned tuna. Bread. Ice cream. Booze.*

His list was way too easy. She had to handle the produce, which would take much longer.

Archer snatched a basket as a cart whizzed by him.

It was Tea, her cart already packed with fruit and vegetables. "I would like Smile Pizza for dinner, please!"

He got moving, his heart already racing. "No way. A ghost kitchen opened up nearby, and I want their tacos!"

Three hours later, he ordered Smile Pizza for delivery.

"So, are we going to open up that carton of Blue Bunny? Or do you have some kind of lunch in mind that involves ice cream?"

Tea nibbled on her leftover crust, her knees tucked close to her chest as they sat on the porch outside of his cabin overlooking the lake. "It's for whenever. A freezer without ice cream is so sad."

"You don't even know what's in my freezer."

"Corn, expired frozen pizza, and a bottle of vodka."

"Never mind, you know what's in my freezer," he grumbled.

She smirked, then took a sip of her pale ale. Archer completely lost track of timing as he distracted himself with all of the microbrew options at the store, leaving him with no chance of winning their race. He picked out beer to go with pizza and accepted his fate.

He stuffed the rest of his crust in his mouth and chewed, watching the way Tea kept her eyes on the sailboats out on the lake, the water a golden peach color from the sun that'd begun to set.

That should be you out there, he wanted to say.

He coughed. "Didn't feel like having dinner with your grandparents tonight?"

She shrugged. "I kind of felt like you needed me."

He furrowed his brow. "Why?"

She brushed the crumbs off her hands, then took a pull of her beer before she answered. "Except for that first night we talked, you've avoided eating with your family, even though your mom is so insistent that you go over there."

Archer clenched his fists, then released them. Clenched, then released.

"You also kind of seem like you have a lot of anxiety about the pandemic."

This time his stomach didn't just churn. It dropped with a *thunk*, like a solid, heavy boulder.

Clench. Unclench.

She pointed to the cabin behind them. "Your place was practically empty of food. I was going to play it off as you being a guy or something, but this past week you kept joking that you couldn't make it over to your folks' place to steal food because they were always there. And you never once mentioned buying food at the store."

His chest flared. He sucked in a breath and looked out at the lake. He wasn't ready to tell her how the pandemic had upended his life.

She scratched at the paper label on her beer bottle, wet with condensation. "I don't think there's anything wrong with that, I also am scared about what's going on. But I can't figure out if the reason you're avoiding your family is because of COVID, or something else. That's why I made a game out of grocery shopping today. I hoped it would get your mind off having to go in."

Archer rested his elbows on his knees, pressing his fists into his eyes *hard*. He didn't want to admit any of his feelings with her. He wanted to keep things surface level and easy. Clear boundaries. Casual. Friends.

He could hear her shifting in her seat. "Arch?"

He sat up straight, eyes on the lake. "Yeah?"

"You mad?"

Yes. He closed his eyes, imagining building a brick wall around his heart. A strong defense. Unbreakable.

When he opened his eyes, he smiled. "I'm really busy. Grocery shopping or spending time with my family is the least of my priorities. As for the pandemic, I'm trying to keep everyone safe."

He knew in his heart he wasn't outright lying, because those *were* the reasons why. But by the way her chest fell at his response, Archer knew Tea wasn't buying it.

"Okay," she replied softly, pulling her gaze away, her eyes on the wet beer label she was scratching off. "Sorry I assumed."

He leaned back and crossed his arms. "All good."

Chapter 9

Tea

Loons prefer lakes with coves and islands for resting and nesting, but enough water for easily taking off in flight. They are excellent indicators of high-quality water, choosing unharmed lakes that haven't been heavily polluted or are free from disturbances such as human activity and motorboats. They also choose habitats with an abundance of fish.

"Nan tells me you're hanging out with Archer again."

Tea was standing on the beach, toes in the water, face shaded by her hat while the rest of her skin burned. She didn't care. Hearing her mom's voice was worth it, and she didn't dare face the reception black hole that existed between the beach and Cabin B. She'd rather burn outside then lose Mom on the phone in an attempt to get more sunscreen.

Unless they would be talking about Archer for too long.

"Yep," she answered, her tone curt. "Can't really avoid him if I'm going to be here for three months."

"Sure, that makes sense. But Nan says you spend every day at his cabin."

Tea sighed. She wasn't surprised in the slightest that Nan made it sound like something it was not. "I'm helping him out with some admin work this summer. Did she tell you that Archer took over as the Wild Pines manager?"

"Already? I thought Astor had another five years before he was going to hand it off."

Did he? Tea wouldn't have any idea, given how she gone mostly noncontact with anyone she knew at Wild Pines. "How did you know that?"

"He used to talk to your father about retiring and said 2025 was the year." Mom sighed. "But I can't blame him. This...*thing* happening right now changes a lot of perspectives."

Tea dug her feet deeper underwater, soft sand lodging between her toes. "I don't know much. Archer hasn't talked about it to me. Or about anything, honestly."

"Are things still weird between the two of you?"

Tea nodded her head, then realized her mother wouldn't be able to see her. "Yeah," she whispered in a soft tone, even though there wasn't anyone around her. It was too early for the cohort to be outside making noise. It was only her and Rhonda, who was down by the docks filling her boat with gas.

"How so?" Mom pried.

She exhaled. "He...doesn't really talk much. It's like he has this mask he puts up when he's around me. He's too nice, in a charming, cornfed-Midwest-boy kind of way. Like how he would act with all of the adults when we were kids."

She flicked some sand underwater, watching it float to the top of the water, then sink back down. "It's unnerving, honestly."

"Well, honey, things between the two of you didn't go so well that summer—"

"I know," she interrupted. She didn't need the reminder.

"Maybe give him some time?"

She squeezed her eyes shut. She really didn't want to be talking about this anymore. "I miss you."

"I miss you too. I'm trying my best to see if I can get some time off and drive up there in August—"

Tea perked up. "*Seriously?*"

She listened to her mom laugh, and it was the most beautiful sound. *God*, she missed her.

"Seriously," Mom replied. "But don't get your hopes up quite yet, okay? Trying to get out of the hospital at all is a challenge these days."

"But there's a chance?"

Mom hummed. "Yes. A chance."

Tea smiled and leaned her head back, the sun touching her face. "This is the best news."

The line went silent on the other end. Tea looked at her phone and realized she lost connection. She held her phone up to the sky, hoping to catch a couple magical bars.

Her phone dinged with a text message from Mom moments later, letting her know she was heading back into her shift.

Tea's shoulders fell, but then she reminded herself that she could potentially see her mother in less than two months. She grinned, tossing her phone on the chair behind her, and skipped to the cabin for sunscreen. She didn't even realize she was skipping until she made it back to the cabin, a moment of deep nostalgia flashing before her eyes. It all felt so familiar. For the first time since arriving at Silver Falls, she didn't hate the feeling.

THEY WERE TIPTOEING around each other.

After the night they ate pizza and Tea left a complacent Archer on his front porch, the two of them slipped into a cordial, surface-level work relationship. It felt weird seeing Archer in this light, especially when she once knew the side of him that would run around Wild Pines with his brother's underwear on his head, or cover his entire chest with body paint for the annual corn hole tournament. Adult Archer was too stoic, and it irked her. Even if Tea hadn't seen him grow up into the man he was now, she was fully convinced that this chill, distant, *nice* demeanor was a mask for whatever was going on behind it. But he told her she was wrong, and she was in no place to push further. Even if she didn't believe him in the slightest.

They used to be inseparable. During the off-season when she was back in New Jersey and he in Saint Paul, they kept in touch by sending ridiculous cards to one another throughout the year. Archer sent her a *Happy Grandparents Day* on her eighth birthday, so she sent a *Happy Bridal Shower* one on his, and the tradition of sending out-of-context cards stuck—until they both received cell phones and could text each other constantly. She knew so much about him then, and now that she was around him every day, she wished she still knew him that way. If only she hadn't messed it up so badly.

Her computer let out a bright *ding*, letting her know she had a new email.

She stood near the lake-facing window as she sipped on the coffee in her mug, her second one of the day thanks to the large, well-insulated carafe that Archer made her every morning. It was one in the afternoon, and the day was cloudy and rainy, but no wind whatsoever. Just a dead, wet, summer day. Everyone was cooped up in their cabins, and after months of having to stay holed up at home, she knew that was likely the last place any of the Wild Pines crew wanted to be.

Another *ding* from her computer.

She made her way back to Archer's desk, which she had turned into her workspace over the past couple of weeks. No more chaotic piles of pens and sticky pads and loose pieces of paper with rimmed coffee stains. Everything was in neat folders and piles, the pens placed inside a plastic University of Minnesota water cup she stole from his kitchen.

The first email was a reply from Rhonda, asking if they could add a debriefing of Silver Fall's new fishing regulations to the agenda that Tea had sent out that morning. She typed a reply, letting her know she would add it to the list.

The second was from the Ten Thousand Lake Loon Committee.

To: Theresa Richards
    (trichards@depaul.edu)

From: The Ten Thousand Lake Loon Committee
    (looncommittee@minnesota.org)

Hello, Theresa Richards!

Thank you for joining our efforts to protect and take care of our loons. Before starting with your local lake committee, we invite all new members to watch this virtual introduction video about our mission and our goals as a committee. We are dedicated to taking care of our loons across all of our ten thousand lakes, and it's because people like you make that possible.

When you are finished, please send your certificate of completion to your local chapter administrator.

We are thrilled to have your help protecting our loons, Theresa Richards!

The Ten Thousand Lake Loon Committee

"What are you reading there?"

Tea jumped, then slammed her laptop shut. She didn't even see him slip in.

Archer was standing rather close behind her, the mask on his face muffling his laugh.

She snatched the cloth mask on her desk and tied it behind her ears. "You can't do that."

"Do what? See what you're doing during precious work hours?"

"Technically, you don't pay me, so I can do whatever I want during work hours."

Even with his mask on, Tea could tell Archer was giving her a *Stop being such a smart-ass* face. He turned toward the kitchen and opened the fridge. "Salad again?"

"You really love that salad, huh?"

After a beat of silence, he closed the door of the fridge with his foot as he balanced the pile of containers with their pre-chopped salad ingredients. "Don't tell my mom. I still have her convinced that I'm allergic to spinach."

"*Still?* How has she not noticed that you're not actually allergic?"

The corners of his eyes crinkled, a clear sign that he was smiling behind that mask. "Can't exactly prove it if we never have it, right?"

She shook her head and opened her laptop back up. "Unbelievable."

They remained in silence for a couple of minutes, her typing away as Archer opened containers and dumped ingredients into two salad bowls.

"Seriously, what are you working on over there?" Archer asked.

At this point, she understood his tone. Before, he'd been playful and unserious, but this tone was adult Archer. Calm and business-like. A "get down to business" and "don't fuck around" kind of tone. The sound of it always made her core twist, and she couldn't decide if it was a bad thing...or a good thing.

"Rhonda requested that we add the new fishing regulations to the agenda for the owners' meeting tomorrow."

"No, we won't have time."

"Yes we will." Tea opened up the agenda document she emailed to the Wild Pines owners that morning. "We can easily talk through the fishing cabin, rental pricing for next season, and hiring maintenance in less than ten minutes, and discussing safety changes for the Fourth of July party shouldn't take more than ten either. The only topic that will probably take a lot of time is—"

"Jet skis."

"—jet skis," she said at the same time. "Right. So if we leave that at the end with minimal time, then we won't have much time to discuss it—"

"You're not accounting for the thirty to forty-five minutes of derailed conversation."

"We won't let that happen this year."

He looked up at her, brow raised. "Good luck with that."

She ignored him and opened up the document design file on her computer. "I'm going to squeeze it in before talking about the party. I'm estimating it will take five minutes."

Archer didn't reply at first. She listened as he unscrewed the bottle of dressing, then to the sound of tossing salads moments later. "Have you done this before? Run meetings?"

She shrugged. "No. But I did learn a bit about business management, which I think will help."

"You seem good at it."

She felt her face flush and quicked a glance at Archer. His eyes were on the bowls and not on her, unaware of the ridiculous way she was reacting to his compliment. Despite their shared lunch hours and the one time they had dinner together, their relationship was a business one. They didn't talk much, and based on the way Archer acted around her after what she said over pizza crusts last week, she had a feeling he wanted it that way.

She shook out of it, watching as he opened his fridge. "I also joined the loon committee."

He paused, the fridge door open. "Seriously?"

Her stomach dropped. "I mean, the association did email everyone saying they would *love* if one person from our resort was represented on the committee, and we all know that really means *do it or you're bear food*, so I thought I could do it that way no one else would..."

Her words faded out as Archer closed the door. He wasn't mad. He looked—amused. Or at least as amused as one could look with a blue mask on their face.

She glared at him. "Don't make fun of me."

He held up his hands. "Hey, I'm not the one walking around with loon books all the time."

She continued to glare. "I think they are fascinating."

"God, you are still *such* a nerd."

"There's nothing wrong with learning!"

"Absolutely. Someone has to love it."

"I do love it, thank you."

"You're welcome." He placed two cans of lemon seltzer on the counter, then opened his silverware drawer and retrieved two forks. "I'm pretty sure you're the only person I've ever seen read a textbook on loons from start to finish in one week."

She felt her face go hot again as she saved the updated document for the meeting's agenda, then hit *print*. "Did you know loons are loyal to their breeding territories and return to the spots where they nest each year?"

Archer looked out at the gray lake that matched the stormy clouds in the sky. "No, I didn't."

The air shifted between them. Her throat tightened. She went to grab her salad, desperate to change the subject. "So it's raining outside."

"Thank you, captain obvious."

She rolled her eyes. "Yes, but we can't eat *outside*, then."

His eyes widened. "Oh, I see." He scanned his cabin. "I'll eat on the couch, you eat at the table."

"I think—" Her words died in her throat.

His brows knitted together. "Think what? Spit it out."

She sighed. "It's been two weeks since I arrived, and I

think we've spent enough time together that we're proba-bly...um...okay?"

Tea watched his jaw work underneath his mask.

"Unless that makes you uncomfortable," she blurted. "But we only went to town once and I tested negative when I arrived—"

"All right."

Her eyes widened. "Yeah?"

She watched him slip his mask off with ease, amazed at how easy he felt to do so. Maybe she was wrong about his anxiety after all. "Yeah," he replied. "Let's eat."

They ate at opposite ends of the table, not exchanging words as they chewed on chicken, spring mix, apples, and goat cheese. They were already out of pecans, but that didn't stop Archer from making it every day. Tea wondered if he made the salad because he truly liked it, or if he made what Tea liked because she was working for free.

Tea bit on a slice of chicken, sneaking looks at Archer as he stared into his salad bowl, brow furrowed, and shoveled food into his mouth. She scanned the snake tattoo on his arm, then the skeleton one underneath it.

"How many tattoos do you have?"

A smirk curled at the corner of his lips. "One hundred and twelve."

Her mouth fell open.

He chuckled, pointing to his right arm. "This arm has twenty-three." He pointed to his left. "This one has nine-teen." He placed his hands on his legs. She ignored how big they looked on his thighs. "Forty-seven on my legs."

She nodded. "Okay...so that's ninety-one."

His smirk inched closer to a smile. "Twenty on my chest, and one on my back."

"Only one?"

"It's...kind of a big one."

Her eyes grew wide. "How big?"

"It's more ink than back at this point."

She whistled. "That's..."

His head cocked to the side. "Too many?"

She flushed. "*No.* No, no. You're just...really passionate about tattoos."

He shrugged. "A friend of mine owns a parlor in Minneapolis. When she started her apprenticeship back in college, I was happy being a person she could practice on. Prices were a lot cheaper, and she's never raised them on me since, even after opening up her own place."

Tea fished her fork around her salad, pretending like she was looking for an apple or something, even though her brain was spinning on the "she" in that sentence. She tattooed him one-hundred and twelve times? That was a lot of time to spend with someone of the opposite sex.

She coughed. "Minneapolis, huh?"

He nodded. "Been there since I finished undergrad. Well, except for my summer in New York."

She dropped her fork in her bowl. "You were in New York?"

Archer ran a hand down his face, looking like he very much regretted speaking.

"When?" she pried.

He scratched the back of his neck, then leaned his head up to look her in the eyes. "I interned at Mint Club three summers ago."

She felt like she was going to fall out of her chair. *That* was why he wasn't in those photos of Riley shaving Austin's head. Archer was in New York. He was less than an hour's train ride away from her all summer. They could have run into each other. Except she would have never gone to Mint

Club because it was a cocktail lounge with a massive line of customers and she barely had a budget to afford it anyway.

He continued, committed to explaining himself. "I lived in this shit studio that I rented with another intern in the East Village, but I was never there. I worked all of the time, learning from the mixologists, prepping garnishes and food before shifts, then staying late to clean."

Tea placed her feet on her chair and tucked her legs close.

"I would have called you, but I was..." He sighed, then rubbed his face again. "Scratch that. I wouldn't have called. I thought about it, but the few times I contemplated it, I got too mad to even click on your name."

She rested her chin on her knees, giving up on the filter she'd attempted before. *Who cares.* It was confession time, and she wanted some answers. "The tattoo artist. A friend or...did it ever turn to anything more?"

Archer placed his wrists on the table, then proceeded to open and close his fists, like he was squeezing two invisible stress balls. "Just a friend, Tea."

Tea exhaled.

"But she did introduce me to Janelle."

Her heart sank in her chest.

"Janelle and I dated for two years, but she broke things off in January."

She cleared her throat, keeping her eyes on him as she spoke. "I'm sorry."

He grabbed his fork and tossed it in his empty bowl. "One of her astrology friends told her that our stars didn't align anymore, or whatever bull shit she was fed. So she moved in with her parents, then remained there as things shut down."

She moved her legs to sit crisscross, then clasped her hands and placed them in her lap. "And now?"

"I packed my things, dropped off boxes to her parents when she wasn't there, then moved up here."

"So you left Minneapolis?"

"Temporarily. I'll move back…eventually. Things are too weird right now."

She nodded her head. "That makes sense."

Archer crossed his arms, his biceps flexing with the motion. "Okay, your turn. Spill."

"Spill what?"

"Date anyone?"

She flushed, feeling perplexed that Archer Vincent was sitting across the table, asking about her love life. It was too weird.

"N-no," she finally replied. "No one."

His eyebrows shot northward. "Seriously?"

"Seriously. I focused on school and spent a lot of time with Mom. We moved out of Morristown and I lived with her in a two-bedroom in New Brunswick while I was in undergrad, close to the hospital and to Rutgers, then moved to Chicago for grad school. We spent a lot of our summers in New York."

He cocked his head again, and the way it reminded her of the Archer of *before* made her smile. He may be covered in tattoos and give off a cool demeanor, but he still looked like the boy she once knew. Endlessly curious and playful. Always looking for a way to tease her.

"Why do I not believe you? You're telling me you've dated *no one*?"

"No one. I had…flings, I guess? But when things got too serious I cut it off."

The red that was streaked along his neck now climbed up to his cheeks.

"I...sorry," she rushed out.

He stood up, the chair screeching against the wood floor behind him. "Maybe we get back to work?"

She didn't say anything as she watched him quickly shove his mask into his pocket, then snatched his hat and placed it backward on his head as he left the cabin.

Chapter 10

Archer

ARCHER CARRIED two folded beach chairs to the circle he set up in the middle of the lawn, flinging them open and placing them down. Then he counted again, making sure he had enough chairs for the owners. The Richards. The Cortezes. The Brambles. The Jansens. The Vanderbergs. His parents. Then him, and Tea. He used his feet to measure out the space between each pair, then turned to where he would be sitting. Tea's chair seemed too close for comfort, but apparently they were past social distancing from one another now. Even though every bone in his body told him to *run*.

"Hey, sorry," Tea said from behind him.

He didn't look at her. "You're late."

It was obviously why she was apologizing, but setting up the circle took double the amount of time it should have without her. And he was pissed at her in general, but for reasons he didn't dare voice to her. It was easier to blame the chairs.

"Nan insisted I wait until she finished the muffins."

He whipped around to face her. She held a basket of blueberry muffins, steam rolling off the tops. "No."

She frowned. "Archer, you can't get coronavirus from food, you know that."

He huffed.

"Plus, Nan said she does it every year, and I think having a few things that feel normal will help people feel more comfortable about the things that are not."

He rubbed a hand down his face. "Fuck, fine."

She didn't respond as she handed him the stack of printed agendas. He placed a sheet down on each chair, Tea following from behind and securing each one with a warm muffin. Butter grease seeped from the paper wrappers onto the pages.

He sucked in a sharp breath.

"Comfort," she reminded him. "It's like this every year."

"Oh yeah, and how would you know that?"

She stood up straight, giving him that stubborn Tea expression he knew all too well. "Because Nan and Pop used to come home with a grease-and-coffee stained agenda every year."

He grunted and rolled his eyes.

Her brow pinched. "What's up with you? Can you handle this today?"

"I'm *fine*."

"Are you sure?"

He gave her a curt nod. "I...didn't get a good sleep last night. That's all."

It was actually the past few nights, but he didn't want to admit that to her. *I had a few flings.* Her words made his blood boil after she said them, leaving his anger at a constant simmer. The idea of some other prick putting their hands on her made it impossible to fall asleep. The first night he got out of bed and did seventy-five pushups before collapsing on the floor. Last night was eighty-three. He lay there after, in the dark with only the moonlight streaming through his window, still wide-eyed as the same thought haunted his ability to sleep: *It should have been me.*

She had made her choice, and he already promised himself he wouldn't go through that again. Even if the way she looked in her summer dress made him do a double take. He busied his hands with straightening the chairs when he caught himself counting the freckles dotted across her shoulders.

"Need to make a coffee?" she asked. "I could probably hold down the fort for a bit if you need it."

"No, it's fine." He flashed her a smile that he knew she wouldn't buy, so he ended the conversation by snatching a muffin out of her basket, peeling off the paper wrapper, and shoving the whole thing in his mouth.

She smirked, then took a seat in her chair, unwrapping a muffin herself. She picked at the top as she read through the agenda on her lap.

The Wild Pines crew was punctual, as usual. By ten o'clock, everyone was sitting in their respective spots. Jorge and Lily laughed at Rhonda as she finished off a joke then leaned back in her chair and flung an arm around Steph's shoulders, who was rolling her eyes. Sandy read through the agenda with glasses perched on her nose, tutting at whatever discussion point she was clearly disappointed by. Kelly was shouting the measurements and ingredients for her muffins to Victoria Jansen across the circle. Wayne sat beside her with a comical frown, like a kid who had a lollipop stolen from him. He looked out toward his docked boat and sighed audibly.

Archer coughed, then coughed louder to get people to

shut up. They eventually did. "Morning, everyone. Thank you for coming. I know this year looks a lot different than others—"

"Astor, are you seeing this?" Sandy interrupted. "We're talking about—"

Dad silenced her with a swipe of his hand. "I'm sure Archer has it all under control, Sandy."

His chest tightened. He sounded supportive, but his use of *I'm sure* didn't exactly instill confidence.

Tea cleared her throat. "We only have an hour, so let's get to it. Our first point of business is figuring out who isn't cleaning the fishing cabin."

Joel straightened his shoulders and glared at Archer. "I can't believe you haven't figured it out yet. Your father would have caught the culprit by now."

Archer tightened his grip on the handle of his chair.

"Okay, we're not doing this." Rhonda wagged her finger between Sandy and Joel. "New rule. No one compares Archer to Astor. If you haven't noticed—and you should have, because it's obvious—Archer has been doing an excellent job taking care of this place without any of our usual help."

Soft fingers brushed against his clenched white knuckles. He turned to Tea, who looked back at him with a reassuring smile. She nodded.

He loosened his grip.

Joel squared his shoulders toward Rhonda. "You're probably defending him because we all know it's your sons who are the problem."

Rhonda coughed out a laugh. "My sons? Have you met them? Do you ever seem them fish? Danny is way too busy posting TikTok videos of him dancing to some 'Savage' song, and Chris is too busy making out with Ashley."

Jorge jumped up from his seat. "They're *making out?!*"

A chaotic rush of yelling befell the group. Tea attempted to calm everyone down, but after a few *please calm downs* and *we have a lot to discuss*, she groaned in defeat and leaned back in her chair.

Archer smirked. "Still think we don't need to account for derailed conversation?"

She rolled her eyes.

THE DERAILED CONVERSATION cost them thirty-seven minutes of meeting time. Archer was also highly amused at how flustered Tea was when she realized she underestimated how long the Fourth of July party planning would take (twenty-six minutes). After concluding that they would proceed with the party outside as normal, the meeting had coasted past an hour and a half. They hadn't even touched on jet skis yet, and to Archer's dismay, they didn't find a solution for whoever was wreaking havoc in the finishing cabin.

They finally called for a vote by noon. Archer raised his hand in favor of jet skis, holding his promise to stand in solidarity with the twins. Tea, to his surprise, raised hers to be in solidarity with him. It made him look like less of a loser when everyone else voted against them for the umpteenth year in a row.

He was already dreading the horrifying fire pit he would wake up to in the morning.

Archer tucked his hands behind his head and reclined in his chair as the owners dispersed. Wayne was the first to bolt out of his seat and head straight for his boat. Kelly made her way to Victoria and Lily to talk more about who was cooking what for the party, the three of them standing a little too close for his comfort. But he lost all of his ability to fight them on anything, especially after they voted on continuing to pause the cleaning services that summer. It meant he was still on his own for all of it, and he desperately wanted a reprieve.

Tea sat silently next to him, legs tucked under her dress as she finished scribbling the meeting minutes in a spiral-bound notebook.

Rhonda crossed the circle, stepping up to Archer and blocking his view of the sun. "Beer?"

He cocked a brow. "A little too early for one, don't you think?"

"We're living through a global pandemic and you survived your first owners' meeting. I think we're past following societal norms."

He hesitated for a moment, then decided *fuck it*. He swiped his hands down his legs and grinned. "Yeah, okay. I'm in. Your porch?"

"No, we're going out."

He froze.

Rhonda pointed to Tea. "You coming?"

"For a drink?" she asked.

"No, for the rodeo. *Yes*, for a drink."

"The rodeo sounds unsanitary." Tea eyed him, under-standing painted clearly on her face. "And so does a bar."

"I promise, this one is outside and safe." She made her way backward toward Steph. "Meet us at my car in twenty."

He exhaled a low hum.

"Hey."

He turned to Tea, her face full of concern. He hated it.

"If you're not comfortable, you don't have to. We can say no."

Archer clenched his fists, then cracked his knuckles. "Are you comfortable?"

She shrugged. "Only if you are."

He wasn't comfortable with any of it. The owners standing close. A public bar. A global pandemic. The girl he'd thought he was in love with sitting next to him after all of these years.

But he wanted to get her to stop looking at him like that, like he was broken and needed fixing. He didn't need fixing. He was *fine*.

Archer hopped up and reached out his hands. "Give me your things. I'll drop them in the office."

She hesitated, some sort of thought flashing before her eyes. But then she smoothed out her features and handed him her notebook, laptop, extra agendas, and pens.

Twenty minutes later they sat in the back seat of Rhonda and Steph's Hatchback, the four of them masked up with windows down as they pulled away from the gravel driveway of Wild Pines.

Steph dragged the sunshade down in her front seat, then examined herself as she pulled her cropped hair into a small bun at the top of her head. "So, Tea, how does it feel to be back?"

"Odd."

"You're going to have to shout, I can't hear you with the windows open," Rhonda yelled.

"*Odd*," she repeated louder. "Most days I feel like it's all a dream."

"A good dream, or a bad one?" Steph asked.

"Both."

Archer turned his head a fraction so he could see her in

his periphery. Her legs were tucked close again, her dress draped over her thighs. She pinched the skin at her ankle with her thumb and pointer finger. It was the first time she admitted to how she was really feeling. Up until then, Archer had to pretend that everything was fine with her. He knew it wasn't. How could it be after everything?

Steph turned around in her seat to face Tea. "You know you can talk to us, right? We're always here for you."

She nodded. "Yeah, I know."

Rhonda lifted a finger, her other hand on the steering wheel. "But we understand if you would like us to keep our mouths shut until then."

Archer watched with bated breath as color flooded Tea's cheeks. "I appreciate that. Thank you."

They didn't say anything for the next fifteen minutes, not until they pulled into the dirt lot of a shit-colored shack in the middle of the woods. Music blared from speakers hanging at haphazard angles along the awning, and the place was packed. His chest tightened as he read a message painted in blue on the side wall.

Save yourself from the heat and get a drink!

"This feels like a bad idea," he grumbled low.

Rhonda parked and pointed to a picnic table on the lawn, far from the crowd. "We can snag that spot over there."

He unbuckled slowly. "And we get drinks...how? Do we have to go *in* there?"

A crowd of people spilled from inside the bar and out onto the patio underneath the awning, fans blasting cool air on their faces. The lawn was dotted with picnic tables, giving people enough space in case they wanted it.

"There's a walk-up bar on the other side for people who

don't want to go in." Steph unbuckled and opened her door. "I'll grab the first round."

"Are you sure? I can—"

"Archer, we watched you get fed to the wolves for two hours. Seriously. Drinks on me."

"I'll help you," Rhonda declared. "You guys grab the table."

Archer followed Tea across the lawn, distracted by the number of people around him. *How does anyone find this safe?* he thought. When he was in Minneapolis during the first few months of the pandemic, he measured every action he took, weighing the pros and cons and if it was worth putting other people at risk.

He heard someone call his name in the distance. He scanned the lawn, leaving Tea to herself as she sat down at the table.

"Archer!"

He turned, then felt his heart fall to his feet.

Janelle stood before him in a black tank top and cropped shorts, her dewy brown skin exposed and her braids hung loose by her shoulders.

His eyes widened. He felt like he couldn't breathe.

Clench. Unclench.

She smirked and crossed her arms. She didn't wear a mask, and he was thankful he still had his on. "What a coincidence, huh?"

He cleared his throat and looked down at his sneakers. "Not really. You know my family has a cabin up here, and yours isn't far either."

When he looked back up at her, Janelle's head was tilted to the side, that smirk still on her face. *Of course she knew.* This run-in didn't seem like a coincidence in the slightest. She looked...pleased. Like she meant for this to happen. She reached up and squeezed his arm, then stroked her thumb back and forth against his bicep. "You look good, Archie."

Clench. Unclench.

He rubbed the back of his neck to stop himself. He could have told her everything—about Dad handing resort management to him, about everything that happened at Hermes Lounge before lockdown—but he didn't feel the need to. Even if Janelle's demeanor was warm and inviting, their relationship felt safe. Comfortable. *Easy.* Drama free. Plus, if she didn't want to play any part in his life back in January, why would he expect her to care now?

He stepped out of her grasp. She slipped her hands in her back pockets. "Are you taking care of yourself, Archie?"

Archer dropped his hands to his sides. *Clench. Unclench.* Hearing her say his nickname made this entire interaction even more unsettling. When he opened his hands again to clench his fists, his left hand came around slender fingers.

Archer whirled his head around, finding Tea beside him. She stood there with that stubborn look in her eyes, mask still on as she held his hand. "Your beer is getting warm."

He looked above Tea's head and found Rhonda and Steph, four bottles of beer on the table. Rhonda did a little shimmy. Steph gave him a thumbs-up.

"And...you are?"

Archer turned back to Janelle. "This is Tea," he answered for her.

Janelle's eyes widened. "Tea? As in your childhood friend Tea?"

Heat crawled up his neck. Janelle didn't know *everything* about Tea, but she knew enough. Like how she was one of his closest friends growing up. How he developed a crush on her, then she disappeared. He'd conveniently left out the rest. "Yep."

Her eyes dipped to their joined hands. "Very...interesting."

Tea stepped back, pulling on Archer's hand. "Nice meeting you," she said to Janelle.

Archer followed Tea, hands still joined as they made their way to the picnic table. When they sat down, Tea made sure to sit right beside him, thigh to thigh, and placed a hand on his knee. He looked across the lawn. Janelle watched them from afar, head tilted. Then she stepped back and vanished into the thick crowd.

Chapter 11

Tea

*Loons can perform territorial rights when gliding
across the lake, by lifting their bodies and flapping
vigorously, which can happen when someone or
something threatening gets too close.*

Tea watched it all happen from a distance with a frog
lodged in her throat. The touch of his arm, the reassuring
smile, the stroke of her thumb. She would have left him
alone if he seemed relaxed by this woman's sudden appearance, but she saw the way his hands worked by his sides and
knew enough. He was uncomfortable and needed saving.
Knowing Archer, he was too polite to save himself.

Rhonda and Steph clinked bottles beside her.

"To making our son's love life more complicated," Steph
said.

Rhonda groaned. "Oh god, do you really think so? I
thought it was common knowledge that they kiss now. I've
seen it *twice*, and I'm afraid it's burned into my memory."

"Do you really think Ashley is running into Cabin G and saying to her father 'hey, guess whose tongue I swallowed today'?"

"Who's that?" Tea interrupted, listening to Rhonda cough out a laugh.

They paused, following Tea's gaze.

Rhonda tutted. "Ah, Janelle. Wondered when she would turn up. Her grandparents have a cabin on Angel Creek Lake. I think it's, what, a twenty-minute drive from here?"

Tea turned to the two of them and watched as Steph nodded, her eyes on Tea instead of her wife. Tea's face flushed at the silent examination—and the words unspoken.

"She certainly looks chummy for a woman who broke his heart six months ago," Rhonda continued.

"That bad, huh?" Tea whispered.

"Not like he would admit it. Archer is always hiding behind that mask of his. Metaphorically and *literally*." She tutted again. "According to Austin, things weren't nearly as bad as..."

Tea remained silent through her pause, watching the way Rhonda's cheeks flushed as she reached for her beer.

"Well, you know," Rhonda muttered.

She looked down at her hands, then up at Steph.

Steph nodded, then cocked her head in Archer's direction.

She nodded back, then got up from the picnic table and sidled up next to Archer, not allowing herself a moment to second-guess herself. Not when she heard Rhonda mumble "You're playing with fire, hon" as she walked away, and not when she stepped behind Archer and slipped her hand in his.

His head whipped around, and the look on his face was

shock before it smoothed into something relaxed but undeniably confused. He finished his niceties and then she dragged him away, making sure he sat close, keeping a hand on him in case Janelle came back. She hadn't a clue what his situation was like with Janelle and if she'd made a huge mistake by advancing on him like that, but by the way he relaxed under her touch and his eyes softened with gratitude at her saving him, she had a feeling he didn't want to give her another chance where he was alone.

Rhonda and Steph left to grab another round, but Tea remained, hand on his leg.

Archer loosened his clasped hands, slipping one underneath the table. He brushed her knuckles delicately with his thumb, and her stomach somersaulted. "You didn't have to pretend to be my girlfriend, you know."

"I know." She liked the way his hand felt on hers, his gentle touch and soft voice. "You looked like you were sinking out there."

"I was."

She lifted a brow. "Wow, you actually admitted a *feeling* to me."

The corner of his mouth dipped into his cheek, his eyes on their hands. "I have feelings."

"Not like you allow anyone to see them."

Archer peered up at her. "Maybe I find it easier that way."

"And then you sink and drown."

He removed his hand and didn't say anything.

Feeling bold, Tea grabbed for it before he could pull away further and squeezed his palm between her two hands, pressing them into the top of his thigh. "Allow *me* to see them, Arch."

He sighed, and for those couple breathes, Tea wondered

if she'd stepped too far. Then he looked down at their joined hands and relaxed, brushing his thumb against hers. "I've missed you."

The frog hopped back into her throat. "Me too," she whispered.

"There's so much I've wanted to tell you over the years, but I—" His exhale was deep and long. "I couldn't get myself to do it, and I'm sorry."

"You're not the one who needs to apologize, you know that."

His eyes were soft as he looked up at her and scanned her face. He opened his mouth, like he was going to actually invite the conversation, then snapped it shut. She decided to push it a little further.

"I'm sorry. About all of it." She looked away from him. It was too painful to see the expression on his face. The hurt that was all her doing. "I ran and I didn't talk to you and I let you think that I didn't care. I lost our friendship that day, and I would do anything to get it back."

When he didn't respond, she peered up at him. She expected hurt and anger, but was only met with a familiar gentleness.

"Let me *in*. Please," she whispered.

He sighed, shifting his head back, the brim of his hat shading his eyes from the bright sun. "What does that mean?"

She squeezed his hands. "Friendship, like the old days. You actually tell me things. Catch me up on the last eight years. *Talk to me.* You're so surface level, and it's killing me."

"Maybe I feel like I have to be. What if you run again?"

When she didn't respond, he shifted toward her and looked into her eyes. "Low blow, sorry."

"You're right, low blow. Does that mean you're ready to talk about it?"

He shook his head. "But I can give you friendship. Only if you promise me something."

"Anything."

"You have to get in the sailboat by the end of the summer."

She pursed her lips. "Okay, maybe not *anything*."

"You can't ignore it forever, Tea bag."

She scowled. "That's not my nickname."

He frowned. "I don't have a nickname for you."

She pointed a finger in his face. "Yes you do. Don't pretend like you forgot."

He shrugged. "I did forget."

"You son of a—"

"*Promise me*, Tea."

She exhaled.

He cocked his head. "If you're going to make me get uncomfortable with you and *let you in*, then it seems only fair, don't you think?"

She squeezed her eyes shut. "By the end of the summer?"

This time his hand squeezed hers. "Yes. You have all summer. And we'll do it whenever you want."

She inhaled sharply, letting it out slowly as she blinked her eyes open. Then she nodded.

His face split into a smile, but his response was cut off by Rhonda and Steph returning with four more bottles of beer.

"Favorite cocktail?"

Archer gave her a face. "That's like asking if I have a favorite child."

"Everyone *does* have a favorite child. They just don't want to admit it."

"Says the only-child kid."

Tea cocked her head. "But am I wrong?"

He grinned as he pressed his hands back on the dock, his legs dangling along the edge, bare feet trimming the water. "Naked and Famous. But it has to be made with Chichicapa or it's not worth it."

She smirked. "Not only do you have a favorite, but you're a *snob* about it."

Archer leaned over and bumped her with his shoulder, his pinky finger brushing against hers with the motion. His close proximity made her dizzy.

Since their conversation at the bar, Archer had unlocked an old part of himself, allowing Tea to get to know him again. They spent their evenings after work like this, finishing a bottle of wine as they rattled off endless questions to one another. Favorite class in college? Where did you spend your twenty-first birthday? What are you listening to right now? Do you still hate hot dogs? (Archer to Tea.) Do you still hate scary movies? (Tea to Archer.) They sat there on the dock, two empty jars and half a bottle of Sauvignon Blanc. It was nice to have him so close again, to hear him joke and laugh and *relax*. Even if conversation remained friendly and they skated around anything too deep. She wondered if Archer would always hold himself at a distance.

She pulled her feet close and itched the tops of them. "Your turn."

"Hmmmm." Archer scanned the lake, the orange glow

of the sunset gleaming off the silvery, sleek water. "Have you water skied since you were last here?"

She frowned. "No, unfortunately."

"Do you want to?"

Her feet throbbed. She scratched them again, her nails leaving red streaks. *God, they're itchy.* "It's been so long, I probably won't be able to get up."

His eyes blew wide. "Shall we test that theory?"

"Right *now*?"

He motioned a hand across the lake. "It's *glass* out there. No better time than the present."

"God, I don't—"

Archer hopped up. "Go get your suit on, and grab a life jacket."

Her chest flared with panic. "Arch, wait—"

"One ski, or two?" He walked away from her. "Who am I kidding? One."

"I really, *really* don't think—"

"Ten minutes!" he shouted, jogging his way to Rhonda's cabin.

Tea looked out at the lake, a deep frown settled on her mouth. The last time she water skied, her father was the one pulling her from Pop's boat. Archer sat at the rear, keeping an eye on her as she glided across the lake, cheering her on.

She gripped the end of the dock as she observed the water. It *was* like glass. She could practically hear her father shouting from the cabin, telling her to get her suit on already.

She turned her head, realizing it was actually Archer bellowing at her. She rubbed at her feet once more, then stood up slowly, eyes scanning the golden sky sprinkled with tall pine trees.

"I miss you," she whispered, then made her way down the dock.

Rhonda cut the engine of her boat as Archer tossed the water ski into the water. "Now remember, grip the handle hard and lean back, then—"

"Archer, please shut up. It may have been eight years, but I haven't forgotten what to do."

He held up his hands. "All right, all right, just helping you out."

She grumbled as she eyed the water. Since arriving at Silver Falls, Tea hadn't allowed herself to go in the water beyond getting her feet wet. Jumping in felt like a *commitment*. It meant finally facing the inevitable.

"Don't make me push you."

She whipped her head around and glared at him. "Don't make me push *you*."

"I'm ready to push *both* of you in if one of you doesn't shut up and get in the water," Rhonda chimed in.

Archer raised a brow. "Let's go, Tea bag."

She squinted her eyes. "Still not the nickname."

He shrugged, that condescending smirk never leaving his face. "What nickname?"

Rhonda helped up three fingers. "Three." She dropped one into her palm. "Two."

Tea sucked in a breath, held her arms tight to her life jacket, then jumped in.

The water felt like ice. Cold licked her skin as she surfaced for air, tiny droplets of water running down her lashes. "*So cold!*" she squealed.

Archer crossed his arms as he looked down at her from the boat. "When did you become such a wimp?"

Tea snatched the water ski. "When did you become such a tyrant?" she grumbled.

"I always have been." He tossed the bright blue handle into the water. "You ready for this?"

"Not even in the slightest."

She slipped her right foot into the ski as Rhonda aligned the boat, the handle dragging behind it. Tea snatched it and grasped tightly, feeling the tug of the boat as Rhonda inched forward.

"Ready!?" Archer yelled.

The pull of the boat had her leaning sideways, water catching in her mouth. She spit it out and flicked wet hair out of her face, her stomach tight with nerves. Once she righted herself, feeling like she had a firm grasp, she yelled *"Ready!"*

The boat roared to life and the pull was agonizing, but she kept leaning back, pressing the water with the ski to try to right herself. The handle slipped from her grip, and she fell backward into the lake, the ski flying off her foot and slapping down on the lake a couple of yards in the distance.

The boat puttered toward her as she scrambled to grab the ski.

Archer was kneeling down, leaning over the edge. "It's okay, the first try is always the hardest."

She brushed wet hair from her face. "I'm also twenty-five pounds heavier than I was as a teenager. Makes it more difficult."

"You mean twenty-five pounds curvier."

She blinked at him, droplets of water running down her cheek.

Archer smirked. "Curvy is good."

"I didn't say it wasn't," she replied.

"Good. Just making sure."

Tea slipped the ski back on her foot, consciously averting her eyes. Was he...*flirting?* Or simply being insufferable? "Let's go again."

"You sure? Do you want to try with a second ski?"

She glared at him. "Never. I'm not giving up."

He grinned. "There's the stubborn Tea I missed so much."

She rolled her eyes as she grabbed for the handle and Rhonda righted the boat.

"Ready!?" Rhonda yelled.

Tea nodded. "Go!"

The handle slipped from her hands again. Then again. And again. The fifth time around, she gripped the handle so tightly, she ended up falling forward and face planting into the water. Her foot slipped out of the ski, the tip of it slamming into her upper thigh.

She rolled over in the water, face to the sky, and groaned as the boat approached.

"You all right?" Archer asked, his face tight with concern.

"No. This is impossible."

"Want to try one more time?"

She shook her head. "It's pointless now. My arms are goo."

Archer reached a hand out to her. She stepped onto the back ladder and let him pull her into the boat, then wrapped a towel around her arms. "Proud of you," he murmured.

She brushed hair out of her face and noticed he was also wearing a life jacket. "You're going?"

"Duh?"

She sat down and watched Archer hop in, completely unfazed by the cold. He slipped on the ski with practiced ease, then slicked his hair back from his forehead as he grappled the handle. Without any hesitation, he yelled, *"Go!"*

The engine bellowed, and in less than three seconds, he popped out of the water. He flicked hair out of his face as Rhonda steered the boat and Archer began to fly.

Tea sat there in stunned silence as she watched him skim the surface of the lake, the sun glistening along the water as he rode the boat's wake, making sharp turns as water sprinkled along his path.

Rhonda made a swinging motion with her hand, signaling a sharp turn. When she steered the boat in almost a full one-eighty, Archer glided along with it, allowing the swing of the boat to steer him past the wake and along the side where the water was calm. He grinned as he leaned back, skimming a hand along the lake's surface, then brushed his hair back with his hand.

Then he looked at her, and he had the audacity to *wink*.

Tea's mouth fell open. Archer was always the best water skier of the group, yet somehow, he was even *better* now. She could tell he'd practiced over the years. It was equally thrilling and devastating to watch. It reminded her of all that she missed, and all that she lost. It also reminded her how much she loved this place and being out on the water. It stirred something deep inside her heart. She didn't hate the feeling of it. She let it marinate as she watched him ride the waves.

She rubbed her thigh, already bruising from her last fall, and promised herself that she would pop out of the water with her ski this summer. Even if it took her weeks of trying and failing again and again, she would do it. For Archer. For her father. For herself.

Archer eventually let go and sank in the water. He climbed on the boat and unhooked his life jacket, giving Tea a full view of his tattooed chest and arms. When he turned to grab a towel, Tea's mouth fell open once more.

The tattoo on his back was a replica of the view from his family's cabin window. The grass of Wild Pines with clovers dotted along the lawn. A sailboat rode across the glistening lake with a glowing sun. Two loons swam in the water and in the distance, two kids jumped from the dock, hands grasped tightly.

Archer rubbed his wet hair with his towel as he turned to her. He looked at her expression, and his grin from earlier melted into a knowing soft smile. He took a seat next to her as Rhonda steered their boat in the direction of Wild Pines.

Tea wrapped her towel tight around her shoulders and brought her knees to her chest. "Was that your first tattoo?"

He shook his head. "It was one of the first though."

She tilted her head and pressed a cheek to her knee. "When did you get it?"

He sighed, his eyes not leaving her face. "October 2012."

Tea squeezed her eyes shut, emotion stealing her breath away. She understood his meaning. It was the month Dad died.

Chapter 12

Archer

Archer shucked off his soaked-through T-shirt and swung open the door to his cabin. "Let me wash up first, then I'll make us some lunch—"

"*Arrggggghhh!*"

He stopped moving, and turned to Tea on the couch. Her legs were curled up close to her chest and she was scratching her feet so aggressively, he felt alarmed. "Uh, everything okay over there?"

"My. Feet. Are. *Killing. Me.*"

Archer took a tentative step toward her and eyed the tops of her bare feet. They were covered with small, splotchy red spots and streaked marks from her nails.

"Uh oh," he whispered.

Her gaze snapped to him. "What?"

"You...well, um—"

"Bug bites, I know." She kept itching. "They're eating me alive."

"No, that's not bug bites." He took a seat next to her.

She stopped her itching. "It's not?"

"No, it's not. And I would stop itching. It's only going to make it worse."

"That's like putting a fishing pole in front of Pop and telling him he's not allowed to touch it all day." She touched her feet again.

"Tea, don't." He lunged forward and grasped her wrists to stop her. "You have swimmer's itch."

Her eyes went wide. "No."

He nodded slowly. "I'm sorry, but yes. It looks like you do."

She looked down at her feet, then back up to him in horror. "But I've *never* had swimmer's itch."

"Sure, when you were a teenager with the immune system of a steel wall."

Tea squirmed, looking rather panicked.

He squeezed her wrists. The pressure seemed to have distracted her from sudden panic. She fixed her stare on the placement of his hands. He brushed his thumbs across her pulse, watching her shoulders relax with each stroke.

"What do I do?" she asked, desperation etched in her voice.

"Well, for starters, don't panic."

"Too late for that."

He squeezed again. "Secondly, don't scratch."

"Also too late for that."

"I have a cream you can use that will help with the itching."

"Sure, yeah, okay."

He lifted her arms. "I'm going to give these back to you. Can you handle it?"

She nodded. Archer stood up and made his way for the bathroom, grabbing hydrocortisone cream and aloe. He settled back on the couch and held them out to her.

Tea stared at them with wide eyes, looking shocked.

"It's not going to kill you, Tea, I promise."

She remained silent and stunned.

He sighed, grabbing her feet and placing them on his lap. He then unscrewed the ointment and dotted the tops before massaging it in. Then he repeated the same with the aloe.

Tea bit her bottom lip. "This is so embarrassing."

Archer shook his head. "It's okay, I was freaked out the first time I got it."

"When did it happen to you?"

"Hmm, five summers ago? You have it easy. I had it all over my legs and my ass."

She coughed a laugh and covered her mouth. Then her head dipped down as she let out a soft moan.

He looked down at his lap, realizing he was still massaging her feet, even after the aloe was thoroughly worked into her skin. He dropped his hands.

She looked up at him, then tilted her head. "You're not wearing a shirt."

Archer looked down at his bare chest. "Sorry, I was in the process of changing it."

He didn't move at first, watching the way she scanned the tattoos on his chest. He hesitated, enjoying the way her eyes roamed over him. Then he caught himself, moving her feet off his lap and returning to his room. "Any updates?" he called after her, sliding open the top dresser drawer.

"Nothing important. The loon committee is meeting in a few weeks over Zoom, and the association said our fee payments went through."

He slipped the shirt on. "Remind me how we were able to manage the payment without asking the owners for it?"

"We're not paying for help, which means we have a

little bit of savings we can work with from last summer. We can remind owners after the Fourth of July, and offer small payment plans if we think people can't afford it in full this year."

He swiped on deodorant. "And the party?"

"We're going to get *hammered,* that's for sure."

Archer stood up straight. That voice wasn't soft or bright. It was burly and rich...and recognizable.

He lunged from his room, finding Austin standing on his porch, nose pressed into the screen door. Riley was tucked underneath his arm beside him, a lollipop dangling from her mouth.

"Holy mother fucking shit," Archer breathed.

"Holy mother fucking shit right back at ya," Austin replied, grinning ear to ear. He swung the door open of the cabin and the two of them stumbled in. Austin released his hold on his wife, then wrapped his arms around Archer and slapped his back.

Archer gripped tight. "Why the hell are you here and not in Fargo?"

"*Fuck* Fargo." Austin squeezed tighter. "I haven't missed a Wild Pines Fourth of July party *ever*, and I'm not letting some fucking pandemic ruin my streak."

Archer stepped back, realizing he wasn't wearing a mask. "Oh crap, I—"

Riley reached out and squeezed his arm, pulling him down so she could kiss him on the cheek. "Don't worry, BILF, we quarantined and drove here. And got tested. Larissa was *persistent*."

"BILF?"

Austin and Riley looked at each other with confusion, then both turned their gaze to the couch.

Tea held tightly to her knees, watching the entire interaction unfold with a look that seemed to be a mixture of fear...and longing.

Riley placed a hand over her mouth.

"Holy mother fucking shit indeed," Austin said.

"Were you really not going to tell me that Tea was here and that you guys made up?"

Archer scratched his neck, watching Tea and Riley set up chairs on the beach. Two bottles of wine and four glasses sat on the table close by. "I never said I wasn't going to tell you."

"Yet she's been here, what, a month?" Austin pulled on the beer in his hand. "I love how Riley grabbed me a glass like she thinks I'll magically turn into a wine person at this exact moment."

"What do you have against wine?"

"You're changing the subject."

"You're the one who changed it."

Austin turned around to face Archer, his back to the women. "Seriously, Arch, what the hell? I had to pull you out of your bed every goddamn day after everything went down, and you're letting her waltz right back into your life like she didn't rip your heart out and feed it to the bears?"

He glared at his brother. "Hey, it's not my fault that she had nowhere else to go."

"But it *is* your fault to have her working for you."

"We're *friends*, Austin."

"Can you actually be friends with her? Have you ever truly only been friends with her?"

Archer rolled his jaw.

"I watched you *obsess* over Tea my whole life. Friends don't stare out the window of the cabin during dinner, watching someone read and drink tea. Friends don't make sure they always sit next to each other at the bonfire, or send those damn cards—"

"And what, you were so much better with Riley?"

"Dude, I've *always* been obsessed with Riley. You're proving my point."

Archer turned away from his brother, staring right into the sun. He removed his flat brim and scratched his head.

"Still haven't lost your hair, huh?" Austin asked.

"Still bald as fuck, huh?"

Austin grinned as he lifted his fraying tucker cap. "Bald as fuck and very sunburnt."

Archer shook his head.

"Dude." Austin placed his beer on the lawn, then gripped Archer's shoulders. "I love you like a brother."

"I *am* your brother, fuckface."

Austin tapped Archer's cheek *hard*, enough that it could be defined as a slap. Archer let it slide—he would get him back later. "I say that because I love you like a friend *and* a brother, and I really don't want to watch you fall apart again. It was scary."

"I won't, we're just—"

The lift of his brow silenced Archer, draining the fight from him.

"Promise me something," Austin replied roughly.

He squinted his eyes.

"Promise me that when things go down—"

"*If* they go down—"

"Don't fucking play me, I'm not blind."

Archer swallowed.

"Promise me *when* things go down, you'll actually take care of yourself. Put yourself first."

"What does that mean?"

Austin dropped his hands then scratched his beard, which covered a lot more of his face compared to the last time Archer saw him at Christmas. "It means that you'll stand up for yourself and what you want. Don't give up on the dream."

Clench. Unclench. "The dream."

"You know, opening up your own cocktail spot in Minneapolis, maybe starting a cocktail school, expanding to a few more locations in the city—"

He gave his brother the glare of death. "I didn't forget my own dream."

Austin threw up his hands. "All right, calm down. I'm not sure these days."

Archer gestured toward Wild Pines, sweeping his hand across the line of cabins. "If you haven't noticed, I'm kind of busy."

"With Wild Pines shit? Seriously, you don't have to be the person running this place."

Heat flared in his chest. "Then who *will* Austin?! There's *no one*!"

His voice echoed across the lawn.

Tea and Riley startled in their chairs, turning their heads in their direction.

Austin grabbed his arm and pulled him away from their gaze, to the shadows of his cabin. "Is that really how you feel? That there's no one else so you have to do the job?"

Archer hesitated. It was enough to send a message to his brother.

"Why didn't you tell me?" Austin pried. "I thought you loved this place. I thought this was *part* of your dream."

"Because I knew you never wanted it, and I couldn't let Dad down."

"You could have. I didn't allow myself to be burdened by it, and neither should you."

Archer flipped his hat backward and rubbed his eyes. "It's...fine. For now. It's not like cocktail lounges are open."

Austin squinted his eyes. "Fine. But when they reopen —because they *will*, man—I want a thorough update. It's not like Dad sat around twiddling his thumbs during the off season, he helped manage that Hy-Vee in Saint Paul during the winter. You'll have the opportunity to still do your thing." He pointed to the women, now back to settling in their chairs, avoiding them. "And I mean, of course you're fine right now. You have some smoking hot help to keep you company."

Archer flipped him off.

Austin's laugh felt like it rumbled the earth beneath them. "I knew you were still sweet on her."

Archer looked up to the sky and didn't say anything. He wanted to tell his asshole of a brother that he was wrong, but the words wouldn't surface. *Was* he still sweet on her?

Austin poked a finger to the center of his chest, then pressed hard. "No compromising. No falling apart."

"You're not going to tell me to stay away from her after everything that happened, or some other kind of big brotherly bullshit?"

Austin slapped his back. "That's like telling my bald as fuck head to grow some goddamn hair."

ARCHER KEPT quiet as he listened to Tea catch up with Riley and Austin. She asked about their wedding, about their home and their friends in Fargo, and the day that Austin decided to give up on his hair entirely and shave his head. Her face flushed as she chuckled along with Riley and Austin's persistent bickering, which Archer *unfortunately* knew was his brother and sister-in-law's favorite version of foreplay.

Tea reached to itch her feet, then stopped herself, eyes sliding to him. She smiled like she got caught, then sat on her hands.

His body hummed. He wanted to reach out and touch her again, to hear those soft moans escape her lips one more time. He wondered what kind of foreplay she enjoyed.

Fuck. Less than a week into being "friends" and he was already imagining taking her clothes off. He hated admitting when his brother was right. It was horrid for Austin's ego.

Chapter 13

Tea

Loons will choose quiet, protected places for their nests, which are built in bays or sheltered islands close to the water. The male loon will select the nesting site before a female mate is chosen.

"So, what's a BILF?"

Riley spread the plastic cloth across the folding table. "Brother-in-law for life, obviously."

Tea taped down the corners, but she wasn't even sure it was needed. The day was hot and the wind was coming from the south. Or, lack *of* wind. It was dead without a cloud in the sky. "That makes more sense," she replied.

"Why, what did *you* think it stood for?"

Her face flushed. "Oh...you know. When people say stuff like MILF or DILF, they mean..."

Riley frowned. "No, I don't know what you mean."

Her flush deepened. "You know...brother I'd like to..."

Riley smirked at her.

Tea grumbled. "You're messing with me."

She whipped her head back and laughed so hard birds flew away from the trees across the lawn. She wiped her eyes, still laughing. "Oh no, honey. You're the only one blessed with that honor."

Tea ripped open the package of patriotic paper plates. "Not the only one," she grumbled.

She knew she had absolutely no right to be jealous, but being hit with how gorgeous Janelle was and hearing that Archer dated her for *two years* never seemed to leave her head.

Friends. We're supposed to be friends. I should be happy for his relationships.

Her stomach soured at the thought.

Riley seemed unfazed as she opened boxes of plasticware. "Well, the only one at Wild Pines. Hey, do you ever hear from Quentin and Deanna? I miss those losers."

"No, never." Tea pulled her hair into a ponytail, thankful for Riley's quick change of subject. "You?"

"Nah. Quentin moved to San Diego and I think Deanna is in Austin? Kind of bums me out. We were all so close." Riley glanced out at the water and paused, her eyes on the teenagers out on the raft. She pursed her lips, then did a scan of the lawn before reaching for her vape in her pocket and taking a pull. "Listen, Tea. I know you guys are chummy and all that again, but I need you to know how bad it was after what you did."

Tea sucked in a breath. "I get it. I broke his heart."

"You didn't break his heart. You eviscerated it. I have never seen anyone fall apart like that before."

She winced. "That bad?"

"Worse than bad." Riley coughed. "Don't fuck with him again, okay?"

She didn't even know how to respond to that except with a nod.

Riley nodded back. "You could have texted me back, you know. A Facebook message or *something*."

Emotion clogged her throat. "I know."

She sighed. "Listen, I get it. You lost your dad, and I am still so sorry about that. He made every summer here *better*." She took another pull of her vape, then exhaled a long puff. "I wish you didn't shut us all out though."

"And learn about all the ways Archer was falling apart?"

The door of Cabin F swung open. Archer was carrying a slow cooker, his mother tucking serving utensils under his arm to carry. Austin followed, balancing two trays in his hands, bellowing out a laugh at something Astor said from inside.

Archer scanned the lawn, then locked eyes with her. He tilted his head, clocking her expression from yards away.

"Just friends my ass," Riley mumbled next to her. "And I thought Austin and I were complicated."

Tea kept her eyes on them as they strode across the lawn. "What do you mean you guys are complicated? You were always meant to be together."

"So were you."

Tea faced Riley to retort, but was cut off by Austin. He plopped the trays of pulled pork sliders and finger Jell-O on the table, then grabbed for his wife, kissing her hard on the mouth.

A hand grabbed for her shoulder and turned her around. "No need to watch that."

She flushed, her mind melting down to one single focal point: the warm tattooed hand on her skin.

"How are your feet?" he asked.

She looked down at her bare feet in the grass, her mind drawing a blank.

He squeezed her shoulder. "Are my creams helping, or...?"

"Oh, right." She nodded her head, snapping out of it. "Yes, thank you. Nan is also making me take Benadryl around the clock, which makes me a little drowsy, but it's helping."

"Good." He looked down at her leg. "Your bruise doesn't look as scary as yesterday."

She looked down at the spot breaking out of her denim cut-offs. The bruise was yellowing, but it still was obvious enough to be utterly embarrassing—a physical reminder that after her second and third attempts out on the water this week, she still couldn't manage to get up. "Maybe I can't water ski anymore."

"You will. We just need to practice."

She bit her bottom lip and looked out at the lake.

"You okay?"

She turned, and his face was wrinkled with concern.

"Yeah," she replied. "Why wouldn't I be?"

"You kind of looked like you saw a ghost when we made our way over here."

Because I did. The ghost of summers' past, telling her how much she screwed everything up. With her grandparents. With Riley. With Archer.

"I think I'm tired," she lied.

"Too tired to be my teammate for the corn hole tournament?"

She narrowed her eyes. "Never."

He grinned. "Good. Because I haven't won in eight fucking years, and I'm in the mood to whip some ass."

THERE WAS something nice about having traditions in such an unprecedented time, or at least that's how Tea felt as she watched the rest of the Wild Pines crew gather at the center of the lawn, placing their trays of potluck items on the table before assembling around the flagpole. Everyone had come dressed in their red, white, and blue best, some in swimsuits, some in summer dresses and shorts. No one wore shoes. Gathering together for the Fourth of July felt like slipping into a worn pair of comfortable jeans. It was familiar, and as she scanned the faces of everyone in the circle, she could see plainly that the others felt the same. There were smiles and lots of laughing as old inside jokes were thrown around. Even if it was a risk, she knew this moment was much needed. People weren't meant to be kept at a social distance. They needed each other.

She felt a twinge in her heart at the thought. Hadn't she been keeping herself at a social distance already, even before the pandemic? Except for her mom, she didn't have anyone else in her life to share her moments with, or even talk to about her father.

At the thought of her father, she turned to face Archer. He stood close beside her, his hands cupped in front of him, the tendons in them clenching and unclenching, as he scanned the crowd. After almost a month of working for him, Tea knew this was his usual response when he was stressed about something but didn't want to raise his voice.

"Arch."

He turned to her, his gaze like ice.

"Traditions like these hold us together. We need each other. It's going to be okay."

He exhaled, his arms still tense. "Then why do I feel like this is a very bad idea?"

"Do you want to leave?"

He sucked in a breath and looked at the cloudless sky.

"We're taking every precaution we possibly can."

"I know," he murmured. "I simply want to protect everyone. Keep them safe. I don't want to be the cause of any more spread, or to create any threats for those who are immunocompromised."

Tea felt in her gut yet again that there was more to Archer's words then he was letting on. She reached for his arm and squeezed it, watched him track the movement. "You've kept everyone safe, and if people didn't feel that way, they wouldn't be here today."

He nodded, his eyes still on her hand on his bicep.

"Should we start this thing?" Rhonda boomed from across the circle.

Archer stepped away from her grasp and turned around. "Yes, let's do it."

The Wild Pines crew remained silent as Danny and Chris unfolded the flag, then helped their moms connect it to the flagpole. Steph lifted it to the top, then pressed her hand to her heart and led everyone in the Pledge of Allegiance. Ashley sang a soft "Star Spangled Banner," and Jorge's face was covered in tears as his daughter finished, the group hollering and cheering by the end of it.

Archer cleared his throat. The noise settled as he stepped forward. "Okay everyone, please go to the table in small groups so we all don't crowd—"

Austin bolted for the food table. Danny and Chris followed, as well as the rest of the teenager gang.

"—at once." He sighed. "Dig in."

The table spread was an impressive feat of Midwest potluck staples. Pulled pork sandwiches, grilled brats with sauerkraut, corn on the cob, slow cookers full of mac and cheese and cocktail wieners swimming in a sweet and sour sauce, fried fish, Scotcharoos, finger Jello, mini strawberry Rhubarb hand pies, peanut butter Buckeyes, and every possible kind of whipped or creamy salad imaginable. Macaroni salad, potato salad, Snickers salad. It was more than enough food for all of them, almost as if the crew was trying to make up for all of the lost potlucks of the year. By the looks on their shining faces, it was the right move. Everyone was happy and laughing as they sat down at picnic tables to eat lunch. Someone had flicked on music from a Bluetooth speaker, a few people dancing as they went to take their seats.

Archer and Tea sat at a distance with Austin and Riley. They listened to Austin rattle off ridiculous stories about summers of the past, recalling the heinous things he and Archer got up to. She sat there with a smile on her face, listening to Archer belly laugh to Austin's retelling of the time they filled Astor's Yeti cooler with broasted chicken and swam it to the dock to eat it, the cooler bag smelling like greasy chicken for weeks after. His shoulders relaxed as the hour passed. At one point he placed his hands down on the bench, his fingers brushing against Tea's thigh. She knew it probably didn't mean anything—the bench was small and he was big and there was barely any room between the two of them. But that didn't stop her heart from hammering in her chest from the small amount of contact.

Eventually people got up from their seats and mingled, watching as Danny and Chris set up the eight boards and bean bags for the tournament. Archer took names of the different pairs and began putting them in brackets, doing his best to remain calm as Austin argued loudly with him. Archer kept shaking his head at him.

Tea tied her hair into a ponytail and walked up to them.

Austin's eyes narrowed into slits as she approached. "You're ruining the dream team."

Archer scoffed. "The dream team? Austin, I have lost the past eight summers paired with you. There's no dream team if there isn't even a *dream*."

Austin threw up his arms. "But I'm your brother!"

"That doesn't make you the best partner." Archer cocked his head at Tea. "She's the dream."

Her face flushed.

"D-dream *team*," he stuttered. "She's the dream team."

Austin rolled his eyes, told Archer to put him down with Riley, then stalked off.

She glanced up at Archer, noticing the pink in his cheeks.

She smirked. "I'm *the dream*, huh?"

"Shove it," he grumbled.

She framed her face with her hands, feigning inno-cence, ready to mess with him. "Am I really *that dreamy?*"

He rolled his eyes and dropped his clipboard on the picnic table beside him, then grabbed her chin, giving her a small yank toward him.

She gasped at his assertive touch. Her lips parted as she looked up at him.

He glared back at her. "It's time to get your game face on. We can't lose."

She squinted. "My game face *is* on."

He shook his head then his other hand was on her face, his thumb drawing two lines underneath her eyes.

She smiled. "War paint."

He nodded, then added two black strikes under his eyes. "You better be as good as you were eight years ago."

She cocked a brow.

He rolled his eyes. "At *corn hole*, Tea. Get your mind out of the gutter."

She laughed, then fixed him with her game time face. "Are you kidding? I went to a big ten school and got *even better* at corn hole. Let's sink these suckers."

THEY WON EVERY SINGLE GAME, to no one's surprise. She and Archer slipped right back into being teammates with ease, like no time had passed at all. They cheered each other on and made faces and sly distractions as their opponents took their turns. Austin called it cheating; Archer called it strategy.

During the final round, as they played against Danny and Chris, it was neck-and-neck. The twins sat at twenty points, while Archer and Tea had eighteen. They only needed one more three-pointer in the target hole to win. The twins needed only one bag on the board.

Danny narrowed his eyes at the board, tossing a bean bag back and forth in his hand.

"Come on, man, you got this," Chris said from across the lawn.

"Yeah man, don't miss," Archer teased next to Danny.

"Shut the fuck up," Danny snapped.

"*Daniel Bramble*, language!" Rhonda hollered.

"Yeah Daniel, listen to your mom," Tea teased.

Danny glared at her. "I agree with Austin. You guys cheat."

She lifted her hands. "Didn't know talking was cheating."

"Yeah man, don't be a sore loser," Archer added.

Danny grumbled something under his breath, then squared his shoulders, took a step, and tossed.

The bag landed on the board, but the throw was too harsh. It glided across the wood and landed on the grass behind it.

"*Noooo!*" Chris screamed next to her.

Danny sank to his knees.

Archer pointed to Tea. "You got this."

She nodded and relaxed her shoulders, eyeing the target, envisioning what angle she would need to throw the bag at the perfect shot. She let out a long breath, then tossed the bag.

It sank right in.

Cheers erupted across the lawn.

Tea held up her arms in triumph.

Archer swerved around a sulking Danny and Chris and ran up to her, bending low and grabbing her legs with his arms.

Fear plagued her chest. "Archer, *NO!*"

He laughed as he stood up, his grip on her legs tight as he threw her over his shoulder, then ran to the dock.

She pounded on his back. "Let me *down!*"

"You said it's good to have traditions!" he yelled back.

"No, no, no, *no—*"

She was cut off by the cold water as he plunged them into the lake. She felt him squeeze his hands around her thighs before letting her go and making his way to the surface.

Tea came up for air, spitting water out of her mouth and onto his face. "You monster."

He barked a laugh. "We do this every time we win, Tea bag!"

"*Not my nickname!*"

He laughed again as he climbed the ladder at the dock, then reached an arm to help her up.

She ignored his hand and climbed up, then stood on the dock before him, soaking wet.

He grinned back at her, his war paint dripping down his face, his eyes glistening with mischief.

It was hard to pretend to be mad at him when he looked that happy. Looked like *her* Archer.

She crossed her arms. "You better make me a s'more tonight."

He loped an arm around her shoulder and led her back to the party. "Already have the supplies."

Chapter 14

Archer

ARCHER STOOD on his porch the following day, cup of coffee in hand, listening to the pure nothingness of a Minnesota morning. The air smelt of pine tree sap and the dew that blanketed the grass. He sipped his drink, his eyes moving to Cabin B next door. The back window on the second floor was cracked open, the room still dark. He'd given her the rest of the week off, so he knew she would be sleeping in today. Besides, after the way she'd tackled her to-do list the past month, there really weren't many other administrative tasks for her to complete. But that didn't stop him from brainstorming other ways to keep her around, tasks that would keep her in his cabin, sitting at his desk when he returned for lunch, crinkle in her brow as she concentrated on whatever was on her screen.

Yesterday with her felt like stepping back in time. He watched her come out of the timid, reserved shell she arrived in earlier that summer, showing sides of herself he hadn't seen in far too long. The playful, teasing sides of her. His mind ran through all of the things she said to him *—traditions hold us together, we need each other.* Even the smallest traditions with her, like sitting with a drink watching the sunset every night or playing corn hole, made it even more obvious how much he missed her. Worse...it made him realize how much he still craved her.

He couldn't deny that his mind was constantly playing through the few moments when she touched him. Holding his hand at the outdoor bar, or squeezing his arm yesterday before the ceremony. He instinctively went to reach for her hand yesterday at the picnic table, then caught himself before he could do something embarrassing, placing his hand next to her leg instead. He yearned to touch her skin, almost refusing to let go when he threw them into the lake. He watched her come up for air, her red hair slicked back, black paint a mess on her cheeks, and he felt the violent urge to grab her waist under the water and kiss her wet, pink lips. Draw his tongue down her neck and rip the strap of her tank top with his teeth.

Archer closed his eyes and took a long, deep breath, doing his best to ignore the tightness in his pants. *God*, he wanted her. He knew it was a terrible idea. He wanted her, yet he wasn't sure if he could trust her again. Not after how she ended things the last time. Not when she ran away from him and said she never wanted to see him again.

"You look far too stressed for this gorgeous morning."

Archer blinked his eyes open. His father stood before him, holding his Babe the Blue Ox mug.

He gave Astor a shy smile. "A lot on my mind."

"Well, of course there is." Astor tipped his head to the Adirondack chairs across the lawn. "Want to talk about it?"

Archer hesitated. *No*, he did not want to talk about it. He'd been able to keep his father at a distance all summer, and would prefer not to dive into the details. But Astor didn't even wait for a reply and walked toward the chairs, expecting his son to follow. So he did.

The two of them sat in silence for a couple of moments, eyes out on the water and the early morning golden sun.

Astor let out a contented sigh, like sitting in this chair overlooking the lake, next to his son, was where he was meant to be. Archer couldn't help but think it was the *wrong* son, though.

"Let me guess," Astor started. "You don't want to be here."

He shifted uncomfortably in his seat. "I beg your pardon?"

"Here, at Wild Pines."

"What makes you say that?"

"Austin talked to me."

Archer exhaled, dropping his head back. "I will kill him."

"But he didn't have to tell me, son. He was only confirming what I already saw."

He looked back at his father. "And what's that?"

"Your heart's not in it. You don't love the lake like you used to."

Archer frowned. "Dad, it's kind of a stressful time."

"I know it is. I wonder if I screwed up by handing things off to you. I feel like I'm the reason you don't love it."

He shook his head. "No, that's not it—"

"Then what is it?"

He swallowed. Was he really about to do this? He knew he should tell his father that managing Wild Pines hadn't ever been his dream. Astor wasn't wrong; he did love this place. He loved water skiing and sailing on the water, cold drinks at sunset and late nights around the bonfire. He missed the way everyone walked in and out of each other's cabins, like it was one giant party, a never-ending summer camp. He also loved having his favorite person back home, making him laugh while also making him think deeply. Even if that person was a major source of his stress.

Yet his father was also right. Managing this place was taking the joy out of it. He knew that would be his fate though. Austin was adamant about not wanting to take it, and when Astor announced he was ready to retire, Archer didn't want to hold his father back from finally getting his well-earned rest. So he said yes, packed his things, and left Minneapolis. Besides, he had nothing else holding him back at the time.

He cracked his knuckles, resigning to it. He could talk to his father. Thanks to his fuckhead of a brother, it was already out in the open anyway. "This job is exhausting and hard to manage."

"Oh I know, I did it for years."

Archer scratched his neck. "Some days I feel like I'm not good enough for it and wonder if Austin would have been the better choice."

"No he wouldn't have."

He eyed Astor. "Dad, we both know Austin was made for the job. He's equally good at physical labor and all of the administrative shit. It's why he does so well at John Deere."

Austin landed his job as an engineer at John Deere before he even graduated college, which moved him and Riley to Fargo shortly after. Archer acted like he didn't care, but his brother had always been naturally smart. He would plop down with Tea and her textbooks and solve equations with her, while Archer bent over their books and couldn't read the language of numbers and lines that came so easily to them.

"I don't agree," Astor commented. "I actually think Austin would have been terrible at it."

Archer coughed out a laugh. Never once had he heard his father make a negative comment about his brother. "Funny, good joke. Stop lying to me."

"I'm not." Astor took a sip from his mug. "Sure, your brother has the technical skills and is good with numbers, but he isn't the best with people."

"That's not true. Did you see him yesterday? He practically had Joel eating out the palm of his hand. He would have never been mad at him for not catching the damn fishing cabin culprit."

"A charmer, sure. But what about empathy?"

His shoulders slumped. "Empathy?"

"Do you really think Austin would have fixed Jorge's boat for free? Or set up payment plans so people didn't have to stress about paying association fees outright this summer?"

"The second one was Tea's idea—"

"Sure, but the only reason you were delayed is because you didn't want people worrying about it quite yet. You care for everyone here."

He worked his jaw, not able to meet his father's eye.

"Son."

Archer blinked up at his father.

"If you really hate it, I don't mind hopping back in—"

"*No.*"

"Are you sure?"

Of course he was sure. The last thing he wanted to do was disappoint his father completely and give up. He'd seen what his father was like without the stress of constantly having to work while he's here. He'd laughed and enjoyed himself yesterday, even kissed his mother square on the mouth in front of everyone, her playful slap in response slightly sickening to watch—but also delightful.

He couldn't take that away from them. Plus, what else did he have right now? It wasn't like Hermes Lounge was open. He wasn't even sure if they would take him back. Not after...

He shook his head, ran his hands down his legs. "Yes, I'm very sure."

"We could also look for new management, if you're not."

Archer's eyes widened. "New management? Dad, no. This is your life's work. Our family's legacy."

"It is. But it's not my only job." He sighed. "My first job and top priority has been to my kids. I worked hard because I knew how much you loved this place, and how much it meant to our family. But that doesn't mean we have to keep it in the family."

He hesitated. "Won't that make you sad?"

Astor shook his head. "It would make me even more sad to see my son unhappy every single year."

Archer swallowed, unsure of what to say. It's not like managing the resort was an all-year thing. He planned on living in Minneapolis during the off season, and he could still have a future in cocktails...if Hermes Lounge let him come back. But that did mean giving up his whole summer, for a job that in the deepest parts of his heart he knew he couldn't do all on his own.

"You don't have to give me an answer now, but I would consider it and bring it to the owners by the end of the summer if you decide it's time to move on."

Archer rubbed his neck. "You really think I should give it up? Didn't you say I was doing a good job?"

"You are. You're *excellent* for the job. But that doesn't

mean it has to be yours forever. Not if you're not passionate about it."

He took a minute to think it through. The truth was, once Tea began to help him, his feelings about managing Wild Pines had shifted. It was easier to have a partner to handle the tasks with. "Tea has been a really big help," Archer replied, not sure how else to respond to his father.

Astor scratched his beard. "If you stayed, do you think she would come back to help next summer?"

His forehead wrinkled as he shook his head. "No. Her dream is to work in New York, to be closer to Molly."

The thought of not seeing her every day left a pang in his heart.

Astor shrugged. "The pandemic changed my perspective on a lot of things. Who knows, maybe she'll find herself with a new dream."

Hope flared in his chest at the thought. Could her mind be changed...and could he be the one to change it?

No, I couldn't do that to her. He wouldn't hold her back from being close to her mom, from following her dream. Not after losing Gareth way too soon.

But that didn't stop him from letting the hope take shape, and for the most dangerous word to take root in his heart.

Maybe.

ARCHER DIDN'T HAVE time to work through his conflicting emotions about Tea, so he ended up carrying them onto the boat. He and Austin promised the girls a day out on his father's motorboat before their long drive back to Fargo, just like old times. The four of them swimming and tanning, picnic lunches and beers. This time they were ice-cold in coolers, not warm from the box, hidden inside wrapped-up towels.

Tea was the first to show, wearing her denim cut-offs and that striped one-piece suit he couldn't take his eyes off weeks ago. Her wavy hair hung loose by her shoulders, tucked inside a fading Silver Falls cap. Her nose was pink from being out in the sun yesterday during the party.

He felt like he couldn't breathe.

She didn't seem to notice as she stepped in, plopping her bag down on the bench seat. "Need a hand with anything?"

He blinked, then shook his head. *Snap out of it.* "Nope, all good." He tossed life jackets into the lazarette, then snapped it shut a little too loudly.

She flinched.

"*Sorry.*"

"Are you still stressed about yesterday?"

The party and all of its risks hadn't even crossed his mind. His thoughts were elsewhere. On his conversation with his father and the *maybe* that clanged around his head...and that damn blue-and-white-striped swimsuit.

He couldn't unload any of it, though. She'd asked to be friends, and he said yes. He would have to swallow whatever he was feeling. He finally had Tea back in his life, and he really didn't want to lose her again after taking things too far like last time.

He shook his head. "You're right. I think everyone needed yesterday after these crazy, fucked-up five months."

"Completely agree."

They stood there in the boat, underneath the canopy, staring at one another. A strand of her hair was out of place, blocking the corner of her eye. He wanted to tuck it behind her ear. Then tip back her hat and—

"*I'M DRIVING!*"

Archer closed his fists, turning toward his brother. "No, you're not. Also, you and I have beef."

Austin frowned as he helped Riley into the boat. "Is it a good kind of beef, like Omaha steaks? Or we talking Hy-Vee chuck roast—"

He reached the helm of the boat, grabbing the dangling remote and sinking the boat into the water. "You talked to Dad about the resort."

"Dude, I thought it was a known fact," Austin defended himself, looking befuddled as he stepped into the boat. "Why didn't you tell him anything?"

His eyes were slitted. "Do I really need to spell this out for you? Dad finally retired, I couldn't just—"

"Archer, it's your goddamn *life*. You can't live it doing something you don't love."

"Watch me."

Archer ignored the way Tea's eyes went wide at his response, or how she pressed her lips into a thin line and moved to the back, taking a seat next to Riley, who was already pulling on her vape.

"Jesus, Archer. You can't possibly think I'm going to let you—"

Archer cut him off. "You will. You made your decision, and I made mine."

The four of them remained silent as Archer backed the boat out of the dock, then turned it to open water.

Austin popped into the passenger seat and crossed his arms, shaking his head.

"You know what, no." Riley popped up and stepped between the two boys. "If we're going to act like this all day, we're turning this boat around and going back. I'm not dealing with this shit."

Austin sighed, then turned to Archer. "Okay, I'm sorry. It wasn't my place."

"It wasn't."

"But if this is going to hold you back from actually pursuing your dream, then I will make it my place."

"What dream?" Tea asked behind him.

Riley's brows shot skyward as she looked between Tea and Archer. She settled on the latter with a face that clearly stated *You haven't told her yet?*

Archer reached for the key to crank up the engine.

Austin grabbed his wrist. "Give me a timeline."

He glared at him.

"How long do I give you until I make it my place again?"

"Will someone please tell me what's going on?" Tea pleaded.

He, Austin, and Riley didn't respond to her, the three of them in a silent war.

He yanked his wrist back. "Five years."

"*Five?* That's—"

"A reasonable amount of time to try to do what I want to." He reached for the key. "If it doesn't work out, then so be it."

Before he could hear what Tea was saying behind him, Archer turned the key and took off, the boat soaring down the lake.

"Fine, fuckface, I'll leave you alone for five years!" Austin screamed over the motor. He plugged in his phone. "Now for some Dua Lipa!"

"Levitating" blasted through the speakers of the boat. Riley took a seat on Austin's lap as they made their way to

Silverstone Lagoon. She held up her arms, her sunglasses gleaming under the sun. *"Just like old times!"*

Archer sneaked a glace at Tea. She already had a beer popped open and was moving to the music, a smile on her face.

He turned back to the water, allowing his mind to drift to what his life could look like five years from now. In every version he envisioned, he couldn't deny the truth: Tea was a part of them all.

The lagoon was quiet when they arrived, but that was to be expected. Silverstone Lagoon was usually where boats congregated during the summer, but no one was out the day after the Fourth.

He cut the ignition, then walked to the back of the boat and let down the ladder.

Austin already stripped off his T-shirt and hat before stepping up the edge of the boat and cannonballing in. Riley squealed and did the same, stripping down to a black bikini he heard Austin make inappropriate sounds over earlier.

He turned away from his brother and sister-in-law, now attached at the mouth in the water, and looked toward Tea. She was in the process of shimmying out of her shorts.

His face flushed, unable to keep his eyes from her creamy-white freckled legs. When her face lifted he jerked his head in a different direction.

"Are you going to swim in that T-shirt?" she teased.

"Yes, I actually think I might."

She tossed her hat on the seat, then stepped right up to him, her body practically flush with his.

His cheeks burned. "What are you doing?"

"Um, you're kind of in the way of the ladder?"

"Oh, right." He sidestepped. "Sorry."

Tea smirked as she stepped around him, then climbed her way down, letting out small breathy gasps with each step into the cold water.

He was in *way* over his head.

"Take it off, Vincent!" Austin screamed from the water.

Archer shook his head as he reached for his back collar, grabbing a fistful and tearing it off in one motion. Before Tea could get a proper look at the tattoos on his chest, he stepped up and jumped, somersaulting into the cold water he prayed would cool him off from the heat crawling up his thighs.

THE AFTERNOON WENT by as it usually did—dips in the lake, beers in hand, music blasting as they lay out in the sun.

At one point Austin and Riley were back in the water, leaving him and Tea alone on the boat.

She was reclined in the helm seat beside him, her face to the sun, her cheeks even more pink.

Archer dotted sunscreen on his pointer finger, then reached out and swiped it on her nose. "You'll thank me later."

She smiled. "Or I'll just thank you now."

He lay back in his chair, ignoring the squeezing feeling in his chest from her smile. Another book about loons was open and face-down on her belly. Her arm was outstretched beside her, her hand dangling off the chair. He felt the aggressive urge to touch it.

Archer reached his arm out, his fingers practically brushing hers. But he didn't move further. He stared at their hands, imagining what it would be like to lace his fingers with hers.

She blinked her eyes open and turned to face him. A knowing expression crossed her face, like she could read his mind. She closed her eyes again, and after a beat, her arm moved an inch, her knuckles bumping into his.

Damn the consequences. Archer brushed his fingers inside her palm. Her skin felt dry and warm and soft. He turned his palm, and sealed their hands.

The smile on her lips widened. Her face was back to the sky as she let out a satisfied sigh.

He brushed his thumb against her hand, giving himself only a moment to rake his gaze over her body. *God*, she was stunning. Her curves, her red hair dried from the sun, those pink lips and the freckles he wanted to bite into. She hadn't flinched from his touch, and it filled his chest with hope.

Maybe. The word hammered in his mind. *Maybe. Maybe. Maybe.*

Chapter 15

Tea

Courting a mate is a quiet affair. The male loon will return to their territory and establish where nesting will take place. The female follows weeks later, joining the same male after the previous year in their familiar territory. Then comes the subtle dance of courtship—side-by-side swimming, bill dipping, circling, and calls between mates to solidify their new home.

"What's the dream, Arch?"

She felt him tense and hardened her grip, refusing to let him steal his hand back. It seemed like it took him a considerable amount of effort to even make the move on her; there was no way she was going to let him end it that soon.

He closed his eyes and let out a breath. He squeezed her hand, then squeezed it again.

She squeezed back, hoping that it would reassure him. *It's okay*, she wanted to tell him. *You can trust me.*

He cleared his throat. "When I started in cocktail bars, I always had this dream in the back of my mind about opening my own spot."

He didn't say anything after that. She rubbed her pointer finger into his skin. *Keep going.*

"Not just a cocktail bar, but an actual school. Somewhere people can train, or take short courses. I had my eye on a spot for a while, but then..." He sighed. "Well, you know."

"Arch, that's—"

"Crazy, I know."

"*Awesome.* It's awesome."

He looked into her eyes. "Tea, you've seen me try to manage the resort. I'm horrible at admin of any kind, and I can't get myself locked in to any consistent schedule."

"Thankfully you don't have to do it alone."

His head tilted in confusion.

"Obviously you have me right now," she continued. "But the miraculous thing about starting a business? You can *hire* people to do the things you aren't good at. People who have those strengths."

He loosened his grip on her hand. She thought she'd completely blown it, that he was going to retreat into himself. Instead, he brushed his hand up her wrist and arm, then back down. He continued his pattern in soft, methodical strokes. "I wish I had your confidence."

She scoffed. "Confidence? Try again."

"Yes, confidence. You came to me determined to work this summer. You knew exactly what you wanted, and you went for it. Nothing will stop you. I...admire it. I wish I had some more of it."

She sighed. *I wouldn't exactly put it that way.* She didn't have anything to do, and offering to work with Archer felt more like a relief than a burden. Even though Wild Pines didn't pay—thankfully all of her student loan payments were put on pause—it'd become her favorite job yet. She contemplated if it was the work...or the man she worked *with*.

She concluded it was the work. She liked numbers, but she also liked people. She needed both. Even though she spent years avoiding the latter.

A *thunk* came from below and seconds later, a large splash of water crested the boat and splattered all over Archer, spraying Tea in the process.

He growled, hanging his head in defeat. Then he bolted upright, dropping his hand from her skin, and screamed to his brother. "All right, asshole, get ready to be *cooked* beef."

Austin cackled as Archer ran off the boat and jumped in close enough to his brother that he could have hit his head, splashing Riley in the process.

Austin and Riley left two days later. Riley made her promise that she would actually talk to her and keep in touch. Tea agreed, but deep down, she felt like she was going to fail Riley all over again. Especially after that day on the boat, when Archer reached for her hand and touched her skin in a way that was obviously more than friendly. She didn't even *try* to push him away. She'd practically egged him on.

She knew she shouldn't have. Things with Archer could go south *fast*. She still planned on driving back to the east coast at the end of the summer and finding a job close to Mom. If she let herself get involved, she would leave him heartbroken and shattered like last time, and any mended friendships she made would likely be done for good.

And yet that didn't stop her from thinking about the feel of his hand in hers.

Tea sat in her usual Adirondack chair overlooking the lake, sipping her wine and reading her next book on loons: *Voices of the Water: The Mating Patterns of Loons.* She found their mating behaviors fascinating, like how both the male and female incubate the eggs before hatching, and how nests are built close to the water. She kept mulling over their migration patterns, how it was natural for loons to be settled in the same spot every summer, then traveling somewhere else for the cold season ahead. It made her think of her own summer migrations, spending long days under the sun at the lake, then long nights back in New Jersey for the winter. New Jersey had never really felt like home. For Tea, it was merely a period of time to endure before returning back to the place that felt most natural to her.

She slammed her book shut, rattling the wine glass perched on the armrest next to her. It was these kinds of thoughts that were the most dangerous. It opened a chasm in her heart when she thought about what this place really meant to her. It made her miss her dad. It made her regret all the wasted summers after his death. It made her anxious about finding a job and realizing she may never be able to have another full summer at Wild Pines ever again.

Never in life did she imagine being jealous of a *bird*.

"Let me guess, the loon broke up with the other loon and now they're trying to divide their twigs and leaves properly, but they still love each other."

Tea rolled her eyes as she turned toward a smirking Archer. He was in his swimsuit, his chest covered by a life jacket.

She lifted the book in her hand. "Guessing you've read this before."

He let out a breath. "It's a steamy one."

Her mouth split into a grin. "No breakups. They actually incubate for twenty-eight days once they make a nest."

"Sounds dirty."

"*Archer*. They're birds."

"Where do you think baby loons come from, Tea?" His eyes gleamed with mischief. "You know, when a mommy loon and a daddy loon love each other very much—"

She tossed her book at him. It bounced off his jacket and tumbled to the grass.

He chuckled as he picked up the book. "Want to go water skiing, or do you want to sit here and read more about bird sex?"

"You're insufferable."

"I'll take that as a yes." He cocked his head. "Go get your suit on."

She sighed, then stood up and peeled off her sundress, stripping down to her suit.

Archer stood before her in complete silence, his eyes wide.

She placed her hands on her hips. "Archer, I know you too well." She pointed to the lake. "It's smooth as glass out there. I knew you were going to ask me."

He cleared his throat, then nodded as he looked down at the grass.

She tilted her head. "Something wrong?"

He coughed a laugh and shook his head, looking back up at her after a beat.

Dilated pupils. Flushed cheeks. Clenched jaw. *Good god.*

Archer covered his mouth and scratched his face. "Nice bikini," he muttered.

He didn't give her the chance to say anything in response as he walked straight for the water.

Moments later, as she clicked on her life jacket and sank into a seat on Rhonda's boat, a small smile crept up her left cheek.

"You got this!"

Her hands fumbled as she attempted to slip the ski on underwater. "No, I really don't think I do!"

Archer grasped the end of the boat, the muscles in his arms flexing as he leaned over.

"*Cheap shot*," she grumbled to herself.

"What was that?" he called to her.

She snatched the rope and pulled the handle toward her. "Put the guns away!" she called back at him.

He looked down at his arms then back up at her, arching a brow.

"Guns?!" Rhonda yelled.

"She's kidding," Archer replied, still not looking away from Tea. "Ready?"

"Not even in the slightest!"

Rhonda roared the engine. Tea kept a tight grip on the handle and locked in her legs, using the pressure of the water against the ski to pop herself up. For a few glorious seconds, she was upright, her hair whipping behind her, the sun on her face.

Until she realized her bikini bottoms were down by her ankles.

Shit! She let go of the handle and crouched down, falling into the water on her side. The water ski slipped off. She reached into the water for her feet, scrambling for her bottoms.

But they were nowhere to be found.

The boat puttered over to her.

Archer lifted his arms. "What happened? You were up!"

Tea frantically scanned the water around her. "You didn't see what happened?"

"Um, no? Did you slip?" He noticed her panicked expression. "What's wrong?"

She felt her cheeks flush. "Um, wearing a bikini was probably not the right call."

"I beg to differ, I think it was an excellent call—" He paused. "*Oh.* Oh no."

"My bottoms slipped off and now I don't know where they are."

Archer froze, then tipped his head back and let out a booming laugh.

She glared at him. "Shut up and help me."

He kept laughing as he removed the towel from around his shoulders.

Rhonda stepped up to him, hands on her hips. "What's going on?"

"Tea's nude."

"I'm not *nude.* I lost my swimsuit bottoms."

"So you're nude," Rhonda teased.

Archer kept laughing as he stepped to the edge of the boat and dived in, facing the opposite direction to give her privacy. Thankfully the lake water was dark enough that she was shaded from him as they swam around the vicinity looking for her bottoms.

After several minutes of unsuccessful searching, Archer swam up to her. "Okay, it's looking like your swimsuit has been sacrificed to the lake."

"This is so embarrassing," she bemoaned.

Archer lifted an arm, reaching for a wet strand of her hair and tucking it behind her ear. "I'm going to get on the boat and hold up my towel, then you climb on and you can wrap it around yourself."

She frowned. "I liked this swimsuit."

"Trust me, I did, too."

If she hadn't been swimming commando in freezing cold water, that comment probably would have left her feeling *a little* too warm.

Archer did as promised and was a gentleman about it. She wrapped the towel around her waist tight as he unbuckled her life jacket. Rhonda maneuvered the boat back in the direction of Wild Pines.

He sat down and covered his mouth, doing a terrible job at hiding the goofy smile on his face.

She sat down in a huff. "Shove it."

He tipped his head back and laughed again.

NAN WAS WAITING for them on the dock. As they got closer and closer to the sandy shore, Tea noticed her grandmother had a mask on her face.

Her stomach plummeted.

She popped out of the boat as soon as they docked, Archer close at her heels.

"Nan? Everything okay?"

Her grandmother sighed. "Not exactly, my angel. Your

grandfather said he wasn't feeling well, so I took his temperature."

She sucked in a breath. She knew what would follow, but she wasn't sure if she was ready for it.

"And?" Archer asked from her side, his voice tight.

Nan let out a long breath. "It's a hundred and one."

Chapter 16

Archer

ARCHER PULLED his truck into the drive-through line at the testing clinic in Ashland. Every muscle in his body felt tight, and the pounding in his head hadn't subsided even hours after finding out about Wayne's fever. A line of cars followed him, all residents of Wild Pines heading for testing.

Tea sat next to him, mask on, legs tucked close to her chest and arms around her knees. She'd panicked when Kelly told them the news, and his heart split in two at the sight of her. Without hesitating, he told her to change and get in his truck, then knocked on cabin doors to spread the news—only to find out that a few others were showing symptoms as well. Coughing, body aches, fever, and chills. The entire resort was on the verge of an outbreak, and it was likely all his fault. Again.

A woman in blue scrubs sat at the window, mask and plastic gloves on. "Hi, sir. Have either of you been showing any symptoms of COVID?"

Archer turned to Tea. She shook her head.

"No," he replied.

"All right. We have the PCR tests, but if you want, we got those new rapid antigen tests in—"

"We'll take them both."

The woman handed them the kits. Archer stepped out of the car and did his test outside, leaving Tea alone in the truck to do hers.

They individually handed them back.

"You should get an email in the next two hours with your rapid results, and the PCR tests in a few days," she said.

Archer nodded, then pulled his truck away from the clinic and back onto the main road. He didn't bother waiting for the other cars. They would all find out each other's results soon enough.

They drove back in silence. Ten minutes into the drive, Archer stopped at a red light. The sun was almost set, the night sky turning to dusk.

The light took a lifetime to turn. His chest flared in annoyance. He gripped the steering wheel hard and took a deep breath and closed his eyes. But no amount of deep breathing was releasing the tight pain in his chest, or in his head.

He slammed his hand against the wheel. *"Fuck!"*

Tea tightened her arms around her legs. "It'll be okay, Arch."

He rubbed his eyes, making sure not to move the mask on his face. "How can you say that? What if someone gets really sick and we can't get them to a hospital in time? All because I said yes to that fucking party."

"This isn't all on you," she countered. "Everyone made their choice. We all took a risk."

He white-knuckled the wheel again and checked the

light. Still red. "But it wouldn't have happened at all if I shut it down and said no from the start."

"Are you really going to blame yourself for this? That's ludicrous."

"Yeah, well, I should have known better. I clearly did not learn from my previous mistakes."

The light finally turned green. He pressed hard on the gas, jerking the truck forward.

Tea's face was pinched into a scowl. "What does that mean?"

He shook his head.

"No, absolutely not." Tea twisted her body so she was facing him. "Archer, what's going on with you? Tell me right now."

"No."

"Why *not*?"

"Because it is the single most horrific thing I've done in my entire life."

She sucked in a breath.

"If I tell you, I don't think you'll be able to look at me the same way ever again."

"I highly doubt that," she murmured.

The sound of her soft confidence in him left a pang in his heart.

They pulled up to another red light. He growled.

"*Archer.*"

He exhaled and tilted his head back, then rolled it to look at her. "Remember when you said that you think I have anxiety about COVID?"

She nodded.

He rubbed his neck. Was he really going to tell her about this?

She placed a hand down on the console between them.

She didn't reach for him all the way, like there was an invisible barrier between them. But the movement was clear enough. *I'm here for you.*

The light above them turned green, and still he didn't move. They were in the middle of the woods, and there wasn't a car in sight. "It's not anxiety about *getting* it, it's about spreading it to others. Back in March—" The word caught in his throat. He cleared it, ignoring the stinging in his eyes. "I was on the schedule to work at Hermes Lounge one night, and I wasn't feeling too great, but I went to work anyway."

Her eyes widened.

"I kept mixing drinks and handing them off to people, thinking it was a cold coming on or something. Days later, I woke up with chills and a fever. That was the day everything shut down in Minneapolis. I couldn't get a test or anything because hospitals and clinics were so backed up. But I knew. I had every symptom in the book."

The light turned yellow, then back to red. "I called my boss to tell him I had it, and he came back to me days later with some n-news." Tears welled in his eyes. He swiped them away with the back of his hand. "Apparently three guests at the bar that night ended up in the hospital. Two of them did not make it."

"*Archer*," she whispered.

"I shouldn't have gone in for my shift. If I had stayed home, they would probably be alive, and—" He couldn't continue. His chest heaved as he let out a sob.

"Hey, hey, *hey*." Tea stretched her hand.

He wanted to grab it—*desperately*—but how could he? How could he risk it? How could she even look at him?

"Arch, it is *not* your fault. They could have picked it up from someone or someplace else. It was spreading like crazy in the beginning, and we still don't know much about *how* this thing spreads."

He snatched an old napkin in his glove compartment and wiped his eyes. "Tea, I was making them *drinks.* Without a mask on."

"And they were probably talking in very close proximity to each other, and to others earlier in the day—"

He shook his head. He knew she was only trying to make him feel better, but it felt like taking a small pickaxe to his mountain of guilt. "What if someone gets really sick at Wild Pines?"

"Then we'll figure it out, one day at a time. Together."

He nodded. The light turned green and this time, he tapped on the gas.

THEIR RESULTS CAME in an hour later. Both negative.

Wayne tested positive, which was to be expected. But Kelly tested positive as well, despite seeming perfectly healthy earlier that day.

He called his mom. "What were your test results?"

She sighed. "Not great, sweetheart."

Both of his parents tested positive too. Along with Steph, Chris, Danny, Ashley, Jorge, and Victoria Jansen.

He sat on the steps of his porch, watching Tea pace back and forth. She was on the phone with Molly, her tone too low for him to capture what she was saying.

She eventually hung up and slipped her phone in the back pocket of her jeans.

Archer leaned forward. "What did she say?"

"She said I could isolate upstairs and leave them downstairs, but that's still a risk. I could go to the inn in town and quarantine for two weeks, but that *also* feels super risky."

Archer pressed his hands together. "I don't like the sound of either of those."

"Me neither, but what other option do I have?"

"Stay with me."

The words slipped out of his mouth before he could even comprehend what he was saying.

Her eyes widened.

Well, I'm in it now. He kept talking. "I have an extra bedroom in there, and technically half the food in the fridge is yours. You could quarantine with me."

She crossed her arms over her stomach. "And if either of us ends up getting sick?"

"Tea, we already spend a lot of time together unmasked. At this point, if you get sick, I'm probably going to get sick."

"That doesn't freak you out?"

"Oh, I'm fucking terrified," he admitted. "But I sure as hell am not letting you stay at the inn, and you will not be spending two weeks locked up in your bedroom."

Her shoulders relaxed. He wanted to reach out and pull her into his arms. Hold her tight and protect her from everything else going on in the world.

She exhaled, then looked up at his cabin behind him. "Do you have good pillows?"

THEY MADE quick work of packing her things at Cabin B. Wayne and Kelly waited outside while Tea stuffed clothes in tote bags. He snatched her pillows and extra blankets, as well as the books she had on her nightstand she told him to grab. Before he pulled away, he noticed a small framed photo by her bed.

It was of the two of them, smiling wide with blue teeth and lips from the snow cones they made. Tea had been obsessed with her disposable camera that summer. She took photos of everything. He still had one himself, a picture she took of him fishing off the edge of the dock. She'd mailed it to him in a *Congrats on your new baby!* card later that year. It was deep in his sock drawer.

He snatched the picture frame and stuffed it in the bag he held, then grabbed a few of her other bags and helped her carry everything back to his place.

When they stepped into the cabin, they both froze in the entryway. It was pitch-black except for the moonlight peeking in from the window. It was eerily quiet outside. No teenage gang around the bonfire. No boats voyaging out for night fishing.

The only sound he could hear was Tea's soft breathing.

He took a step forward. "Your room is this way. Want to settle in?"

"No." She dropped everything she was holding onto the solid wood floor. "I want you to grab that bottle of vodka in your freezer."

He laughed, watching as she opened his cabinets and grabbed two plastic cups. "I think drinking vodka straight would be a bad idea?"

"We'll mix it with the cranberry juice I bought."

He lifted a brow, placing her things on the couch, then flicked on the lamps. "You bought cranberry juice?"

"I figured a mixer would be good to have on hand." She reached for the fridge handle. "Oh crap, I should have grabbed some of my wine."

He smirked. "Open the fridge."

She tilted her head in confusion, then opened it. Her mouth split into a grin. "*Six* bottles?"

He shrugged, making his way to the kitchen to join her. "I grabbed them a few days ago. Figured having a few bottles would be good to have on hand."

She shook her head. "So we're stocked for a quarantine, aren't we?"

"I guess so."

The two of them stood there, staring at each other. They had yet to remove their masks since the drive to the clinic.

Tea seemed to be thinking the same thing. "Should we take them off?"

He swallowed. "Only if you're comfortable."

She didn't move for a beat, then slowly lifted her hand to his face. Archer stood still as she undid the elastics around his ears.

He smiled, stepping closer to her. He removed her mask, placed it on the counter, then cupped her face in his hands. "Are you doing okay?"

She nodded. "I'm a little scared that I won't be around them. But thank you for letting me stay."

"Of course. Anything you need."

She bit her lip. It took everything in his power not to lean down and kiss her. He knew if he did and she rejected him, a two-week quarantine would *not* go well.

Or, if she didn't reject him...it could go *very* well.

He didn't let himself fantasize about it.

She grinned, and for the second time tonight, Archer wondered if Tea was reading his thoughts. "Ready to get shitfaced?"

He grinned back at her. "Frozen pizza for dinner?"

"Sounds immaculate."

Chapter 17

Tea

To assemble their nests, mated pairs will gather twigs, leaves, and other vegetation from the lake. A nesting pair of loons will return to the same sight each year, refurbishing the original nest instead of building a new one.

SHE WOKE up with a blinding headache, in a room that wasn't her own. The guest bedroom in Archer's cabin was small but quaint, the twin bed covered in a worn quilt made with patterns of trees and boats and loons. Tea remembered Archer telling her his grandmother made it for him when they finally maneuvered her few things to the room. It was one of the only things she remembered from the night before.

She groaned as she turned onto her side to check her phone for the time. Before she could tap the screen, she saw the tall glass of water by her bedside, along with a few painkillers.

She grumbled and took the medicine, washing it down with water. Her mouth tasted stale. She sat up as she placed the water back on the nightstand, then realized a familiar picture frame was propped up next to her phone. She squinted at the photo of her and Archer, wondering how it got there. Then she remembered snippets of the night before; Archer tucking her in, plugging in her phone, and fidgeting with something as she closed her eyes.

He must have grabbed it for me. Her heart raced at the idea of him seeing that photo. She wondered what he would think if he knew she'd kept it by her bed all these years. That she'd driven it the eight hour and forty-seven minutes from Chicago that gray day in May. It made her feel embarrassed. Besides the large tattoo on his back, which was more of a tribute to her father rather than her, Archer didn't seem to hold on to any mementos from their past. He picked himself up and he moved on.

He confused her. After that day on the boat, Tea thought Archer would make another move. She'd certainly hoped so when he cupped her face last night. She wanted him to dip down and kiss her. To make up for all of those years apart. Yet he didn't budge, and the rest of the night, he acted *friendly*. They ate frozen pizza and played *Super Mario Brothers* and drank way too many cranberry vodkas, laughing themselves almost sick. Now she was in bed, unable to piece together how she even got there.

She looked down at her clothes, realizing she was in a pair of sweatpants and a shirt that weren't her own.

Oh god, she thought. Did he change her? She felt for her undergarments, exhaling when she found she still had on her bra and underwear. But her clothes from yesterday were on the floor beside her, and she was wearing his clothes instead.

A soft knock broke her away from her thoughts.

"You okay in there?" Archer asked on the other side of the door.

She groaned loudly, then listened to him chuckle in response.

"Yeah, I kind of figured that would be the case," he replied. "Did you take the meds?"

"*Yeah*," she croaked.

"Good." He waited for a beat. "Are you going to come out, or...?"

"That requires moving," she quipped.

"Okay, well, I carried you into that bed. I'm not carrying you out as well."

She palmed her face. *He carried me to bed?* "I think I'll disintegrate into the sheets instead."

"But I have coffeeeee."

Coffee. She kicked the quilt away and stood up, then threw open the door.

Archer was leaning against the frame. He was in shorts and a worn white T-shirt, his hair tousled from sleep. But his smile was wide. He looked like he actually got some rest.

God damn him. She scowled. "No one should look that happy hungover."

He shrugged. "I'm not hungover."

Her mouth fell open. "*How* are you not hungover?"

"Practice? Tea, I work in beverages. I have a bit of a tolerance."

She squinted her eyes. "No more vodka the rest of this quarantine."

He smirked, then cocked his head to the left. "Bathroom is that way. I put your stuff in there last night, and there's a stack of towels next to it."

She glanced around him. "I was promised coffee."

He gave her that cocky smirk again, then reached for the steaming cup sitting on the desk outside her room and handed it to her. "Someone's grumpy."

She flipped him off as she went to the bathroom, listening to his laugh the entire way there. She brushed her teeth and rinsed her mouth, then took a few sips of coffee before washing her face. She leaned back as she soaked the washcloth in her hands, eyeing Archer. He stood in his living room, eyes out the window to the dock and the sunny day that welcomed them. She dropped her eyes to his arms, then the rest of his body. She let them linger on his calves and his thighs; underneath all of those tattoos was a lot of lean muscle. When he shifted and turned she jerked forward, splashing some of her coffee on the counter.

Shit. She wiped the counter, reminding herself she *finally* had Archer back in her life. Was she really going to screw all of that up?

She pulled her hair into a ponytail, taking her time finishing up in the bathroom while giving herself a pep talk. *Just friends. Keep it casual.*

Archer stood at the counter. Two plates of freshly scrambled eggs and toast sat in front of him. He picked one up as she approached and handed it to her. "Want to eat on the dock?"

"You made me breakfast?"

"Carbs and butter usually help with hangovers. So does vitamin D."

"Is that scientific fact?"

"It's anecdotal." He picked up his own plate. "Nice sweatpants, by the way."

She looked down at his clothes on her body. "*Please* don't tell me you had to change me."

He grinned, didn't respond, then exited the cabin.

"*Archer!*" She groaned, feeling mortified as she followed him out, balancing her mug and plate of eggs.

They sat at the edge of the dock, knees propped up so they could balance their plates. She briefly forgot about her mortification as she scarfed down her breakfast, feeling better after having something in her stomach.

Archer watched her, looking bemused.

"Shove it," she grumbled, wiping the butter grease from her chin. "Seriously you should have let me sleep in my clothes. There was no need to change me."

"You told me you left your pajamas at the other cabin, so I offered you some."

She set down her fork. "I said I forgot my pajamas?"

"Um...yes?"

Her face flushed. "Oh. Interesting."

"What's interesting?"

She tucked her knees to her chest. "I can't exactly forget pajamas if I don't own them."

"I am...so lost."

"Archer," she said, widening her eyes at him, "I don't wear pajamas to bed."

His mouth fell open before he snapped it shut a second later.

"No pajamas," he repeated. "Then why would you say that?"

"Probably because I was embarrassed?"

He shook his head. "Why? It's only me."

"*Right!* It's you."

"Tea, I've seen you in bikinis my whole life. I saw you in one *yesterday*."

She hung her head, realizing how blissful it had been not to remember what happened to her bikini bottoms yesterday. Then the rest of the night hit her. Nan's news.

Driving to Ashland. Taking a test. Agreeing to quarantine with Archer.

Archer caged her chin with his thumb and pointer finger, lifting her face to his. "Hey, look at me."

She blinked, then did.

"They're okay. We're okay."

She cleared her throat. "*Are* you okay?"

He sighed, dropping his hand. "I'm still a bit on edge, but I have to admit, last night helped a lot."

"It did?"

He nodded. "It was nice to clear my head and not focus on it so much. And...you're probably right."

"I usually am, but what about this time?"

"*Fucking smart-ass*," he grumbled under his breath. "You said last night that we should focus on the things that make us feel alive."

Her eyes widened. "I did?"

He grinned. "You don't remember, miss *I had a little too much to drink?*"

She hummed, her cheeks flushing. "Remind me. What makes you feel alive, Archer Vincent?"

He leaned back, eyes out to the lake. "Being on the water. Making cocktails. Hearing my brother laugh. Hanging out with you." He turned his face to hers. "Really anything with you."

She leaned back as well, crossing her arm over his and tilting her face to the sun, the ghost of a smile on her lips.

"What makes *you* feel alive, Theresa Richards?"

Her smile widened. "Sailing."

Archer knocked his arm against hers. "Feeling ready yet?"

She released a long breath, letting her mind drift to her father. What would he be doing on a morning such as this?

He'd probably be right here on the dock, sipping on a coffee with Mom, maybe even having a conversation similar to this one. Or he'd be readying the sails, getting ready to take her out on the water.

The thought of her father and this place no longer made her feel like she wanted to scream and run. It felt like a balm on her soul. A patching of her heart. A coming home.

"Almost," she whispered. "Almost."

BESIDES THE OBSCENE amount of vodka they consumed the first night, Tea's days with Archer progressed in similar ways. She woke up to coffee and breakfast, which they would take down to the dock and talk about anything and nothing. He told her more about what happened at Hermes Lounge, about how he was worried they wouldn't take him back.

"Archer, come one. They know it's not your fault."

His face pinched into disappointment. "Do they?"

"Have you spoken to them at all? Since March?"

He shook his head. "Not really. Just a little bit about their plans to expand outdoor seating and maybe open things up this fall."

"See? They're keeping you in the loop. I don't think they would do that if they were planning on firing you."

"Yeah...I guess you're right."

They also talked about his plans to open up his own spot in Minneapolis. He admitted the only thing holding him back was figuring out all of the logistics—applying for a business and liquor license, figuring out taxes and payroll. Tea listened, making lists in her head on how she could make *all* of that so much easier for him. Then she caught herself. What could she possibly offer him if her plan was to go back to the east coast?

After breakfast, which was a two-hour affair every morning, they would get to work on *something*—anything to keep them occupied and busy and *not* thinking about the outbreak around them. Archer didn't work on the property, intent on keeping his distance from everyone quarantining, so they tackled the things in his cabin. She sewed the ripped couch cushions while he changed the lightbulbs, swapping bright white lights with warmer golden ones. They sanded down the spots of chipped paint, then primed his living room using paint they found in the resort's storage shed. They only had two options for a color so he let her choose. She went with a muted sandy hue that she felt softened the room. Archer clicked on one of their old shared playlists of high school hits—Ed Sheeran, Maroon 5, Mumford and Sons, Lumineers, Alabama Shakes—and sang along to the lyrics, using paint brushes as microphones. He accidentally splattered her with paint during a guitar riff, so she got back at him moments later by rolling a streak on the back of his T-shirt. All-out war ensued, leaving them covered in paint and bright with laughter.

Nights later, she tossed together a pasta salad. It was far too hot to turn on the oven to cook anything—a sweltering ninety-degree sunny day, the lawn at Wild Pines still empty as everyone quarantined.

Archer lay on the floor, a half bottle of cold beer next to him, staring up at the ceiling fan that was incessantly clicking. It'd started making that noise two days earlier, and it was driving him mad.

"You could turn it off," Tea suggested. "Then you wouldn't have to hear it."

"But then it would be hot as hell in here."

She sighed and walked up to him, holding the bowl in one hand and her beer in the other. "I know. But you're acting like a crazy person staring at that thing."

"I wish I knew what the fuck was making that noise."

"*I know*." She turned toward the table. "Are we eating on the floor, or—?"

"Yes."

She waited a beat, then realized he was being serious.

He sat up and patted the ground. "It's cooler down here. Trust me."

She sighed, placing the bowl down and handing him a fork. She pulled on her beer.

Archer dug into the salad. "Hey, do you remember that one summer we made dessert nachos?"

"Oh my god, *yes*." She took a forkful herself. "We put so much garbage on those, I can't remember what the chips were."

"Graham crackers."

She snapped. "*Right*. We melted chocolate and peanut butter and marshmallow fluff."

"I'm pretty sure we sprinkled on every kind of candy we could find in our cabins." Archer smirked. "Austin was puking all night."

"I didn't feel too good after that either. Although it wasn't nearly as bad as the time we attempted to make snow cones."

He grimaced. "*Way* too much sugar. My tongue was blue for a week."

"I'm pretty sure it was two weeks."

"I remember your dad gave me this charcoal toothpaste to try to get it off. That shit was nasty."

She gave him a shy smile but didn't look him directly in the eye.

Archer was silent at first, then he cleared his throat. "Too much?"

She dug around the pasta. "Still not ready."

Tea could feel the tension rolling off him, but she ignored it as she continued to eat.

Later that night, she called Nan to check in.

"I only have a cough, but still no fever," Nan filled her in. "Although your grandfather isn't doing so well. He's had a hard time breathing."

She gasped. "Is he okay? Does he need anything?"

"We're going to go to the clinic and see if we can get him an inhaler or something tomorrow." Nan tutted. "Do not worry, angel. Your grandfather is a strong man. We will be fine."

She called Mom right after, but it went to voicemail. They opened all the windows in the cabin to let in the cool breeze, and both of their rooms were too unbearably hot to close their bedroom doors. The sheets felt sticky on her skin, so she ripped them off and lay there in her underwear. It was past midnight but she was still awake, listening to the clicking fan, and...the sound of grunting and heavy breathing.

She sat up. "What the hell are you doing over there?"

Archer grunted and heaved a sigh. A *thump* sounded. "Pushups."

"You're *exercising* right now? In this heat?"

"I do pushups every night."

"Why?"

"Takes my mind off things."

She pursued her lips and lay back down, listening to the

creaking sounds of Archer's bed as he climbed back in it. "What things?"

More creaking in his bed. "Nothing important."

She waited for him to elaborate. A warm wind rushed through the window, followed by the soft patter of rain. The creaking in the bed next door slowed, followed by the sound of deep breathing. She covered herself with her sheet and accepted defeat.

WHEN TEA AWOKE HOURS LATER, she was in her own bedroom in Cabin B.

"What the—"

She heard slamming cabinets downstairs.

"Wayne! Be quiet. Our girl is still sleeping."

"If she keeps sleeping she'll miss the blueberry muffins!"

Blueberry muffins. She jumped out of bed, wrapping herself in her robe, and ran down the stairs. But when she got there, the kitchen was dark and empty. No muffins. No coffee. No slamming cabinets. No Pop standing at the counter with a cup of coffee, butter and jam in his beard.

She bolted upright from her bed in Archer's cabin, skin prickling in sweat and goosebumps. It was cloudy outside and the heat had finally dissipated. She threw on a tank top and shorts, then stepped out of the cabin for fresh air. The grass was wet from the rain that swept through the night before, the clouds refusing to let go of the sky. She looked over at Cabin B, her eyes on the dark windows, wondering how Pop was sleeping.

"Hey, you're up early."

Tea didn't budge. "Weird dreams."

The screen door swung open, then snapped shut. She turned to Archer as he descended his porch steps. He was wearing gym shorts, running shoes, and a tight dri-fit shirt that hugged his biceps.

His face pinched with concern. "Is it the bed? We could swap if you're not sleeping well—"

She cut him off. "No. Pop's been having a hard time breathing. Nan has to take him to urgent care today to see what they can do."

Archer hooked an arm around Tea's neck and pulled her to him. She stumbled from the motion, but he steadied her with his other hand, keeping her upright.

He pressed his lips to the top of her head. "He's going to be okay, Tea."

Her chest ached. "But what if he isn't?" Her lips brushed against his shirt as she spoke. "What if something goes really wrong and everything goes downhill...and I'm not there to help?"

"Wayne is active and healthy—and incredibly stubborn. Just like someone else I know."

She harrumphed, which made him chuckle, his warm breath in her hair soothing her nerves. She relaxed and wrapped her arms around his waist. "So you're saying he'll be too stubborn to get too sick?"

"Precisely."

"I'm not sure that's how it works."

"I'm not sure how *any* of this works." His hand trailed up her back, and he tucked it behind the crook of her neck, pulling her head closer toward him, inviting her to rest her cheek on his chest. She did willingly as he placed his chin to her crown. "If things go downhill in the next few days, we'll handle it, all right?"

Tea squeezed her arms around Archer's body, holding

back tears. She knew what he was saying was right. Pop was healthy enough to fight something like this. But so were a lot of other people who'd caught the disease—very healthy in one moment, gone the next. She couldn't fathom not being allowed around him if something went wrong. She also knew she didn't have the power to save him. Same as the cancer that had speedily spread throughout her father's body. No amount of willing or praying could stop it from taking over.

Archer must have picked up on her tension because his hand was at her neck massaging her skin, his thumbs adding enough pressure to calm her down. When her arms relaxed, he tightened his grip at her nape and moved her to face him.

"Better?" he asked.

She nodded. They stood there for a beat, his hands drawing circles in her skin, her shoulders relaxing with each motion. She dipped her eyes to his lips. It was hard not to. His body crowded every inch of hers. She blinked up to look at all of his face.

His gaze was also drawn to her lips. His breath smelt of mint from his toothpaste and the coffee he abandoned inside. His hand moved into her hair, fingertips working at the soft space between her ears.

"Tell me to stop," he whispered.

She knew he wanted to keep that firm boundary between them, like the way he shut her down last night. But today, as the sun finally broke through the clouds across the lake, the resort quiet except for the soft call of the loons, nothing had ever felt more right. She selfishly didn't want him to stop. She wanted to keep feeling this way.

"Tell me you don't want this," he continued. "Tell me it's a mistake."

Her eyes trailed back down to his lips. "That would be lying."

His other hand, which had found the small of her back, moved to cup her cheek, his hands cradling her head like it was a precious gift. She moved her own hands as well, placing them on his chest, feeling his heart rattle between his ribcage, running at the same tempo as her own.

"*Arch*," she whispered. The tone of her voice came off more as a plea than a reassurance. Everything else about her life may not make sense—where she would live or work, whether this pandemic would truly upend everyday life like all of the scientists and newscasters predicted, thrusting them into a new normal—but at least she could rely on this. On the constant Archer Vincent had always been for her. And how much she needed him to close the distance.

He brushed his nose against hers. For a moment, she was convinced that was all she was going to get, and she accepted in her heart that she would be okay with it, that having Archer in her life as a friend again was enough. But then he dipped down and took the plunge, his lips soft but the pressure firm as he kissed her for the first time in years.

And Tea admitted the truth: Being *just friends* with Archer Vincent would never be enough.

Tea lifted to her toes and wound her arms around his neck. Without breaking the kiss, he moved a hand to her waist and lifted her to him, his other hand lost in her unruly morning hair. He gripped a fistful and tilted her head back, deepening the kiss as he slid his tongue into her mouth. A low growl escaped his chest.

It made her go molten all over, and too soon, she wanted every part of her body touching his. She dipped a hand inside the collar of his compression shirt, running it against his warm skin, and the tattoo that covered it. The thought of it—of *all* of it—had tears welling in her eyes.

She broke apart from him and stepped down to the grass, wiping her tears.

Red cheeks, swollen lips, and fear in his eyes, Archer looked at her with concern.

"It's okay," she sputtered. "I'm—I just feel—" She couldn't say the rest, the words stuck, unable to break free.

Archer leaned in and caught her tears with the pad of his thumb. "I can't be your friend, Tea."

She blinked up at him with watery eyes, still tongue-tied.

"Not when this is how I've always felt about you."

It's like he read her own thoughts out loud. She swallowed, unsure of what else to say. "Like you always wanted to kiss me?"

"Like I want *everything* with you."

She fisted his shirt, bringing him closer. "You are a very special person to me, Archer Vincent."

He smiled then kissed her again, this time soft and slow and full of unspoken words.

Similar to the last time she kissed him, enclosed by the dark, surrounded by pine trees and away from prying eyes, Tea let herself get lost in him. She dialed up the intensity, biting his lip as she fused her body firmly to his, moving her hands to his neck.

"Take me inside, Arch."

He moaned, slipping his hands to the backs of her legs. He lifted her in one swift motion, then carried her up the porch steps.

Tea trailed kisses down his neck as he swung the door wide. He sat down on the couch, shifting Tea to the center of his lap, then wrapped her hair with his hand and yanked her toward him.

She gasped.

He grinned. "You like that?"

"V-very much," she breathed.

"Good." He released his grip and hooked his thumb inside her spaghetti strap, guiding it down her shoulder. He dipped down and gently bit her neck, then licked her skin.

Dear god. "That too," she whimpered.

He laughed into her neck, his warm breath and the stubble on his chin leaving goose bumps dotted across her skin. She clenched her thighs around his hips.

"You are needy, aren't you?" He chuckled again. "I have to admit, I'm *really* into it."

She flushed. "You already knew that about me."

The words slipped out of her mouth too quickly. The flush of her cheeks deepened into a bashful ruby red.

He didn't seem to notice or care. He hummed, dragging his lips up her neck and back to her mouth, his hands squeezing her waist as his thumbs dug into the tender spots above her hips.

She was the one to moan this time. The last time Archer touched her like this, it was all desperate, with nervous hands and shaky breaths. This time he was certain, his hands firm against her body as he held her to him. She sucked on his bottom lip, the other strap of her tank top falling past her shoulders.

A phone buzzed on the table.

Tea broke apart from Archer, turning around.

"*Jesus,*" he whispered. She felt his hand on her collarbone, his thumb dipping into her cleavage. "You are..."

Another buzz. Then another.

"Arch."

His hand kept exploring her skin.

"*Archer.*" She popped up and went straight for her phone, fixing her straps on the way.

She fumbled as she swiped it open. "Hello?"

"Tea? I saw you called. Is everything okay?"

It was Mom. "Y-yes." She shook her head. "Actually, no. Nan says she has to take Pop to urgent care? Apparently he's having a hard time breathing?"

"Oh honey, he'll be okay. It's only…"

She was unable to focus on her mother's words, the sound of her heart hammering in her ears drowning them out. Tea turned to face Archer, but found an empty seat instead. A full cup of coffee sitting on the end table.

Chapter 18

Archer

ARCHER ABANDONED his earbuds in his pursuit to get the fuck out of the cabin. His sneakers slapped against pavement as he increased the pace, the sound of his harsh breathing and the pounding in his chest the only distraction he had on his run. That, and the sound of Tea's whimpering as he tasted her skin, the feel of her thighs clenching against his.

Fuck.

He slowed and placed his hands on his knees, breathing hard. What the hell was he thinking, kissing her like that? She looked so vulnerable and scared, and his immediate reaction was to protect her, then kiss her senseless? He hadn't even thought of the repercussions. Seeing her every morning, like a ruffled kitten with that unruly hair and sleep in her eyes, he felt his careful boundaries slowly unfurl at the seams. He didn't want to wait for her in the kitchen every morning. He wanted to see her first thing when he opened his eyes. Curl his body around hers and bury his face in her hair.

"No," he reminded himself. "No, no, *no*."

He thought about the last time he opened himself up to her, how horrible it was, how she made him feel.

It was the last night of summer, before he was set to leave for the University of Minnesota. They were all gathered in the basement of Cabin F when it was owned by Quentin's parents, playing truth or dare. He'd sat next to Tea that night, their bodies only a couple of inches apart. They did that a lot—sit close, but never touch. Like they were on the brink of something new, both of them too scared to make the first move.

Riley finished confessing a "truth" about why she liked Austin so much. "His hair," she confessed. Then she turned to Tea. "Okay, sweetie pie, truth or dare?"

Tea tucked her knees close. "Truth."

Her lips curled into an evil smile. "Who's your crush?"

Archer's chest tightened. He *really* wanted to look at her, but he didn't want to be so obvious. Instead, he sat there and held his breath.

"Um, never mind. I choose dare," Tea replied.

That smile grew bigger. "Great. Kiss your crush."

Archer glared at Riley, who was no longer being nonchalant about the whole thing. She stared right back at him, like she was doing him a goddamn favor.

It's not supposed to be like this. He looked in his periphery to see what Tea would do.

She didn't do anything except stand and run up the stairs.

When the door slammed, Archer stood and pointed at Riley. "Fuck you."

"Hey, watch your tongue around my girlfriend," Austin snapped.

He gave Austin a death glare. "Maybe I would if your girlfriend minded her own damn business."

"Oh *come on*, Archer. I was setting you up!" Riley pleaded. "You clearly need the nudge, you're horrible at making the move."

He puffed his chest. Then he was off, running up the stairs after Tea.

It was pitch-black outside, the moon the only light glistening over Silver Lake. He found her moments later, curled up underneath a pine tree, tears in her eyes.

He knelt in front of her. "Hey, what's wrong?"

She wiped her nose with the back of her hand. "Nothing."

"I'm sorry Riley pressured you. That was mean."

She shook her head. "I'm not crying about that."

At the time, Archer had no idea she was crying about her father, about the news that'd dropped on her earlier that night. Gareth Richards had stage four testicular cancer. He only had weeks to live.

Instead, he was an eighteen-year-old with raging hormones, and the most beautiful girl in the world sat crying in front of him. He lifted her to her feet and hugged her tight, telling her that whatever it was, he was there for her. "You can tell me what's wrong, Tea. Best friends forever, remember?"

She tilted her head back and gave him a watery, apologetic smile. "Even if your best friend has a secret crush on you?"

Every single part of his body *burned*. "R-really?"

"I would have kissed my crush, but down there didn't seem like the right—"

Archer lunged for her, fusing his mouth to hers. She kissed him back with the same intensity. They were *terrible* at it. Archer wasn't sure what to do with his hands or his tongue. Tea was shaking with nerves, her fingers fumbling as she pulled on his sweatshirt. She took a couple of steps back, deeper into the woods, and he followed. She leaned against a tree and pulled him toward her. He placed a hand on the trunk, and the feel of *all* of him pressed against her made his vision go black. He skimmed his free hand inside her tank top and up her belly. She didn't stop him as he tucked it inside her bra.

She moaned, and he practically lost himself to the sound of it. Years of tension finally snapped, and they couldn't get enough of one another. They went from zero to sixty in a matter of minutes. She undid his jeans and slid a hand inside his briefs, grabbing for him.

He broke his lips from hers. "Tea, *crap*. Is this too fast? Should we—"

She squeezed and he groaned, dipping his face into her neck.

"I'll stop if you want me to," she whispered.

"No, I absolutely don't want you to stop. I-I just don't know what I'm doing."

"Me neither," she confessed.

"You're awfully good at that for not knowing what you're doing." He released his hands and cupped her face. "Tea, are you sure?"

Her eyes were on his lips. At the time, he was so lost in her he couldn't see what was plainly on her face: She was hurting. She wanted to forget for a little while.

And Archer handed it to her far too easily.

"Yes," she whispered. "I'm on birth control."

Moments later, clothes abandoned and deep in the woods, Archer took her first, and she took his.

They dressed in silence afterward. She wouldn't look him in the eye.

Archer glided the strap of her tank top to the side and kissed her bare shoulder. "Everything okay?"

She stepped out of his grip. "That was a mistake."

His face darkened. "What do you mean that was a mistake? I thought you said you wanted it."

She hesitated, then shook her head, backing away from him.

Archer felt his stomach plummet. "Wh-what is going on?"

"We shouldn't have done that." She still wouldn't look him in the eye. "It was mistake."

"*Why?* Why do you keep saying that?"

Tears streamed down her cheeks again. "Because you are my best friend. We're moving way too fast and I feel like I just ruined everything."

"*Tea.*" He attempted to reach for her, but she stepped back. Then stepped back again.

He stilled, his skin prickly from the cold—and the distance between them. He held up his hands. "How could you have ruined everything? We *both* wanted this, remember?"

"I don't think I actually want this," she whispered.

He rubbed his face, ignoring the pinch in his nose and cheeks. He wanted to cry, but he wouldn't let himself in front of her. He didn't want her to experience how broken she was making him feel.

"I need some time," she continued.

Then she ran.

Archer had spent too many moments since that night wondering if he should have run after her, forced her to talk about what was *really* going on. But instead, he stood there, broken hearted, wondering what the fuck he did to ruin it between them so badly.

The Richards left unexpectedly the next morning. And out of respect, he gave her the space she wanted. He waited for her to reach out. She never did.

A truck honked behind him, bringing him back to reality. Archer stepped to the side of the road and sat in the grass, dropping his head in his hands.

It was a mistake. He'd asked her if she felt that way still, right before he kissed her earlier. Practically *begged* her to say it again. To remind him that he shouldn't go down that road. But she wouldn't say it.

That would be lying.

He rubbed his temples. Even after years of telling himself he would never again give Tea Richards his heart, in less than two months, he'd fallen right back into it.

He stood up and wiped the sweat on his forehead with the bottom of his shirt. Kiss or not, Tea still planned on leaving at the end of the summer. Leaving Wild Pines, and leaving him. There was no need to do this to himself all over again. Not when he had a community of people he needed to look after. Not when he had his own plans and dreams he needed to focus on.

He waited for his breathing to even out, then continued at his usual pace.

Tea was sitting on the porch when he returned, knees tucked close. He made it back to Wild Pines a while ago, but went for a walk to cool down and clear his head. He would handle this calmly. He would not let his emotions get in the way.

She lifted her face when she heard his approach. "Hey."

He nodded once. "Everything good with Molly?"

"She's good, yeah. Nan also called. They gave Pop an inhaler."

"Good." He climbed the porch steps, walking around her. "I'm going to take a shower—"

She popped up. "Archer."

He couldn't look her in the eye. Instead, he set his gaze on the screen door. "Yeah?"

"Please tell me what you're thinking."

He paused for a beat. "Was it a mistake this time too?"

"Hey," she whispered.

He shook his head. "It's a yes or no, Tea."

She didn't respond.

He felt like he wanted to puke. How could he let this happen again?

Archer climbed the last step and swung open the door.

Tea chased after him. "Archer, come on. We need to talk about it."

"No, I really don't think we do." He ripped off his shirt and tossed it in the laundry basket, then grabbed his towel and stepped into the bathroom. When he went to close the door, Tea stopped it with her hands.

He closed his eyes, took a deep breath. Stepped away from her to turn on the shower head. "Listen. It's a weird time right now. We're both scared and lonely and forced to be around each other. We got ahead of ourselves. Let's not do something we'll both regret."

Her eyes dimmed. "Is that really how you feel?"

Not even close. But he nodded, because what else was he supposed to do? He had to protect himself against her, or he would lose himself all over again.

He watched her hesitate, watched the range of emotions cross her face, until she settled for a complacent, blank expression. "Fine. Then that is how we leave it."

She grabbed the handle and slammed the bathroom door.

Archer stripped down and got in the shower, turning the spigot from hot to very, very cold.

They quickly slipped back to being cordial with one another. They were like roommates—maybe worse. They didn't hang out or talk. Archer spent his days working himself to the bone, doing any task he could possibly think of, even offering to buy groceries for anyone with COVID who couldn't leave their cabins. He spent his evenings in his bed, imagining how easy it would be to crawl into hers, then cursed himself for being such a goddamn fool and punished himself with a brutal round of pushups.

When they hit day fourteen of their quarantine, Archer came back to his cabin to find Tea packing her things.

He frowned. "Are they good?"

"No fever or symptoms for five days, so things should be safe now." She slung two tote bags over her shoulder, then made her way out of the room.

He stepped to the side to give her space, then realized the picture frame was still on the shelf. He picked it up and followed her out. "Wait, you forgot this."

Tea turned to him, looking at the photo in his hands. Then she looked up at him, her face like stone. "You can keep it."

She left without another word. She didn't even glance back in his direction.

Chapter 19

Tea

Loons are expert fishers, moving at lightning-fast speeds. They use their large webbed feet to propel themselves like torpedoes through the water, while easily breaking and kicking to make abrupt turns when needed. They also use their wings for quick escapes when they feel threatened, known as "wing rowing."

TEA SAT on the couch in Cabin B, half listening to the meeting for the Ten Thousand Lake Loon Committee on Zoom. The other half of her was listening to her grandparents fight about what they should have for dinner.

"Wayne, it's not hard. *Pick* something," Nan pleaded. "Tater tot hotdish? Tuna macaroni salad? Fried fish?"

"Anything will be fine, darling." Pop sucked on his inhaler, then placed his fishing cap on his head and kissed her cheek. "Whatever works."

Nan growled, slamming her fists on the counter "You

say that every night, then complain when I make something you don't like!"

"I'm sure it will be brilliant!" He was out the door and beelining toward his boat. Nothing would stop him from fishing after almost two weeks of being confined to the house. Their entire cabin smelt like bleach after Nan washed it thoroughly, the smell still lingering three days after Tea had settled back in her room.

Nan shook her head, muttering under her breath.

"We could have burgers," Tea said.

Nan huffed. "You know what, fine. At least someone will make a decision."

Tea sat up. "*Really?* You never say yes to burgers for dinner!"

"Tonight, I'm willing to make an exception for my girl." Nan reached into the freezer and pulled plastic-sealed burger patties out of boxes and placed them in the sink, then walked to the cabinet. "Although I don't have any burger buns, and I'm pretty sure we're out of ketchup."

She tilted her screen down. "Want me to run out and get stuff?"

"Oh, no, angel, you don't have to. You're busy with something."

She closed her laptop. "It's all good, this is kind of boring anyway."

It wasn't completely boring—the committee was talking about how the quality of water helped to enhance loon life, something she'd already read in one of her books. But she'd been cooped up in the house for three days and needed something to do. After her blowup with Archer, she didn't bother going over to the cabin and asking if he had any work for her. She also didn't go out to the beach, in case he was out and about working on things. Eventually she would have to rise from her hibernation, and a trip to the grocery store sounded like as good an opportunity as any.

"Are you sure? Going to town is so far—"

Tea rose from her seat, then slipped her sandals on. "It's only twenty minutes. Really, I don't mind. Anything else you need me to pick up?"

Nan scribbled a small list of other items they would need, then pressed a fifty in Tea's hand. Tea tried to give it back to her, but she refused, saying it was only fair if she was going to drive the twenty minutes to town.

She eventually conceded, and minutes later, was on the winding road heading to town. She hadn't been in her car since she arrived that summer. Besides grabbing groceries, or going to the clinic in Ashland, Tea had no reason to be in a car. When she was, it was with Archer in his truck.

It felt good to be behind the wheel of her father's Chevy Classic again. If she concentrated hard enough on the smell of the leather seats or the heat of the plastic dashboard, it almost felt like her father was back in this car, driving with the windows down, David Bowie blasting through the speakers.

She patted the dashboard. As if it were responding, the engine puttered, then made a gurgling noise.

She gave the dash another love tap. "Come on, buddy, almost there."

It puttered again, then the car slowed. She pulled over and parked, wincing as she heard the car make a final groan. She tried revving the engine again, but it wouldn't kick. The car made another groaning sound that, unfortunately, did not sound pleasant.

After a few panicked seconds of ferociously turning the key to get the engine going, a plume of black smoke rose from underneath the hood.

"Oh no," she whispered. "No. *No.*"

She got out of the car and lifted the hood, and was welcomed by the unmistakable smell of oil, metal, and a dead engine.

Tea ran back to the driver seat and called Nan.

"Angel, so glad you called, I was wondering if you could also grab some milk—"

"Nan, Dad's car. It…it died."

"It *died?* Where are you?!"

She frantically looked around. "Um, oh god, I actually don't know. I'm still on Route 63, near a big sign for—" She squinted her eyes. "I think that says Moose Lane?"

"Okay, I know where that is, I'll come get you." She listened to Nan frantically rifling through her purse. Then there was silence. "Uh oh."

"What's *uh oh.*"

"Your grandfather has the car keys in his pocket, and his phone is here—oh, I always tell him to bring it and he never does."

"No other set of keys?"

"Not on us, no. I think we left the other set at the farm."

By "the farm," Nan meant their two-story farmhouse surrounded by fields of corn and soybeans that was a six-hour drive away.

"Oh, wait I see Archer, let me see if he can get you."

Panic rose in her chest. "No, Nan, it's okay—"

"*ARCHER!* We need your help!"

Tea continued to plead for her grandmother to stop immediately, but it was useless. She heard her explaining to Archer what had happened and eventually gave up, settling into the driver's seat, legs dangling outside the open door. She strained to hear something—*anything*—from him. But he was silent until Nan finished explaining what happened.

Eventually, he spoke. "Where is she?"

"Route 63, outside the entrance for Moose Lane."

"Tell her I'll be there in ten."

"Did you hear that, Tea? Archer will come help you out."

"Tell him it's okay, he really doesn't have to—"

"He's already gone."

Tea hung up and rested her forehead against the steering wheel. She looked at her phone, the battery almost dead. She called her mom anyway.

It went to voicemail.

"M-mom." Her voice croaked. She wanted to unload all of it. Dad's car. Not being able to get up on a water ski. The COVID outbreak. The quarantine. The kiss. But her guilt seeped in, blocking her from speaking any of her truths. "I miss you," was the only thing she could manage before she hung up.

Ten minutes later, Tea watched as Archer's truck approached from her rearview mirror. She got out of the car and watched him park in front of her. He didn't look in her direction as he rounded the Chevy.

He stopped in front of the hood and placed his hands on his hips. "Yeah, this is toast."

Her gut twisted. "So it's not fixable?"

His gaze flicked to her, his expression soft. Apologetic. "I'm not sure. I called the mechanics in town; they're coming this way with a tow truck."

She pursued her lips and turned away from him.

"*Thank you, Archer,*" he mocked in a high-pitched tone.

She scowled at him. "I didn't ask you to come."

"Oh, well in that case." He pointed to his truck. "I'll head out then."

Tea narrowed her eyes into slits.

He shoved his hands in his pockets. "Come on, you needed someone, and I'm happy to help."

"Classic Midwest boy, doing the nice thing."

"Hey, there's nothing wrong with *being nice*."

"Except when he's not being honest about how he really feels."

He took a few steps toward her. "All right, you know what—"

His thoughts were cut off by the tow truck that pulled up next to them. The man leaned out his window, a cigarette dangling from his frowning lips as he eyed her car. "Well, that certainly doesn't look good."

TEA AND ARCHER sat side by side at Northern Auto Mechanics, neither speaking a word, when Larson, the man from the tow truck, appeared in front of them.

He looked at Tea, then slowly shook his head. "Sorry, darling. It's not looking like we're going to be able to save this one."

She leaned her elbows on her knees and placed her face in her hands.

"Completely totaled?" Archer asked.

"More than that. I'm surprised the car was even running. This thing was pretty dangerous to have on the road."

"How much would it cost to repair?" Tea mumbled.

She heard the man hesitate.

Archer placed a hand on her back. "It's not smart to repair it, Tea. It's going to cost you a fortune, and at that point, you might as well get yourself a new car."

"But I don't want a new one," she whispered. "I want that one."

She heard scratching of a pen on a clipboard, then listened as Archer thanked Larson for helping them out. The door to the auto shop swung open and shut, then they were enveloped by silence again.

Archer knelt before her and gently pulled her hands away from her face. "Hey, talk to me."

She exhaled a long, frustrated breath. "About what?"

"About the fact that you have to give up your father's car."

Her chest flared as she looked up at him. *Talk* to him? The man who kept putting up all of these walls between them? She was tired of watching Archer open up small bits of himself, only to abruptly slam the door in her face, like none of it mattered. Like *she* didn't matter.

She looked into his brown eyes, soft around the edges. His cap was backward on his head, and she could see the lines of a tan around his collar, likely from working under the blistering ninety-degree heat the past three days. The fight drained out of her.

He pulled her out of her seat, then cupped her hands as he led her out of the auto shop and into the July sun. He didn't let go until they reached his truck, parked on the side of the road.

"I'm stuck," she whispered.

Archer dropped her hands and pulled his mask down as he turned to face her. "What do you mean you're stuck?"

"I'm stuck *here*. I have to keep spending my summer here without any kind of escape." Her voice rose with every word she revealed. "I can't fly home, I now can't drive home. I don't have a car. I don't have money. I don't have a job or a place to live." Her words were frantic as she rattled them out. She ripped her mask off. "And there's literally *nothing* I can do but sit here and I have absolutely no idea what I should be doing next, or where I should go. And I miss my mom and I feel like—"

The words clogged in her throat, tight with emotion. She blinked away tears and shook her head. She'd said too much.

"Tea, what can I do? What do you want right now?"

"I want my *car*."

"No." Archer reached for her wrists again and pulled her toward him, his grip tight. "What do you *want*?"

I want to go home. But where was home? New Jersey hadn't felt like home in a long time, maybe even ever. Being with Mom was her only real reason for being there. She didn't have an apartment to call home either, and her place in Chicago made her feel like she lived in a shoebox. Wild Pines felt the most like home, but even if being in Cabin B or out on the docks felt familiar, there was still something missing. Still something she was longing for.

What she really wanted was Dad. She wanted his booming laugh and his grilled burgers. She wanted another long road trip to the lake, or a run to the grocery store with the windows down, singing "Under Pressure." She wanted to watch him dance with Mom in the kitchen and kiss her in a way that made Nan scream at them to get a room. She wanted to go out on their boat and fish or water ski. She wanted just *one* more early morning of him waking her up, telling her to get ready for a sail.

Archer squeezed her wrists. "What do you want, Tea?"

"I want to go sailing."

Tea pulled her hair into a ponytail, swimsuit on, life jacket clipped to her chest. She padded over to the beach toward Archer as he tightened the sail for a boat she had never seen before.

"Whose is that?"

Archer guided the boat into the water, not looking her in the eye. "It's mine."

"*Yours?* Since when do you have a boat?"

"Since the only person I knew that had one never came back to the lake."

Emotion seized her chest. It sounded like a dig, but she knew it wasn't. Her father's sailboat was no longer at the lake—Mom sold it a year after he passed, after Tea insisted she would *never* sail again. Mom got a nice chunk of change for it, enough to cover some of their costs until she found her job at the hospital. Secretly, Tea was grateful she would never have to see that boat again. She knew it would make returning to Wild Pines near impossible.

Archer looked up at her, like he was waiting for her to say something on the matter. But she kept her mouth shut as she stepped into the cool lake, inspecting the details of his boat: the sleek white hull with a thin yellow stripe that matched the bright sail securely tied above.

He audibly sighed. "You ready for this?"

Waves splashed around them, the sky a hazy gray. She could see whitecaps out on the lake. Dad used to say a sunny day was deceitful for sailing—the wind may be there, but it could die quickly, then you'd be stuck on the lake until the next gust...or until someone saved you. It was these gray days he loved the most, when the waves were rough and the wind blew at your hair.

Life's an adventure, Tea bear.

She smiled. "Yeah. Let's do it."

They hopped on. Archer sat in the front, Tea next to him at the back. She positioned her hands on the tiller behind her as Archer handed her the rope.

"Life's an adventure, Tea bear."

Her eyes swelled with tears. "Are you trying to kill me?"

He smiled, but it was sad. "No. Just giving you a nudge."

She wiped her eyes with the backs of her hands, then she let out some of the sail to catch the wind, and they were off.

The boat moved quickly across the water, cresting the waves with ease. Archer's boat was much lighter than her father's. It moved fast. She kept a tight hold on the rope, having to control the wind in the sail as much as she could. She pointed the boat northwest, the sail catching at the *perfect* angle. The boat tilted to the side and soared, making her belly flop.

"Still a daredevil, huh?!" Archer called out to her.

She grinned. They continued like that for she wasn't sure how long, riding each gust of wind with a grace she knew her father would be proud of. When she had the boat at the perfect forty-five-degree angle, she tilted her head back and howled with delight. Water splashed her face and hair, but she didn't care. Sitting behind the wheel of her father's Chevy Classic was *nothing* compared to how sailing made her feel. For the first time in eight years, she could truly sense her father's joy. Hear his booming laugh.

Tea could see Archer grinning, his eyes out on the lake. Then his face fell as he looked up at the sky. Thick charcoal clouds moved from the east, the sky looking angrier as the clouds traveled quickly in their direction.

"I forgot how fast the storms can roll through here," Tea said.

"Huh?" Archer shouted.

She attempted to say it again, but the wind picked up, drowning out her words.

"Maybe we should head back?!" Archer suggested with a yell.

Tea nodded and loosened the sail, allowing some of the wind to catch as she angled the tiller for a turn. A powerful gust came out of nowhere. She pulled the rope to tighten the sail, but it was useless. The wind pushed the sail out and pulled the rope with it, slipping from her hands.

"*Shit!*" she screamed, grasping for purchase.

"PULL!" Archer yelled back at her.

She tried, but the pressure of the wind was too great. She pulled, then a sharp rip came from the sail. The boat swung far to the left, then completely tipped on its side.

Tea tumbled out of the boat. She held onto her life jacket as she came up for air.

The clouds boomed above them, followed by sheets of rain.

Chapter 20

Archer

"TEA! WHERE ARE YOU?"

Archer screamed in the dark, frantically swimming around the boat. The storm that came out of nowhere had blanketed everything in darkness. He couldn't see her pale skin or wild red hair. Panic climbed up his chest as he swam.

"TEA!"

"Right here!"

He whipped around and saw her clutching the mast.

Relief flooded his body.

"Are you okay?! Are you hurt?" He had to shout at her above the booming thunder.

"The boat!"

The two of them attempted to twist the boat upright and push it to shore. But the sharp gusts of howling winds made flipping it impossible. Archer's muscles strained as he pushed with no luck.

"Maybe we should get out of the water?!" Tea yelled at him.

Right. Thunderstorms and water. Not smart.

They abandoned the boat, the two of them making their way to the patch of sand nearby. They weren't close to any of the resorts on the lake.

Tea ripped off her life jacket and threw it on the beach, then paced back and forth. She looked *furious*.

He sat down on the wet sand and unbuckled his own jacket, scanning the torn sail as his boat floated sideways in the water. It was the only part that seemed to have any damage, but it meant they wouldn't be able to sail back to Wild Pines. "There's a patch of blue sky at the northern end of the lake. I bet this storm will pass, and then someone will hopefully come get us."

His reassurance didn't seem to calm her nerves. If anything, she looked more frustrated as she paced, her face pinched into a scowl.

A crack of lightning flashed above.

"Tea!" he shouted. "It's going to be all right!"

"*Of course it is, it always is with you!*"

"What is that supposed to mean?!"

She whipped around to him, her wet hair sticking to her face. "Why are you not angry with me? You had to stop working today to rescue me, and now I ruined your sailboat!"

"Who cares! It's just a boat!"

"*Arrggghhh!!*" She screamed to the sky. It startled him. Never once had he seen her so agitated about something. "You are insufferable sometimes, you know that? You want me to *talk to you* and share my feelings, but you can't ever do the same! I *hate it*. Stop being so Minnesota Nice to me and *be real* for once!"

Anger flared in his chest as he jumped up from the sand. "*Fine.* You want me to be real with you?" He stormed up to her and got in her face. "I *hate* that you don't want to talk about your dad."

Her jaw jutted out, but she didn't respond.

"He was like a second father to me and I miss him *every goddamn day*," Archer admitted. "When I found out he died, I had to cope with the fact that I lost him *and* you in the same month, and it *wrecked* me. Then you come back to Wild Pines and you don't want to talk at all about your grief, which makes me feel like a complete asshole because I'm still grappling with mine."

She swallowed. "Yeah? Well, I hate how *you* don't want to talk about what happened to us that night."

"*Of course, I don't!* You told me I was a mistake."

"I didn't mean it, Arch!"

"Oh yeah? How was I supposed to know that, through radio silence?" He waved his arms in the air. "If you didn't mean it then why didn't you reach out to apologize—or *something* after all of those years?"

"Because I was *hurting*. I lost Dad and I didn't know how to function. The only thing I knew how to do was box up my emotions and put them away for a while. I didn't allow myself to really think about it. Or *feel*." She crossed her arms, not even bothering to wipe the raindrops away; she was soaked. "You should have reached out when you were in New York."

"And what? Hear about all of your *flings*?"

She took a step back. "What? No! I would have wanted to talk things *out*."

He shook his head. "I couldn't. I was still angry that you didn't try reaching out first, and still way too in love with you. I couldn't handle watching you walk away from me again. It was horrible the first time. You *broke* me, Theresa."

She remained silent for a beat. "You were in love with me?"

Panic climbed up his ribcage. "Y-yes."

Her eyes widened. "Are you *still* in love with me?"

Clench. Unclench. He scanned her face.

"Are you?!"

"*I don't know!*"

Her lips parted in shock.

He swallowed. "Was I really a mistake the other day?"

She shook her head. "No," she said, her tone softer, the sound of the storm almost drowning out her words. "No, never."

He felt like he could cry. "And eight years ago?"

Tea looked out toward the furious waves of the lake. "I'm so sorry, Arch. I shouldn't have done or said any of that to you. I was angry that night. My parents told me about Dad's cancer, then I went to Quentin's. I thought they were being selfish for ruining my evening, because all I wanted that summer was to kiss you, and I was determined to do so that night. And then everything felt too good and after we—"

Archer wiped the wet hair from her face and tucked it behind her ear. She flinched at his touch, so he dropped his hand.

"After, when it was done, my only thought was how could I possibly learn to love another person when the pain of losing them would be too great? I was going to lose my dad. I didn't want the same to happen to you."

"You could never lose me," he croaked.

She finally faced him. "Have you seen what's going on in the world? People are dying all around us. Our time together is not guaranteed."

"So that's going to hold you back from living your life? You'd rather live in fear than have what you want?"

"I don't know what I want."

"I don't believe that for a second."

Her face softened.

"Theresa Richards, you are the most stubborn, determined person I know. You spent this summer reading about *loons* because I know you secretly want to find that nest, and you walked into my office and told me you wanted a job and didn't take no for an answer. If you want something, you go for it."

He stepped closer to her, crowding her space. "Now tell me, what do you want?"

"I don't know," she answered.

"Liar. *What do you want?*"

"I-I—"

"Tea!"

"*I want you!*"

He grasped her waist and yanked her toward him, sealing his mouth to hers. Tea wound her arms around his neck and raked her hands in his hair. He rolled his lips against hers as he slid one hand around the small of her back, the other cradling her head. He tilted her so she was at the perfect angle to devour her mouth. She tasted even better than he remembered. Or maybe it was the fact that it felt like a tectonic shift had taken place between them. In a single moment, it felt like everything changed.

She didn't think I was a mistake.

He knew in his heart that there was much more to that evening long ago, that her words were said in anger and in fear because of what was going on at home. But it was ignoring him for eight years that got him. After a year of giving her space and not hearing from her, then another, he wondered if she really did mean it when she said he was a mistake.

But now she was here in his arms, saying she *wanted* him, admitting that he wasn't. That he *never* was.

The rain slowed to a sprinkle, then petered out. It felt like a natural shift to end the kiss, but Archer was greedy. He didn't want it to stop. He grabbed her by the ass and lifted her up. She wrapped her legs around him and cupped his face, the intensity of her kiss letting him know that she wasn't done with him either.

"*Hey, lovebirds!* Need a lift?"

They pulled from each other at the same time and turned toward the voice shouting at them.

Rhonda was in her motorboat, swinging a hook in her hands, smirking like the Cheshire Cat.

ARCHER HOOKED HIS SAILBOAT, then climbed up to sit on the bench, his mind racing. Her confession. Her kiss. It all played out in his head, his swim trunks feeling tighter and tighter as he thought about the whimpers that came from her throat, or the little flicks of her tongue.

He wasn't done with her. He was *far* from done.

Tea hopped out when they got to the dock, then the three of them guided his boat back to the beach. He pulled it out of the water, then untied the sail and released the ropes.

Archer heard Tea thank Rhonda, who replied with a sly "No, thank *you*." He didn't look up, or at least not until Rhonda was sufficiently out of ear shot.

"Archer!"

He groaned and looked in the direction of Sandy Vanderberg, who was standing on the porch of her cabin. "Yes, Sandy?"

"You can't beach your boat! Under the owners' by-laws—"

Oh *hell* no. "Tea is injured!" he lied. "I need to take care of that first."

Tea turned to him, her brow tilted in surprise.

"*Please* go with it," he grumbled low.

She smirked, then reached for her ankle. "I tumbled pretty hard!" she shouted to Sandy.

Archer beamed, then scooped her up in his arms. She clutched her ankle, dedicated to the act.

Sandy kept shouting something, but he ignored her as he carried Tea to his cabin. His mind was on *one* thing. He'd waited almost a decade for it. He wasn't going to waste another second.

Tea played with his hair as he climbed the porch steps. "Not playing dutiful, nice, Midwest boy, are you?"

"What are you talking about? I'm carrying an injured woman to my cabin."

"Hmmmm." she flicked his ear as he swung open the door. "And what injury do I have, sir?"

He looked her in the eye. "The injury of having to deal with *flings* for eight years."

A devious grin spread across her face. "Oh, that *really* bugged you, didn't it?"

"You have no fucking idea."

She laughed, then looked down at the floor. "Are you going to let me down, or?"

"Nope." He walked to the back of the cabin and straight to his bedroom.

WET SUITS WERE DISCARDED to the floor. Soft, creamy skin splayed out on top of his sheets. Red curly hair painted over his pillow. All of it felt like a fever dream.

Archer climbed on top of her, running a hand up her leg, following the slope of her curves.

Tea slipped a hand between them, reaching for him. "Arch, I want you. *Please.*"

He grinned, kissing her neck, moving his hand between her legs. "Patience, love. I rushed with you the first time. I'm going to take my time tonight."

And that he did. Archer savored every single moment, committing every dip of her body and every sound she made to memory.

Then he carried her to the shower, and did it all over again.

Chapter 21

Tea

Once a nesting site is established, loons will make their annual return. Low success rates or changes to the environmental habitat may contribute to a deviation from previous patterns, leading the aquatic birds to canvas for a new site within the territory. The pair may produce one or two eggs in a season, then remain in the nest for an incubation period of twenty-eight days.

TEA STRADDLED ARCHER'S CHEST, pinning him to the bed. A small bedside lamp cast his room in a dim orange glow, but it was still enough light to give Tea the chance to thoroughly examine all of Archer's tattoos.

She traced the snake that coiled around his left bicep with her pointer finger. "How do you decide which tattoo to get?"

He shrugged. "It honestly depends on my mood."

"Do they all have a meaning?"

"Some don't. Some do."

She hummed, drawing a line on his skin to the next one. It was a martini glass, with an olive on a toothpick inside it. "You would have a cocktail tattoo."

He slipped a hand inside the old U of M shirt he let her borrow, his fingers finding her waist. His thumbs dipped into the boxer shorts he lent her as well, drawing circles on her hips. "I have all of the six classics."

"Tattooed on this arm?"

"No, they're all over."

"*All* over, huh?" She teased a finger inside the front of his boxer briefs. "Sounds like I'll need to do a thorough examination."

His grip tightened. "You can find all of them *without* undressing me."

She huffed, crossing her arms in protest.

He chuckled. "Find them first, then I'll give you a prize."

"*Oooh*, I like this game." She rubbed her hands together. "What are the six classics?"

He tapped his fingers on her skin as he listed them off. "Old fashioned, martini, sidecar, daiquiri, whiskey highball, and the flip."

She leaned in, scanning his chest. "All right, I don't know half of those so I'll look for drinks."

"You don't know *half*? Do we need to have a lesson?"

"*Shhh*. I'm studying."

He chuckled again. His hands were still on her body, his fingers massaging her curves. She liked having Archer's hands on her far too much. The thought of what his hands did to her in this bed, in his *shower*...it made her feel warm all over. She blushed as she replayed some of it in her head.

He touched her cheek. "What are you thinking about?" he said, bemused.

"*Shhhhh.*"

He smiled, then closed his eyes, letting her trace the rest of his left arm with her fingertips.

She found a small cocktail with an orange twist. "*Oh!* This looks like a daiquiri!"

He peeked an eye open, then closed it again with a smile. "That's the sidecar. Thinking we do need to have a lesson."

She grumbled, moving on to his right arm, finding a similar looking cocktail, but with a twist of lime. "Okay *this* must be the daiquiri."

"Good girl."

She smirked as she continued. She moved on to his chest, finding another cocktail in a rocks glass. "Old fashioned."

"Two more."

She sat up straight, tapping her lip as she searched for more drinks. She noticed a small mug at the center of his chest, right above his heart. *Are any of these cocktails served in a mug?* She squinted and leaned back in to give it a closer look. Upon inspection, she realized it wasn't a mug.

It was a teacup.

She brushed her pointer finger over the outline. A string dangled from the cup's lip, a tea tag attached to the end. Words were inscribed on the tag, so small that she could have easily missed it.

Sweet Tea

She sucked in a breath.

Archer flinched. "You found it."

"Yeah, I guess I did." She brushed her thumb back and forth on the inscription. "Was this your first tattoo?"

He nodded, tucking her hair from her face so he could look at her. "This was my first, the one on my back was next."

"You remember my nickname," she whispered.

"Of course I do."

"I honestly thought you forgot."

"I would never forget anything about you."

She blinked down at him. She liked seeing him this way, soft around the edges, calm and relaxed. No stress from his job or trying to have some kind of handle on Wild Pines during the pandemic. His jaw loose, his hands gentle, his gaze tender and knowing.

He hooked a hand behind her neck. "Come here," he whispered.

She did as he asked, dipping down to kiss his lips, the feel of his stubble on her chin igniting something deep in her belly. She let her body go pliant as he rolled her to his side, sliding his hand around her waist and to her butt.

He squeezed as he broke their kiss. "I have thought about these curves from the moment you arrived."

She raised a brow. "I'm surprised. I mean, you barely looked at me."

"Trust me, I was looking."

She gave him a smug smile. "Does this mean I get my prize early?"

He bit her bottom lip and sucked on it. "I could be tempted."

She kissed his chin, then left a trail of kisses down his neck, proceeding down to his chest.

He hummed in response. "What are you doing?"

She grinned, then flipped him back over, pinning him down again with her legs, hands on his chest. "Finishing what I started."

He laughed, squeezing her thighs. "You are a tease."

"*Shh.* I have two more cocktails to find."

She eventually found them—one on his right calf, the other on his left ankle. She then became far too interested in examining the rest of his tattoos to claim her prize, brushing her hands on each piece of artwork. "Only one on your back?"

"Just the one." Archer played with her hair, curling it with his fingers. Moments later, he brushed his thumb across her lips. "You miss him?"

She didn't have to ask who he was talking about. She knew. "Every minute."

She wanted to end the conversation right there, but she knew she shouldn't. Not after everything Archer confessed to her on the beach. If he could be brave and talk through the things that hurt, then she could do the same.

She kept her eyes on his tattoos as she spoke. "I didn't want to believe he was gone. It was easier to build up a new kind of life and scrape away the memories of him that felt like scars. We moved out of our house, we created new summer traditions in the city, and I ignored my grief."

Archer sat up, sliding her to his lap, then wrapped his arms around her. He didn't say anything. He gave her space to continue.

She combed a hand through his hair. "I was so nervous coming here this summer," she confessed. "It was the first time I had to really face the memory of him. I thought it would be completely devastating, and some of it has been. I used to have these dreams about him—one moment he's there, then the next he's gone—and they came back with a vengeance once I entered our cabin. But...not all of it has been devastating. There are parts of him that I like to experience, like being on a boat, or skiing on the water." She rolled her eyes. "Or *attempting* to ski."

He smiled, but it was full of sadness. His hands caressed the small of her back.

"I miss the everyday moments the most," she rasped. "Like him singing in the car or listening to *Minnesota Public Radio* while he made his coffee in the kitchen. Or seeing the way he looked at Mom. I hate that she's so lonely now."

"I hate that *you* were lonely," he muttered.

She kept playing with his hair. "I'm not lonely anymore."

He kissed her shoulder, then pulled her in for a tight hug.

She buried her face in his neck. "What do you miss about him?" she asked.

He pecked her shoulder a couple more times. She realized he was kissing her freckles. "My dad spent his summers so busy with the resort that we never had time to do things together, like fishing or water skiing or sailing. But Gareth always had the time. He treated me like his son and taught me everything." He looked up at her. "Do you remember his lake showers?"

She groaned. "Oh god, don't remind me."

Archer grinned. "He refused to take a real shower and only wanted to wash in the lake. I thought he was *so* cool."

"You used to join him a lot."

"I did. Until I realized what his soap was doing for the environment."

She closed her eyes. "He kept doing them though."

"I should have known something was up that last summer. He didn't do a lake shower once."

"It's okay. I wasn't paying attention either. I was too preoccupied with...other things."

"Like your secret crush?"

"Shove it."

He chuckled. "Did you know Gareth was the first one to teach me how to make a cocktail?"

Her eyes blew wide. "Really?"

Archer grinned. "Yeah. He taught me how to make a margarita. Then we snuck out to the dock and drank them. He kept saying how good mine was."

"How old were you?"

"Don't worry about it."

She shook her head and snickered. "Why does this not even surprise me?"

He laughed with her, then kissed her on the lips. "How was that? Talking about it?"

"Awful," she admitted. Because it was. It *was* awful to remember her father and how much she missed him. But it was also wonderful to live through happy memories. Remind herself that he may be gone, but he would never be forgotten. "You're the only person I want to open up to."

He scanned her face. "Why's that?"

She cupped his cheeks. "Even after years of no contact, you still know exactly what to say."

"Okay, well, at this moment, I have *nothing* to say." He reached for his bedside table and switched off his lamp. "Only things I'd like to do."

He kissed her and she melted into it, ready to strip off the limited amount of clothes they had on. She wanted to feel every part of his skin on hers again. She wanted his heavy breathing in her neck and his stubble scraping her skin and the weight of his large body pressing into her.

A low growl bellowed from outside the open window.

They both froze.

"What was that?" Tea panicked.

Archer's arms were tight around her. "Oh *fuck*."

"*Archer*, is that...?"

The sound of a claw scrapping metal came next, followed by the ping of a lid hitting the dirt.

Terror seized her entire body. "Oh my god."

"*Shh*." Archer got up from the bed and peeked outside the window. She followed closely behind, peering around his broad back to get a glimpse. When he felt her behind him, he held his arm out as if to block her and keep her safe.

They watched in silence as a black bear shoved its nose inside the open dumpster.

"B-bear," she muttered, stupidly.

"So...I forgot to secure the dumpster tonight," he whispered.

"You *think*?" she whisper-screamed.

He moved his lips to her right ear. "Yeah, and who's fault was *that*?"

"Yours, obviously."

The bear continued to rummage through the trash, oblivious to the people whispering by the window ten yards away.

She scanned the screen. "Can it rip through this? Should we close the window?"

"I think it will hear us."

"Isn't that a good thing? Won't that scare it away?"

"If it isn't threatened, yes." He loosened his hold on her. "I need to tell everyone."

She followed him out to the living room. "I'll help make some calls."

Fifteen minutes later, the Wild Pines resort was flooded with light. Everyone was making loud noises to scare the bear. Music blasted, wooden spoons banging on pots and pans in kitchens, lots of yelling and shouting.

Archer watched the bear descend deep into the woods before quickly securing the dumpster and running back to the cabin. He locked the door, something they *never* did at Wild Pines—*why would you need to?*—then pointed in her direction. "You are not leaving my sight tonight."

She feigned irritation and droned, "Oh no, how awful."

He shook his head and stormed up to her, then kissed her on the mouth and walked her backward, returning them to his bed.

Chapter 22

Archer

He woke up the next morning feeling like he was still dreaming. Tea lay asleep beside him, her bare back exposed, her hair covering the surface of the pillow. He remained there for a beat, listening to her soft breathing, marveling at how any of this could actually be real.

He slid closer to her, gliding a hand around her stomach and pulling her to his chest. He kissed her shoulder, then her neck, then her cheek.

"*Ergggh*," she groaned.

He smiled. "Morning, sleepyhead."

"Too. Early."

He looked out the window at the sun, already well above the lake, the morning underway. He combed her hair with his fingers. "The princess still loves to sleep in."

"Hard to sleep when you're *talking* to me."

A low laugh rumbled from his chest. He released his hold on her stomach. "I'll leave you alone."

She snatched his hand then shimmied backward, pressing her body against his again. "I didn't say *leave*."

He grinned, settling back in with her, his face buried in

her neck. He let himself lie there, ignoring his to-do list, which was fine; it wasn't that long these days. Tea made sure of that. Plus, when did he ever get the chance to sleep in? Better yet, when did he ever get the chance to sleep in with *her?*

As he listened to her breathing go heavy, Archer's mind wandered. He thought about his summer, about how differently things could have gone. Moving up here was temporary, or at least it was until he could figure out his life in Minneapolis and whether he even had a job at Hermes Lounge anymore. But now, he wondered if maybe that wasn't what he wanted after all.

His brother's words from earlier that summer drifted into his head. *Stand up for yourself and what you want. Don't give up on the dream.*

But what if I have new dreams? he thought as he opened his eyes, examining miles of freckled skin. He kissed her back, and allowed himself the smallest pleasure of *what if.* What if he gave up on Minneapolis? On Wild Pines? What if he packed up his stuff and followed Tea back east? Would he be happy with that? Would *she?*

She rustled, waking back up. "Coffee," she pleaded.

He grinned. "Coffee."

He kissed down her spine, then sat up and got out of bed. He glanced at himself in the mirror and fixed his hair, then watched as Tea wiggled behind him, burrowing herself deeper in his sheets.

The sight of it left a goofy grin on his face that he couldn't control. The entire thing made him inexplicably happy. He wondered why he'd held himself back from having *this* for so long. Then he remembered that it wasn't only him who'd needed the time. Tea needed to work things out as well. If he hadn't given her that space—given *himself* that space—their conversation yesterday likely wouldn't have gone the way it did. It probably wouldn't have happened at all.

He stepped into the kitchen and started his routine for making coffee; grinding the beans, heating the kettle, setting the filter.

"*Psssst!*"

Archer followed the sound to the door. Rhonda stood outside, wearing a sweatshirt and jeans, mug in hand.

"Are you alone, or do you have a visitor?" she whispered through the screen.

He glanced back at the bedroom, the door slightly ajar. He turned back to Rhonda. "I have a visitor," he whispered back. "Also, go away, I'm barely dressed."

Rhonda lifted her arms in silent celebration, then did a little dance.

He rolled his eyes. "*Stop*. This is still really new."

"New my ass. You guys have been tiptoeing around each other for years."

"Yeah, well, *this*"—he pointed at himself, then at his bedroom door—"is very, very new. Go away."

"Do your parents know? Austin? Kelly? Wayne?"

"*No* one knows. And please be quiet about it until I figure out how she feels."

"You guys haven't talked about it yet?"

His face flushed as he poured hot water over coffee grounds. "There wasn't much time for talking," he mumbled.

Rhonda covered her mouth, making a scene of looking scandalized.

He glared. "Get out of here."

She lifted her arms. "All right. Secret's safe with me."

"Thank you."

"Archer?"

He blinked up at her. "Yes?"

Rhonda beamed. "I'm happy for you." Then she was off, down his porch steps and over to Steph on the lawn, the two of them off on their morning ritual of coffee on the dock.

He couldn't help his smile. *Happy.* Moments later, as he poured fresh coffee into two mugs, his bedroom door creaked open.

"She's alive," he teased.

Tea approached him, sliding her body between him and the counter. His smile widened as he held a mug to her, then placed his hands on the counter, bracketing her in.

She took a sip of the coffee and her face relaxed.

"Still a little grumpy in the mornings, are we?"

She took another sip. "Get used to it."

His heart did a backflip. *What did that mean?* Her comment sounded awfully permanent. It didn't bug him—it *thrilled* him—but he reined in his emotions. She only just woke up. Maybe she wasn't thinking clearly yet.

She took another sip, lifting a finger to his chest and tracing her tattoo. When he returned to Minneapolis that fateful summer eight years ago for college and met Kiera a week into classes, who was eager to practice her tattoo skills on someone, Archer volunteered immediately. He'd wanted something tangible to hold with him. Even if Tea wasn't speaking to him, he knew he would always carry a piece of her in his heart, so why not make it permanent? Getting tattoos was easy after that—he collected them like people collected coins or baseball cards. But there were only two on his body that truly meant something to him: Gareth's sailboat on his back, and Sweet Tea on his heart. In his two years with Janelle, she never asked him once if any of his tattoos meant something to him. He wondered if that was one of the reasons he'd fallen into a relationship with her so quickly. They worked well together...but they also kept each other at a comfortable distance. Nothing ever felt too deep with her. Or at least, nothing did compared to how deeply he felt for Tea.

She scanned his face. "Sleep well?"

He nodded. "Very."

"Me too," she whispered. "I've never shared a bed with someone before. I'm surprised I didn't hate it."

"Never? Not even with your *flings*?"

She lifted a brow. "Archer. Drop the flings. I don't bug you about Janelle."

He shrugged. "You could, if you wanted to."

"Hear about your gorgeous ex-girlfriend and the committed relationship you had that I didn't have any idea about? No thanks, I'm good."

He leaned in closer and cupped the back of her neck, angling her face to his. "There's only one thing you really need to know about my past relationship."

She frowned. "Fine, what is it?"

"I never once felt for her the way I feel for you."

Her face softened. "Really?"

"There's never been anyone else like you, Tea. You're it for me."

She placed her mug down, then looped her arms around his shoulders, pulling him into a hug. He squeezed her back, waiting to hear what she would respond. But after a couple beats, he realized she wasn't going to say anything. He felt a snag in his chest, like someone was pulling a string loose. *Does she not feel the same way? Did I say too much?* His mind began to spiral, but he forced himself to quiet it. They had only been together like this for less than twenty-four hours. He wasn't getting far too ahead of himself. She would talk to him about how she felt in time. He needed to be patient.

He squeezed her again. "What are you up to today?" he mumbled in her ear.

"Hmmm." She released her hold and looked at him. "Think you could fix your sail?"

He smirked. "Maybe. Looking for a particular nest?"

She rolled her eyes. "Eight years without sailing is too long. I need to make up for lost time."

He gave her a mischievous grin. "There's *a lot* of lost time to make up for."

She slapped his arm. "It took everything in me to get out of bed. Don't make me do it again."

He groveled, which made her laugh. He loved her laugh, the way it sweetened any room she was in, like honey in a hot cup of tea. He lunged for her waist and tickled her, which made her laugh—then scream. He clenched her waist and lifted her up, depositing her on his couch, his hands smooth on her skin as he crawled on top of her. He moved from one kind of tease to another, listening to the way her laughter shifted into pleading. Archer decided that while he liked hearing her laugh, he liked hearing her *beg* much more. Especially when it was his hands and his body that she begged for.

ARCHER SPENT a majority of the next week doing two things: kissing Tea, or thinking about the next time he'd be able to kiss Tea. Finally having her in the way he always wanted didn't slow down the intensity of his feelings for her —it ramped them up. With Janelle, it hadn't been anything like this. She was an easy girlfriend, a good partner to him… until she wasn't. But with Tea, he felt that constant flame, and he enjoyed every minute of the burn.

During the days, he worked and watched Tea from a distance. After he fixed his sail, she went out on his boat three more times, returning with windswept hair and glowing skin. It took everything in him not to drag her to his cabin and kiss her pink cheeks. Undress her from that striped one-piece and keep her in his bed the rest of the day.

They kept things quiet at first, wanting to keep whatever was happening between the two of them. Rhonda didn't say a word, but that never stopped her from winking every time she saw him.

Tea was cautious about how often she came to the cabin, especially with her grandparents close by. At night, she would wait until Kelly and Wayne went to bed before sneaking over to his place then creeping back even later.

"This is a little ridiculous," he admitted one night as Tea got dressed to go back to Cabin B. "I feel like a teenager. Let's tell them."

She shrugged on her shirt. "If I tell my grandparents, they're going to come at me with twenty million questions."

"Is that so bad?"

She paused. "Kind of? How are we supposed to answer their questions if we're still figuring things out ourselves?"

He sat up and placed his feet on the floor beside his bed, then pulled Tea close. She stepped into the space between his legs and ruffled his hair. He had gotten the sense that Tea was not ready to talk about what would happen after the summer. He'd tried bringing it up once or twice, asking her what kind of job she wanted after all of this, or where she would want to live in New York. Archer wanted to hear her talk about her hopes and dreams, and maybe see if there was a way he could fit into all of it. Go *with* her. But she always changed the subject.

He ran his hands up the backs of her thighs. "What if we said that?"

"Doesn't that seem kind of vague?"

He titled his head. "We're still living through a pandemic, you know. I think there are a lot of other people out there who are also trying to figure things out."

She played with his hair. He closed his eyes, reveling in the feel of her hands, the way her touch made his shoulders relax.

"Doesn't that scare you?" she asked.

Yes. He was scared. At Wild Pines, everything was safe and easy. But outside of his cabin, where it felt like the world was falling apart? The two of them would have to face that reality eventually. It felt like he and Tea were on the edge of the dock, waiting to take the leap.

Yet after years of anger and longing, wishing that things had gone differently with the girl who stole his heart, he didn't want to spend his time with her being scared. He wanted to make the absolute most of it.

"What scares me is not getting the chance to wake up next to you in the morning," he admitted. "I don't want to hide this anymore, Tea. Who cares what everyone thinks."

She scanned his face, allowing the silence to linger between them. Then she crawled into his lap and kissed him. "Okay," she whispered. "Let's tell them."

He moved his hands up her legs, then slipped them inside her shorts.

Chapter 23

Tea

There are four types of loon calls you may hear that communicate different things between pairs. The wail, used for long-distance communication between mates, particularly under stress. The yodel, typically used by the male when he feels threatened by an intruder. The hoot, a soft call that signals communication between the family at short distances. And the tremolo, also known as the "crazy laugh" that is used when threats are perceived. But there is also a fifth and lesser-known call—a soft cooing between two mates when they are close to one another at their nest.

THE LAKE WAS quiet the next morning as Tea blinked her eyes open. She wasn't used to waking up to the quiet. Usually by the time she woke up, people were out on the beach, the teenage cohort playing volleyball or making some kind of ruckus, and Pop was slamming cabinet doors downstairs while Nan pleaded with him to *keep it down*. But this moment was still. Serene.

She reached for her phone and discovered it was six in the morning. Two notifications waited for her. One was a missed call from Mom, likely on a break during her shift. They kept missing each other the past few weeks. She hadn't had the moment to tell her about Archer, yet each time they missed a call, she couldn't help feeling relieved. She liked how safe things felt with Archer at the moment. Inviting the rest of the world into it meant actually facing what came next, and she didn't feel ready to face it.

Even though her second notification forced her to.

It was an email from Bank of America about her internship.

To: Theresa Richards
   (trichards@gmail.com)

From: Bank of America Recruitment Team
   (recruitment@boa.org)

Dear Theresa Richards,

We are pleased to let you know that Bank of America will be shifting our summer internship programs to new programs this fall. We are delighted to welcome you as a Financial Analyst intern at the bank. Given the state of the pandemic, this position will be a hybrid role. This means some of the days you will work remotely, and others will be in-person at our offices in Manhattan. We will send you the proper equipment for at-home work. Your start date is September 15.

Please let us know if you are still interested in this

internship, and we'll send over a contract with salary details.

Thank you for your patience, and we hope you are keeping well during these trying times.

Stacy Gils
Bank of America Intern Program Coordinator

She turned the screen over and placed it on her nightstand, aghast. She lay there for a moment in stunned silence, then got out of bed and bundled up in a sweatshirt and leggings, making her way outside and sliding the screen door gently behind her.

Except for the early morning calls of the crows and the creatures slowly waking up around her, the lake was calm. A family of ducks swam up to the beach, dipping in and out of the water. The remnants of a thunderstorm lingered south of her, soft booms of thunder that passed over the resort late last night, leaving the grass dewy and the benches slick from the rain. She wiped down the seat at the dock then curled into herself, admiring the lake and the majesty it beheld, quiet and serene, leaving her alone with her wandering thoughts.

Streaks of cotton candy–pink covered the sky, blocking the sun as it slowly rose to meet the day. Tea couldn't recall the last time she was up early enough to experience a Silver Lake sunrise, but she never forgot the feeling. It made her feel small in a great big world, like a tiny speck in a grander plan. A pebble on the beach. A pinecone on a tree, moved by the force of the wind. Without the rumble of boats, she could hear the soft hoots from the loons, echoing across the lake and into open windows and screen doors behind her.

What do I do?

She'd worked hard to get that internship. She knew working at a bank wasn't the most appealing career choice, but numbers made sense to her, and eventually the pay would be really good. She chose this internship because it was closer to Mom, and after everything the two of them had been through—the late nights at the hospital, moving out of their home, finding ways to scrape by with only one paycheck coming in—she couldn't fathom leaving her behind. She had to return east.

She rested a cheek on her knee and listened to the loon songs. Yes, this place was special. It was the only place that truly felt like home. But eventually, like the loons, they would all have to migrate elsewhere for the winter. She couldn't stay forever.

NAN, Pop, Larissa, and Astor were exactly where she and Archer expected them to be during an afternoon at the lake; enjoying chips, dip, and margaritas for happy hour. They sat around the picnic table on the porch of Cabin F, already making a ruckus of noise as the two of them approached from across the lawn.

"Can I *please* hold your hand?" Archer begged.

"My god, can you not go a few minutes without touching me?"

"No, I don't think so."

She shook her head. Archer was doing *a lot* of that lately. Sweet little comments that made her heart melt, expressing his need for her while his big hands roamed her body. His mouth showing his need in *other* ways. Her skin prickled at the thought of what that mouth did to her thirty minutes earlier.

"Hey."

She looked up at him, his face soft and serious. "Yeah?"

"It's going to be okay. One day at a time, remember?"

Tea hummed as they reached the porch. "One day at a time," she repeated.

They climbed the steps.

Larissa jumped from her sweet. "Archer! Is that really you? Come to finally join me on my porch?"

He gave his mother a teasing face. "Mom, I've come over for dinner a couple of times now."

"A couple of times a summer is pathetic, son."

"Hey, I've been busy!" He turned and pointed to Tea. "Right? We've been busy?"

Tea shrugged. "I don't know. A couple of times *does* sound pathetic."

His mouth fell open, which had everyone laughing. His eyes thinned into slits, but a smile widened on his cheeks. He liked when she teased him.

"Okay, okay, fine. I have another excuse," Archer announced.

"It better be a good one," Larissa grumbled.

Archer shrugged, then turned to Tea. She nodded once, slight enough for him to get the message. *Go for it.*

His mouth burst into that grin, the one that Tea couldn't help but fall for. Gleaming white teeth, teasing dark-brown eyes, a sharp jawline that made him look less like a boy in his youth and more like the man she had come to know. Somehow in the years apart, Archer Vincent transformed into an even more gorgeous version of himself, and it stole her breath away. She wondered what a man like him could see in someone like her, a woman barely holding on as her life sailed by at top speed.

Archer slipped a hand around her waist, then kissed her on the lips.

Nan and Larissa gasped. Wayne and Astor cheered and clinked glasses.

"Since when?" Larissa asked at the same time Nan shouted, "How long?!"

Tea blushed. "A week."

Astor threw up his hands. "A week?" He pointed to his son. "It took you *that* long to seal the deal?"

Archer shook his head with a smile. "Hey now, that's not fair."

She shrugged. "I don't know, Arch. That *is* a long time to seal the deal."

He squeezed her waist as the others laughed then chattered excitedly amongst themselves. He leaned in close, his lips at her ear. "Good things come to those who wait?" he murmured.

She smirked as she whispered back, "Shall I remind you of that later?"

He chuckled, his breath warm on her skin. "You are not playing nice today."

She turned to look at him, their faces close. "I give you full permission to not play nice later as well."

"You dirty little—"

She stepped out of his grasp, which made him laugh. Tea took a seat at the table. Archer lifted the last chair and placed it close to Tea's so he could put an arm around her shoulders, his fingers gliding across her skin.

Larissa clapped her hands together. "I want every detail."

"No, you don't. That's gross," Archer quipped.

She rolled her eyes. "Not *that* kind of information."

Nan furrowed her brow. "I'm confused."

Astor chuckled. Wayne scanned the group, also looking confused.

"When did you first kiss her?" Larissa asked her son.

Archer looked at Tea with a sweet expression, like he was recalling a special memory. "When we quarantined together."

Even the mere thought of that kiss, how it went from sweet to *very* hot in a matter of seconds, made her skin go warm. The way those hands of his took control, making her beg for more and more.

He rubbed her arm.

Larissa looked confused. "That was more than a week ago."

Archer frowned as he responded to his mother. "Okay, relationship police. We had some things to work out."

"And what did you work out?" Nan asked.

Archer moved his hand from her arm to her hair, combing sections of it with his fingers. "That I don't want to leave her side."

Butterflies took flight in her belly at his words. *Not leave her side?* What did that mean? Her thoughts spiraled as the *awws* and *how sweets* came from the group.

"Tea?"

She looked at Nan across the table.

"Have you told your mom yet?"

She hesitated, then shook her head. "She's been, um, really busy at the hospital. Haven't been able to get her on the phone."

Archer's hand paused for a brief moment, then continued playing with her hair.

Astor popped up from his chair. "This calls for more

margaritas!"

Larissa and Wayne lifted their glasses and cheered. Nan kept a close eye on Tea, hands in her lap.

Archer pointed to his father as he stood up. "Don't you dare touch that shaker. I'm making it." He then turned to Tea and held out his hands. "Time to learn how to make a proper margarita."

She took his hands and let him lead her into the cabin. He slid the door shut, then pulled her deeper into the cabin, away from listening ears. He cupped her face with his big hand. "Hey, you good?"

She hesitated.

He brushed his thumb across her cheekbone. "*Talk* to me, Tea. Tell me what you're thinking."

She leaned into his palm. "You don't want to leave my side?"

"Does that scare you?"

She could have said *no* and kept things good between them. She wasn't ready to tell him the truth about what she woke up to that morning. But this was Archer in front of her, her best friend of many, many years. She knew she could trust him to hold her honest thoughts.

"Yes," she whispered. "I'm scared."

He leaned down to kiss her cheek. "We'll figure it out. One day at a time, remember?"

She didn't say anything at first, then simply nodded. Her thoughts were too muddled in her head. The look of Nan's face across the table. The fact that she still hadn't talked to Mom. The internship. New York. The man in front of her who wanted to be by her side but also had big dreams of his own. Did this mean Archer wanted to give up his dreams? What did he actually mean when he'd said that?

He laced his fingers through hers with a beaming smile. "Come on, let's have your first cocktail lesson."

Tea stood at the counter as Archer grabbed all of the ingredients, as well as a cocktail shaker, a jigger, a small cutting board, and a knife.

She pointed to the latter two. "What are those for? I thought we are making drinks?"

"For the lime juice."

"Can't we use the bottled stuff?"

He looked at her like she'd just committed a major crime. "And this is why we're having a lesson."

She shook her head.

He chuckled. "What?"

Tea shrugged. "It's fun to see you passionate about something."

He beamed, then moved to stand behind her and kiss her shoulder. "I'm passionate about *a lot* of things."

She rolled her eyes. "Okay, Casanova, show me how to margarita."

He remained behind her as he pointed to the different objects and bottles. "Most people assume when making a cocktail that you put the spirit in first, but you actually want to do it last. It's the most expensive product going in the shaker. So if you screwed up your measurements and the tequila was already in there, then you wasted quite a bit of money."

"Got it. So what's first?"

He had her cut and juice a fresh lime, then add in the simple syrup and orange liquor.

Archer stepped up to the counter beside her. "You could use blue agave instead of simple in margaritas, but we're working with what we got." He lifted the bottle of silver tequila. "Now this is the part where we add the spirit."

"*Finally.*"

He barked out a laugh, then uncorked the bottle and handed it to her. "Two ounces, so two pours in the smaller part of the jigger."

She did as instructed, pouring in her measurements as Archer scooped ice from the freezer. He tossed it in. Then he sealed the shaker with the top and handed it to her. "Now shake really hard until the outside is so cold you can't stand it."

Tea went to shake, then hesitated and slid it over to him. "Why don't you show me?"

He smirked. "Getting lazy?"

She leaned her elbows against the counter. "I want to see you in action."

He shrugged then lifted his arm and shook, his biceps flexing with each shake. He was mesmerizing to watch, moving from two hands to one as he grabbed more ice for her glass, then reached for the strainer. He popped it open and strained her drink, topping it with a lime wheel.

The entire moment was less than a minute, but it was enough for Tea to surmise that she could not be the reason Archer walked away from all of his connections in Minneapolis, or even his work at Wild Pines. He was naturally good at all of it, and it was clear by the pleased expression on his face as he slid his glass to her that he loved it with his whole heart.

I don't want to leave her side.

Her heart sank as she took a sip of the drink and watched him make another for himself, knowing deep down that while everything about their summer felt perfect, at some point she would have to say goodbye.

Chapter 24

Archer

WORD SPREAD FAST about the two of them. Archer couldn't go a day working at the resort without someone stopping to congratulate him—or to tell him it took him long enough. Sandy was particularly vocal about Archer's inability to lock her down long ago. Joel remained confused, stating that he was certain they had been together all this time. Their comments didn't matter to him though. Archer Vincent was the happiest he had ever been.

He walked back from the storage unit, putting on his work gloves. It was four o'clock and he still had a few more things to do. The docks needed another power wash, and weeds were starting to build up along the beach.

He scanned the lawn, hoping to find Tea sitting in her usual chair, reading another book about loons. He teased her about them constantly, but mostly because he wanted to hear her talk about it. He liked listening to the things she was learning, experiencing that smart, incredible brain of hers working in real time.

He stepped in a circle looking for her, then found a flash of red hair in his cabin window. She sat on his couch, her hair loose around her shoulders, book perched on her knees. She twirled a scrunchie with her finger before placing it on her wrist, then leaned back on the couch.

He removed his work gloves and dropped them on the deck of his cabin, then swung the door open.

Piercing blue eyes peeked at him over her book. "Done for the day?"

He shrugged. "Sure."

She frowned. "How much more do you have to do?"

Archer removed his dirty Silver Falls T-shirt and tossed it to the ground before climbing onto the couch. Tea shimmied over to make room for him, like it was the most natural thing in the world for him to come home to her. To lie on the couch and wrap his arms around her.

He squeezed her waist and nuzzled her neck. "Doesn't matter."

She sighed. "I probably should say it *does* matter, but..." She closed the book and placed it down on the floor. "At this moment, I don't think it matters either."

He grinned. "Good."

They remained there for a long while. He rested his head on her chest and listened to her heartbeat, steady and strong. Golden light streamed in from the window as the day grew later. Small particles of dust danced in the air, moving in their own little orbit. Tea lifted her hand, her fingers playing through the stream of light, the particles of dust swirling around in a tempo of her command.

Archer traced his fingers up her arm, then twined them with hers. He liked the look of their hands together. His, covered in the tattoos that he was fond of. Hers, unblemished freckled skin, bronzed from hours out in the summer sun.

She stretched her fingers wide and played with his

hand, rubbing her thumb across the sword tattoo on his pinky finger. "What are you thinking right now?" she breathed.

"That I like the way our hands fit together," he answered honestly.

She pressed her lips to the top of his head. He could feel her smile. "Okay, Casanova."

"I'm not joking."

"I know you aren't."

The sun set earlier each day, a horrible reminder that summer was coming to end. In three weeks, Wild Pines would close up for the winter, and he would have to figure out his life. Was it back in Minneapolis? Or was he meant to follow her?

He hadn't attempted the conversation with her since they admitted to their families that they were together. There was something in the way she'd looked at him that day, something sad in her expression. He was scared to find out what it meant, especially when it felt like *everything* was on the line. He knew eventually they would have to talk about it.

He cleared his throat. "I'm also thinking about what comes next."

She fidgeted. "As in what we're having for dinner tonight?"

"As in where I'll be going at the end of the month."

She fell silent.

Archer covered her hand with his, then curled their arms close.

"Have you heard from Hermes Lounge at all?"

"No, not yet."

"Have you tried reaching out?"

His heart sank. "I haven't attempted it."

"Do you want to go back?"

He kissed her shoulder. "I don't know what I want anymore."

She hummed. He waited for her to ask what he truly wanted, but she shifted and said, "Tell me about the cocktail school you want to start."

"What do you want to know?"

A hand combed through his hair. "What made you want to do it?"

Archer brushed his hand down her arm, then placed it on her thigh. "I enjoyed taking my classes to get my certification, but I realized that not everyone wants to go through a rigorous program like that, where the focus is more on having a career. Some people just want to learn how to make a decent cocktail. I would have customers come in and ask for the specs on our drinks, but I wasn't allowed to share them. It had me thinking...why not open up the lounge for a few classes during the day? I pitched it to my manager last year, and he didn't hate the idea. As long as I didn't share the secrets for our specialty cocktails and taught the classics and crowd pleasers, like margaritas and espresso martinis, then it could be a cool way to bring in more business. I figured maybe I'd start there and then if it took off, transition it into a business of my own."

He rubbed her soft skin, his thumb pressing into her inner thigh. "Then the pandemic hit. I don't think people are going to take classes in person right now, or who knows if we'll ever get to do anything like that again with the way things are going down. All of these new spikes are making people nervous. I feel like my career in hospitality imploded." He paused, then lifted his head to look at her. "I'm wondering if I need to find something new to work toward."

She pursed her lips. "I highly doubt cocktail lounges and in-person classes will be gone forever."

"Tea, they're talking about kids going remote for the entire next school year. I can't go this whole winter and not work. I'll need to find something new."

She poked his nose. "I think you should reach out to them."

"Why?"

"Why not?" She shrugged. "What's the worst that could happen? They say no and they are closed for good?"

"No, the worst could be them telling me that I should never return because of what I did, and my career going up in flames because no one will ever want to work with me again." He pressed his lips together then blew out a breath. "Or that cocktail lounges will cease to exist after this."

She sat up and snatched his phone off the coffee table. "Stop being dramatic. We're going to write an email together right now."

"Uh...now?"

"Yes, now." She typed in his passcode. He wasn't surprised in the slightest that she knew it—she was obser-vant, and he had nothing to hide. She opened up a new message on his email and handed it to him.

He smirked. "You're the businesswoman. You write the email."

She did a satisfied little wiggle that made him laugh. He tightened his grip on her thigh and moved her leg so it was wrapped around him, then nestled in as she typed. When she was finished, she read it out loud to him to approve before sending it off to his manager.

Despair gripped his heart. He didn't want to think about his manager's response, or the end of the summer. It was too much to handle. He wanted to stay on this couch, under the streaming golden sunlight, wrapped up in her forever. He didn't want to think about the future. He wanted to live in blissful ignorance.

He slid his hand up her leg and kissed the center of her chest, then worked his way up her neck. "Join me in the shower?"

She hummed, her arms making their way around his shoulders as she shimmied into the cushions.

"What the hell do you think you're doing?!"

They both froze. Archer lifted his head to the door, wondering if someone was yelling at *him*. But the sound was coming through the open window of his bedroom, on the other side of the cabin.

A muffled voice responded. He couldn't make out the words.

"*¿Estás chalado?* You've been doing this all this time? *¡Qué locura!*"

It was Jorge.

A door slammed shut. "I don't understand you!"

And that was...Joel?

Archer looked at Tea.

"Fishing cabin," they said at the same time.

They bolted upright. Archer pulled on his shirt as they exited his cabin, then jogged over to the commotion. By the time they reached the small fishing hut, others had congregated as well. Rhonda, Steph, Kelly, Lily, and his father.

Joel stood in front of the door, arms crossed, his face tight with irritation.

Jorge stood at a distance from Joel, shaking his head as he made his way over to his wife, rapidly filling her in on what happened in Spanish. Archer knew a few words from his time in school and working in the service industry, enough to pick up on the gist of what was going on. When

Jorge opened up the door to clean his fish, he found Joel making a mess of it.

He glared at Joel. "You've been angry at me about not catching the culprit, but it's been you all this time?"

Joel crossed his arms. "I was teaching you a lesson on leadership. You clearly couldn't figure out who it was, and it's been *months*."

Rhonda laughed out loud. It wasn't a true laugh though. It was more of a disbelieving one—a *I can't believe you* one. "So you come in here every week and make a mess of everything, then blame *my* kids and get angry at Archer? Joel, I've been waiting years to say this, but I think you're a lunatic."

Steph patted her wife's shoulders. "All right, calm down."

"How can I be calm? The man's insane!"

Joel pointed a finger at Astor. "No, *he's* insane for giving up his position five years before we all agreed he would!"

Dad's brow wrinkled. "You're blaming me for this?"

"*Yes.*"

"Funny." Dad crossed his arms. "I don't remember agreeing to anything, and I didn't think I needed to consult you on my business decisions."

"I think you do. Your family might be managing the resort, but we own our cabins. *We* are the ones in charge."

"And are you dissatisfied by how the place has been run this summer?" Dad breezed a hand around the landscape to make a point. "We don't have our cleaning services coming in and we don't have money from renters and many of us currently don't have jobs. Yet despite all of that, my son has done an excellent job keeping this place in shape while caring for everyone here, and for at least a fourth of what he was paid in Minneapolis."

Many pairs of eyes darted in his direction. He shifted on his feet uncomfortably.

Dad continued. "Let me remind you that I am still an owner, and I know for a fact that without Archer, things could have gone a lot differently this summer. I don't think I would have had the same energy to take care of Wild Pines *and* manage to keep people safe during a global pandemic."

"He helped me fix my boat. For *free*," Jorge added.

"*And* he helped all of us with delayed association fee payments," Lily added.

"Did you see Archer strip and add new varnish to all of our picnic tables?" Rhonda asked him with a sweep of her hand. "We didn't even ask him to do that."

"Or remove all of the clovers from the lawn so the kids don't have to deal with bee stings," Steph chimed in.

The group kept at it, listing off all the things Archer accomplished that summer. His chest swelled with pride. He may have felt way in over his head at the beginning of May, but as he listened to his community list off all of the little things they noticed he did to make their space the best it could be, it made him surprisingly emotional. It made him realize that maybe, after all of this time, he actually did like being the manager of the Wild Pines resort.

"If you are uncomfortable with the way things are changing around here, then you and Sandy are more than welcome to put your cabin up for sale," his father said.

Gasps dotted around the crowd, which had grown bigger during the argument. Every owner was now present, as well as a few of the teenagers pausing from their game of volleyball.

Joel's face was the color of a tomato. "How dare you. We were the first ones here."

"That claim means nothing. In fact, I believe it is in our

by-laws that the owners of other cabins can vote owners out if they are hostile and present a threat to the ecosystem of the resort."

Silent nods followed. Archer felt Tea step close, and he brushed her fingers with his.

Dad unfurled his arms. "So what's it going to be? Should we call a vote, or will you apologize and accept that change is, in fact, very good for our resort to thrive in Silver Falls for years to come?"

Joel kicked a rock with a force that surprised Archer. The man seemed fragile, but he certainly had spunk hidden in there somewhere. Especially if he gutted fish every week and made a point to leave the cabin in a state of disarray.

Joel stilled and looked at him, his expression poisonous rather than apologetic. At this point, Archer would take what he could get. This was already too much of a scene, and the last thing he wanted was to kick Sandy and Joel out of the cabin that they've happily owned for over fifty years.

"I apologize," Joel spat. "I will not interfere again."

Archer nodded. "Apology accepted."

No one said a word as Joel continued to glare at Archer.

He shoved his hands in his pockets. "You are right, Joel. This is as much your home as it is ours. If you have any issues with how things are done, please come talk to me. I would be happy to work out a solution. I don't want you to feel like you need to make a statement to get your point across. If you're unhappy, then let's do something about it. I want you to be happy here—for *all* of us to be happy here— for years to come."

Astor smirked. "Does that mean what I think it means?"

Archer turned to look at Tea as he answered. "Yeah. I'm not going anywhere."

Tea gave him a genuine smile. She was *happy* for him.

And while he felt confident in his decision, the look on her face made him feel torn between two different worlds.

Whoops and hollers sounded off from their small crowd.

Joel nodded, then turned on his heel and left for his cabin. Sandy stood clutching the banister as he approached, then violently whispered at him as they entered Cabin C.

Steph patted Rhonda on the back. "Babe, you can't call an old man a *lunatic*."

People chuckled as they dispersed.

Rhonda held up her arms. "Am I wrong?"

Steph rolled her eyes. "Come on, let's get you a drink."

Jorge rubbed his eyes. "I think we could all use a drink." He pointed at Archer. "Pisco sours?"

Archer grinned, then snaked an arm around Tea's shoulders. "Pisco sours?"

"I have no idea what those are," she admitted. "Cocktail lesson number two?"

"Oh he doesn't know how to make a true one," Jorge quipped.

Lily slapped his arm as they began to walk toward their cabin. "Jorge, be nice."

"It's not my fault his fancy cocktail school taught him all wrong!"

Archer eyed his father, who was chuckling along with the interaction. He hesitated, then turned to Tea. "Hey, go with them, I'll catch up."

Tea kissed him on the cheek, then followed Jorge and Lily.

Astor titled his head. "You okay?"

Archer cracked his knuckles. "Oh yeah. I'm glad we figured out who was doing it. Cleaning that cabin every week was driving me crazy."

"At least you cleaned it. If it were me, I would have left it to rot until the culprit came forward."

"That's...disgusting, Dad."

"And that's why you are the best person for this job."

He paused. "Thank you," he replied gingerly.

Astor patted his back. "I'm proud of you, son. This summer hasn't been easy."

"No, it has not."

They remained there for a beat, Astor's hand on his back, the trees rustling from the warm breeze coming from the east.

Eventually he watched his father walk away, stunned by his words of praise.

His mind raced as he made his way to Jorge's cabin. Four Pisco sours sat on the table beaded with perspiration. Jorge was busy in conversation with Tea, Lily nodding along to whatever her husband was saying.

Archer took the seat next to Tea and reached for a glass, then took a large sip.

Jorge looked smug. "Good, right?"

He shrugged. "Needs more simple."

"You're such an ass."

Archer smirked as he leaned back, throwing an arm around Tea's shoulders and kissing her on the head.

"Hey, Jorge was telling me that he got his job back," Tea said.

Archer's brows shot up. "Seriously? Dude, congrats."

Jorge sighed. "Yes, back to the office three days starting the second week of September. I don't love the idea of going to the office, but I *do* love the idea of making money again." He lifted his glass to the two of them. "Thank you for being kind about my delayed payments. It meant a lot to us."

"We could probably pay you soon," Lily added. "Potentially in a week or so."

Archer swiped his hand. "Don't worry about it. Tea was able to work out finances so we could pay the association in full. As long as you pay what you need to before the next season, we will be good."

Jorge sighed, leaning back in his chair as he took a sip of his drink. "That must be nice. Having someone working for you who actually knows what they're doing with finances."

Tea frowned. "Do you guys not have someone working on your accounts?"

"Oh we do, but he's horrendous at it. I mean, clearly. Half of us were furloughed this summer because he didn't consider the right amount of savings to take care of employees in crises such as this. Which is embarrassing considering the company relies so much on public donation. Me and a few of my colleagues are advocating for new financial management; someone who actually knows what's best for those kinds of resources."

Archer couldn't help himself. His eyes flicked to Tea as Jorge talked. Her face was pinched into a scowl, the crease in her forehead visible, deep in thought.

Financial management? Someone new? *Minneapolis?*

He closed his eyes. *No.* He couldn't hope like that. She had her heart set on being with her mom, and he wouldn't be the one to sway her decision. She'd made it clear that he should move forward with his life in Minneapolis. He just wished she would consider a life where he wasn't only a part of it for three months of the year. He didn't want to settle for only the summer. He wanted the whole year. He wanted years to come. He wanted it all.

Chapter 25

Tea

A week after birth, loon babies can already dive and swim, but their favorite mode of transportation is riding on the backs of their parents. They rely on their parents quite a bit during the first weeks of their life. They are fed by their parents for the first six weeks, and they don't take flight until week eleven or twelve. By the end of the summer, the juvenile loons leave the nest and habitat in coastal regions until they are ready to breed and claim a lake environment of their own.

She wondered if it was a stupid idea. Then she remembered this was *Archer*, whom she would have never hesitated to do this to before. She grinned and stood there in her swimsuit, watching him sleep soundly in his bed. Then she took a deep breath and jumped on him.

Archer bolted upright and grasped her arms, eyes wide,

hair sideways from sleep. When he noticed it was her, he relaxed. "You monster. What time is it?"

"Midnight."

He groaned, letting go of her and falling back onto his pillow. "You better have a good reason for waking me up an hour after I went to bed."

She crossed her arms. "Archer Vincent, what day is it?"

"The day I kill you," he grumbled.

"Nooooo. The *day*."

"Um." He twisted to his right and tapped his phone screen. "August twenty-second?"

"Not the date. The day."

He looked at her with a quizzical expression. Then she watched the lightbulb go off, his face full of glee. "Move."

She did as she was told, giving Archer space to jump out of bed and open up his dresser. When he stripped off his boxers, she slapped his bare butt.

"You little—"

She didn't wait to hear the rest. She bolted from the room and ran out of his cabin. In a matter of seconds she heard the slam of the screen door, then pounding feet as Archer chased her from behind.

It was pitch-black outside. The cabins were dark and no one was out on the lawn. Smoke swelled from the fire pit that had been snuffed out. The moon was the only light to guide her as she ran for the lake, not stopping as her feet reached the water. The water made her slow, but she kept at it until she was able to dive in, Archer close at her heels. When she came up for air, hands grabbed her ankles and yanked.

"*Eeek!*" she shrieked.

Archer pulled her closer and covered her mouth. "First rule of the night swim?"

"Don't wake everyone up," she mumbled into his hand.

The night swim had been their tradition for years. It started when they were ten. Tea had looked out her bedroom window in Cabin B and noticed Archer's lights still on in his room. He waved at her, then made a swimming motion. She cocked her head, then patiently watched as Archer snuck out of the house and ran for the lake. She changed into her suit and joined him for a secret night swim, a tradition they kept going every last Saturday of their summer at Wild Pines.

Archer smirked and dropped his hand. "Second rule?"

"Float under the stars and contemplate how much life is going to suck for nine months until we're back."

He chuckled. "And third?"

She pursed her lips. He lifted a brow.

She sighed. "Confess your deepest, darkest secret."

"Bingo."

"I don't think either of us truly followed that last rule if we were pining for each other for years."

He paused then tipped back. "We eventually got there."

They lost track of time, the two of them floating in the water, eyes on the sky. The lake water felt warm compared to the chilly air, with fall lingering among them like an omen. The night swims were always her favorite part of her summer, but they also made her sad. The same was true even eight years later.

"What's your deepest, darkest secret?" he asked her.

She paddled her feet. "That I want to find the loon nest."

"That's not a secret. Nor is it dark or deep."

"*Fine.*" She thought about it for a minute. "I don't know what having a home feels like anymore."

Archer didn't say anything, giving her room to continue.

"When we moved out of the house, Mom's apartment never really felt like home. It felt like *hers*. My dorm room certainly didn't feel that way, and I barely spent time in my apartment in Chicago because I was so busy with my program. Plus, my bedroom was the size of a matchbox."

"What about here? Silver Falls?"

"There are parts of the cabin that feel familiar, but...I don't know. I'm looking forward to having a place that I can really settle in, like how the loons have their nest they return to every year." She paused. "My life kind of feels like this right now. Floating, not exactly sure where the water will take me."

Tea waited for Archer to say something, but he remained silent. She lifted her head, wondering if she'd floated too far from him and whether he heard any of her last few sentences. He was still right beside her, his face to the sky, deep in thought.

She dipped her hair back in the water. "What's your deepest, darkest secret?"

He didn't respond. After a beat, she heard the rustling of water, then tender hands reaching for her waist. She righted herself as Archer pulled her close and wrapped his arms around her.

He kissed her, his body warm and solid. She kissed him back, taking her time, enjoying the way he cradled her, like holding a precious piece of art.

When they broke apart, he rested his forehead against hers. "I'm still in love with you," he whispered.

The sound of those words bloomed in her chest, warming her to her core. "Still?"

"Still." He pecked her lips. "I did my best to ignore it for so long, tried to move on from you. But then I saw you get out of your car at the beginning of the summer, and I couldn't help it. You're even more beautiful than I remembered, and I felt devastated. I realized that my feelings had never changed. All I did was turn them off for a little while."

She swallowed. "And now?"

"Now...I don't think I'll ever be able to switch them off again."

He kissed her, soft and slow. "Don't say it until you're ready," he continued. "I'm a patient man. I can wait."

She felt every emotion in the book, and she wasn't sure which one to grasp onto. She was ecstatic. Sad. She felt grief. She felt passion. She felt longing. She felt scared. She felt hope. Did all of these things equate to feeling love? Was that what people meant when they said it?

"What is that feeling like?" she asked him cautiously.

He kissed her cheek. "You know that feeling you get in your gut right after you jump in the lake? You're floating in the air, waiting to hit the water?"

"So...feeling love is feeling absolutely terrified?"

"Well, yes." He chuckled. "It's more that freefall feeling. There's exhilaration and excitement, but also fear. It feels like you don't have control. But you have to trust that the water will catch you, that everything will be okay."

"And what about when you hit the water?"

She waited as he thought about it for a moment. "I guess...that's where you'll find the relief, and hopefully, the joy."

She nodded. She understood that feeling well. Tea felt like she had been freefalling since the day her dad died. She waited for some kind of relief, yet still after eight years, she never found it. Or...she wondered if what she was experiencing was more like floating in the lake, completely aimless. At least Archer had taken a leap in a certain direction, and now he was freefalling, waiting to see what would happen. He *went* for it, and she was the only one who could give him that relief.

He grabbed her legs and wrapped them around his waist as they floated in the inky black lake. "What are you thinking?"

"I-I don't really know what I'm thinking."

He kissed her shoulder. "Maybe we should dry off and go to bed?"

"Okay," she whispered, her gut twisting. For some reason, she felt like she'd failed him. Or maybe she failed herself.

The sound of muffled voices echoed from across the lawn.

Archer and Tea turned toward them.

He chuckled. "Hello, Romeo."

The two of them watched as Chris stood underneath a window at Cabin G. His arms were raised, poised to catch Ashley as she crawled out of her window and shimmied down the roof. She grabbed the nearest branch of the tree.

"Why do I feel like this is not going to end well?" Tea mumbled.

"*Shhh.*"

They continued to watch as Ashley attempted to elegantly climb down the tree, until her foot slipped. She dangled from one of the branches as Chris reached up for her waist. She slipped into his arms, the two of them tumbling down to the grass.

"Should have been taller," Archer teased.

"Arch, stop it."

He looked at her with that mischievous grin. "Oh come on, this is *gold.*"

"May I remind you that we used to sneak out? For *years?*"

"Yeah, but it wasn't ever like *this.*" He huffed. "Even though I always wanted it to be like this."

They continued to watch as Chris helped her up, kissed her delicately on the mouth, then grabbed her hand as they raced across the lawn. Ashley was the one who slowed, realizing who was in the water. She pulled on Chris's arm, who stopped. He looked at her and Archer with wide eyes.

The four of them remained silent for a long beat.

Archer then smirked and saluted Chris.

Chris grinned and saluted back, then pulled Ashley to the woods.

"Time to go inside?" Tea suggested.

"Only if you'll slap my butt again."

She dug her toe into his butt cheek, which made him yelp.

He chuckled as he walked to the shore, still carrying her as he stepped out of the water. "Come on, my Sweet Tea. Let's get you to bed."

Tea entered her cabin early the next day. Archer promised his father he would help clean the gutters for Cabin F, which apparently was a job that required Archer's full attention at eight o'clock in the morning. So Tea shuffled over to Cabin B, wearing his T-shirt and sweatpants, ready to crawl into her bed. That was until she stepped inside and found Nan standing at the counter with a cup of coffee, waiting for her.

She stilled. "Sorry," she said reflexively.

"Oh honey, I'm not angry that you stay over there. I'm glad you two are together."

Tea sat on her usual stool, in front of a basket of strawberry rhubarb muffins fresh out of the oven. "You are?"

"Of course. Your father and I were always convinced the two of you were meant for each other."

She felt like she couldn't breathe. "He thought that?"

"Yes. He loved that boy like his own. He knew he was a good one from the start."

Tea glanced at the cabin next door, watching Archer climb up the ladder, his father holding it steady at the bottom. "Yeah, he's a good one."

Nan poured Tea a cup of coffee, then slid it across to her. "What I don't understand is why you still haven't told your mother. It's been, what, a month?"

She wanted to crawl into a hole. "She's been so busy."

"And yet I've had no problems getting her on the phone this week."

Tea paused. "Did you tell her?"

"I didn't mean to."

She placed her face in her hands. "Crap."

"Well, gal dang, kid. I don't get it."

Tea looked up. "Get what?"

Nan placed her hands on her hips. "Why would you not want to tell your mother? Are you angry at her or something?"

"What? No!"

"Are you ashamed of him?"

"No, not at all."

"Then what is it?"

Tea froze, not sure how to respond.

Nan sighed as she stepped around the counter, then took Tea's hands in hers. "Listen, honey. I know these years have been so hard. I knew coming to the cabin was going to be a lot for you. Being in this place helps me to remember all the happy memories of my beautiful son, but I knew that wouldn't feel the same for you and your mom. So I gave you both the space you needed. But now...now I'm going to be Tough Grandma."

Tea looked down at their hands.

"Tough Grandma is going to admit the truth: that your father would not want his death to be the reason you don't live life to the fullest."

Tea blinked up at her grandmother.

She pointed to the window and the man cleaning the gutters outside. "That boy is in love with you. It's clear as day. I think you're sitting here unable to admit to yourself that you love him too. Because you are afraid of what that would require you to do."

"And what would that be?" she muttered.

"To actually go out there and live your dang life."

"My life is back east. With Mom."

Nan shook her head. "No. Your life is what you make it. Only you can decide what you want it to be."

Before she could respond, Nan placed a muffin on a plate and handed it to Tea with a napkin. "Now I will go back to being Nice Grandma. But be warned, Tough Grandma will make an appearance again if you do something stupid."

"Like what?"

She fixed her with a sobering look. "Like make a huge mistake."

Tea knocked on the back door of Cabin F.

Archer stood in the kitchen next to his mother, chopping tomatoes for the salsa she was making. He glanced up at her as he slid them from the cutting board into a bowl, a smile slowly forming across his cheeks. He rinsed his hands.

"Tea, dearest!" Larissa mixed them into the bowl. "Want to join us for tacos tonight?"

"Oh! I think Nan is making hotdish..."

"Nonsense. I'll tell her to put it in the fridge for tomorrow and they can come over too."

"In that case, sure. Thanks missus—"

Larissa looked up and glared at her.

Tea's shoulders relaxed. "Thanks, Mom."

Archer dried his hands with a dish towel, then tossed it to the counter as he approached the door. "Mother, stop harassing my girlfriend."

Girlfriend. Were they using those words now?

"It's not harassment, *son*, it's called manners."

Archer swung it open, then grabbed Tea's face and kissed her hungrily on the mouth.

"Something the two of you should probably learn! My god, chill it out there."

They both laughed and broke apart.

Archer rubbed his thumbs into her cheeks. "I missed you, Sweet Tea," he said softly, only to her.

She rolled her eyes. "You saw me this morning."

"Too long."

"You're ridiculous."

"Mmhmm." He nuzzled her nose. "I'm okay with that."

She tilted her head back and pointed at the lake. "It's glass out there."

Archer lifted a brow. "Are you saying what I think you're saying?"

"If it's to watch me make one last failing attempt at water skiing, then yes, that's what I'm saying."

He slapped her butt with both hands. "Let's go."

SHE RIGHTED herself in the water and gripped the bright blue handle. The sun was gleaming across the lake, making it almost impossible to see Rhonda and Archer in the boat. But she wasn't going to let anything stop her today. She had to get up. She *had* to.

"You got this!" Rhonda cheered.

"Hold on to your bottoms!" Archer yelled.

"I'm in my one piece, jackass!"

His laugh boomed across the lake.

"Ready?" Rhonda yelled.

Tea took a long, deep breath, then nodded to herself. *"Hit it!"*

Rhonda pressed on the gas. Tea kept a firm grip on the handle, the pressure of the water at her feet propelling her up. It felt like too much, enough that she was ready to call it quits for good. Then her body lifted, the grip in her hands gave a little, and she was floating on the lake.

Archer lifted his arms. *"Yeah, baby! You did it!"*

Tea grinned, jerking her head back to get her hair out of her face, and finally—*finally*—glided across her favorite place on earth. It was easy to get back into it, moving across the wake of the boat as it sailed across the water, letting each turn propel her to the side so she could soar along. The feeling was freeing. It felt like heaven. It reminded her of all her happiest moments. Road tripping with Mom and Dad to Silver Falls, the promise of a full summer at Wild Pines ahead. Lying on the couch in Cabin A, tucked tightly in Archer's arms.

Eventually her forearms ached and she couldn't hold on much longer. She let go of the handle and sank slowly as Rhonda killed the engine ahead.

Tea was undoing the water ski on her foot, waiting for them to make it back to her, when she heard a soft cooing on the shore nearby.

She paused, her movements slow and quiet as she turned to the sound and eyed the three loons by the nest at least five yards away on the shore. One of the loons was much smaller, its feather a mix of juvenile brown and black adult colors. The baby. *Pebble*.

"Tea?" Archer called to her.

She abruptly turned to him and held a finger to her mouth, then pointed to the nest.

Archer's mouth fell open, followed by Rhonda who joined him at the side of the boat. The three of them remained quiet, watching as the family settled into the nest. Rhonda snapped a picture with her phone, a big fat smile on her face.

Eventually Archer let down the ladder and silently helped Tea into the boat. He wrapped a towel around her and kissed her wet lips. "You did it."

She tilted her head. "Did what?"

"*All* of it."

They sat down on the back bench as Rhonda slowly puttered the boat away from the loon nest. He kissed her again, and the feel of his arms and his lips made her stomach flip flop.

After they docked the boat, Archer gripped her waist and kept her close as they walked back to his parents' cabin. He kissed her temple, then looked up. His body stiffened.

She pouted. "What? What is it?"

He didn't glance down at her, or even say anything. She turned toward where he was looking.

A petite woman stood on the porch, with short burgundy-colored hair and bangs, looking rumpled in athletic shorts and a tank top with a mustard stain down the center.

Her entire body lit up. "*Mom!*"

Tea jumped out of Archer's grasp and ran for her mother.

Chapter 26

Archer

HE KNEW the summer would come to an end. He just didn't expect it to happen so quickly.

They got good at avoiding what would happen next. Tea hadn't spoken to him about how she was planning on heading back east, and for a while, he wondered if her lack of communication was her considering not going at all. But if she was, if she really wanted to return, he was ready to offer to drive her himself. Until her mom showed up.

Molly Richards tested for COVID, then drove twenty hours to northern Minnesota, only stopping once to sleep in her car and a couple other times for quick burgers, sandwiches, or any other easy meal she could get via a drive-thru on the road.

By the look of her surprised expression, he knew Tea had no idea her mom was driving up to the lake. And by the look her mother was giving *him*, he had a feeling there was a lot that hadn't been said between the two of them.

Archer kept quiet through dinner as everyone caught up around their outdoor table, bubbling with excitement that Molly was back in Silver Falls after eight years. He wanted to be excited for her and for Tea, but the only thing he could muster was a feigned smile to mask his dread.

"Archer."

He looked up from his half-eaten taco and across the table at Molly. They were all sitting outside, the sun tucked away behind the trees, the night getting cooler. Tea sat across from him and next to her mom. He hated how far she was already.

He swallowed. "Yes?"

"Tea tells me you're working in hospitality? Cocktails?"

He leaned forward and faced Molly head on. "Yes, I've been working at one of the top cocktail bars in Minneapolis for a couple years now. But the lounge is closed, and I have no idea if it will open back up."

She shrugged. "It might. I've seen a lot of bars doing some creative things in New Brunswick. Outdoor seating, walking cocktails in bags or plastic cups."

He cringed on the inside. There was no way he was serving his cocktails in *bags* or *plastic cups*. He'd rather find a new job. If that made him sound pretentious, then so be it.

Dad leaned back in his chair, turning to Tea. "And what about you? What will you be doing?"

"Did you ever hear from Bank of America?" Molly asked.

Archer clenched his fists tight.

Tea flicked her gaze in his direction before responding. "Um, yes, actually. They offered me my position back. They want me to start mid-September."

Everything around him went dizzy. Archer released his fists and grasped the chair he sat in, taking long, slow breaths as everyone congratulated and cheered for her with clinked glasses. Everyone except him and her grandmother, who sat next to him with crossed arms and pursed lips.

Tea's smile was tight, her eyes not meeting either of theirs directly.

How could she not tell me?

"So does this mean you're moving back east?" his father asked her.

Tea looked at her mom.

Molly tilted her head. "I heard someone's car broke down and maybe they would need a ride home?"

Her face went red. "You drove all this way to pick me up?"

"If that's what you want, yes. But we'll have to head back tomorrow night. I don't have much leave time..."

Tea's eyes fell to her hands.

Archer wanted to melt into the damp grass beneath them. He remained silent as everyone finished dinner, then helped his mother clear everything and walk it back to the kitchen. He turned the hot water on and washed the dishes, concentrating on the soap and scrubbing and nothing more.

"Arch?"

He looked up from the sink.

"Can we talk?" Tea asked through the screen door.

He placed the dish down and wiped the suds on his shorts as he made his way toward her. He didn't look her in the eye. "What the hell, Tea?"

She stepped into the cabin. "I'm sorry."

"Sorry? Come on. You've had weeks to talk to me about this, and you waited until the last possible *minute?*"

She hugged her stomach. "What did you want me to say? That I was offered my internship back? That I'd eventually head east?"

"*Yes.* You should feel comfortable talking to me about this."

"And watch you fall apart again?"

He growled, then pinched the bridge of his nose, closing his eyes. "I'm not eighteen anymore, Tea. I'm a grown-ass man. I can handle a hard conversation."

She dropped down to the couch near the window. "Riley told me not to mess with you again. I don't want to hurt you."

Archer got to his knees in front of her and reached for her neck. "Not talking to me *does* hurt me, love. You have to communicate. You have to tell me what's on your mind."

She scanned his face. "What's on my mind?"

He nodded.

"Okay." She bit her lip. "I can't be the reason you give up on your dream."

"Literally none of that matters when it comes to you."

"But it *should*, Archer. You can't give up your whole life because of me. You love what you do and you're really good at it."

She sounded an awful lot like Austin, and he absolutely hated it. "I haven't heard anything from them. I could find something else for the winter, maybe out east—?"

Her eyes went wide. "Out east? Like, move there with me?"

His chest squeezed. "Would that be so bad?"

She hesitated. "I-I really don't think that's a good idea."

"Why not?"

"Because your life is *here*. Minneapolis is a lot closer to Wild Pines, which you just committed to, and you're closer to your family. I couldn't tear that away from you."

He sighed, defeated. He dropped his grip on her neck and placed his hands on her thighs. "Then stay."

"B-but—"

"You said you're not sure where home is. So stay. With me."

She covered her mouth with her hands. She looked lost. Uncertain.

"Do you not want to be with me?"

Her shoulders sagged. "Archer."

"Do you?"

Her eyes were glossy with tears. "What if...what if we did long distance? You stay here, and I go back with Mom? I-I can't leave her, Arch. She's all alone out there."

Long distance. The thought churned like acid in his stomach. It would be back to what they were before—three months together, nine months apart. It sounded like literal hell.

"It could be good," she babbled on. "A little space, maybe? To think it through? Figure out what we should do next?"

He stood up. "I need to think. I'm going to take a walk or go for a drive or something."

"Hey, wait—"

He didn't wait. This time, it was *him* who needed a little time to parse through his thoughts. He snatched his keys and left.

ARCHER WANDERED the craft beer aisle at Hector's. It was the only place he could think of, and for some reason, looking at microbrew varieties calmed him. He scanned the labels and took deep breaths and—

"Why am I not surprised to find you here?"

Janelle stood beside him, holding a basket of groceries and two bottles of wine tucked under her arm.

His instinct was to offer to hold them for her, but he

caught himself. He turned back to the fridge. "Yeah, not a surprise."

She stepped in front of him. "You okay, Archie?"

He sighed. "Not really. Came here to clear my head."

"Want to talk about it?"

He eyed her, thankful his mask was hiding the scowl he couldn't help. "With you? No."

"Girl problems?"

He scratched his head. "Janelle, please."

"So you are with her, huh?"

He sighed audibly and looked up at the fluorescent lights, not caring if they temporarily blinded him. "Yes. For now."

"For now?"

His chest flared as he looked back at her. "Yes, for now. She's heading back east like always and leaving me behind. To pretend like whatever is happening between us doesn't exist. Or at least not for nine months of the year."

She hummed. "Sounds like this goes a lot deeper than one summer."

He rubbed his forehead. "Yeah. It does."

"And now do you understand why our stars didn't align?"

Archer hesitated. When he was dating Janelle, he kept quiet about her love for astrology and zodiac signs and reading the stars, because he thought it was all a bunch of bull. Yet now, as she looked at him with a serene and, dare he say, *smug* expression, he wondered if he'd written it off too quickly.

"Sure," he admitted. "I guess our stars don't align."

"Do your stars align with her?"

"No fucking idea." He shifted back and forth. "But in my opinion, they would align in every universe."

"Then it sounds like you know what you need to do."

He squinted at her. "Why are you being so nice to me?"

She shrugged. "Just because we didn't work out doesn't mean I don't care for you, Archie. I will always want the best for you.

He looked into the fluorescent-lit fridge. "We never used to talk like this."

"Probably because it was never really meant to be."

They stood there in silence, both staring ahead.

"You know when you finally open that school, I'll be the first one to sign up for a class."

He rolled his eyes. "You'll need it. You can't make a cocktail to save your life."

She laughed. "Your margaritas are way too weak! I want *double* the amount of tequila."

"Sadist."

She laughed again. The sound of it brought a smile to his face.

"You're still going to do that, right? The cocktail school?"

He exhaled. "Yeah. I think I am."

HE DIDN'T BOTHER TALKING to Tea when he got home that night, or the following morning when he saw her take off in his sailboat with her mom. He gave them their space; they hadn't seen each other since *last year*. Molly meant a lot to Tea, to the point where she was ready to give everything up so her mother wouldn't be alone. He watched from his cabin window as the two of them returned from their morning sail, smiles on their faces and tears in their eyes.

Later that day, he received an email.

To: Archer Vincent

(archer@hermeslounge.com)

From: Lyle Thorne

(lyle@hermeslounge.com)

Archer! Broski!

So good to hear from you, dude, what a crazy time it's been. Reaching out to let you know I'll be opening up Hermes Lounge this fall. Things are going to look a lot different. We're going to utilize outdoor seating with heaters until people physically cannot handle the cold anymore, and plexiglass dividers between tables indoors. More details to come, but would love to have you back around. When do you return from up north? I think you told me this is the weekend you usually head back?

As for your cocktail classes, I had an interesting idea. Given that we can't have as many customers in, and who knows how long we'll be able to utilize the outdoor patio, I was thinking…what if we did the cocktail classes online? Great way to make some dough during the winter. They could log in to classes you teach on Zoom. We'll have to talk through details on how to get them materials and whatnot, still bouncing this around in my head.

Shall we meet next week? Excited to get back into things. Missed you, man.

Lyle

He tossed his phone back and forth in his hand. He didn't hate the idea of teaching classes online. Obviously not ideal, but at least it was something to get him started. He sat there on the couch, imagining what the next season of his life looked like, forcing himself to think through that season *without* Tea for nine months of the year. Getting his stuff out of his storage unit, alone. Finding an apartment, alone. Experiencing another brutal Minnesota winter. Alone.

It was impossible.

He typed out an email and sent it as his door creaked open. He looked up to find Tea in his cabin.

He stood up from the couch. "I can't do it."

She stood before him, silent.

"Long distance," he continued. "I can't, Tea. I watched you walk away at the end of every single summer for eighteen years of my life. I don't want to do that anymore. It's too hard."

She sniffled, then wiped a tear with the back of her sweatshirt sleeve. "I have to go with her, Archer. Being in Chicago so far from her during all of this...I can't leave her alone again, not with everything going on. I'm sorry."

Archer worked his jaw, watching as she cried in front of him. Tears filled his own eyes. Right now, he was his own demise. *He* was the one causing the pain. Yet deep in his gut, in the heart of who he was down to his core, Archer Vincent knew this couldn't be it. It was always him and Tea. *Always.*

Their stars were aligned in every universe.

He knew he would never experience love in the ways he'd grown to deeply love Theresa Richards. Now that he had her again, was even more deeply in love with her than his teenage under-developed brain could have comprehended, he refused to believe this was the end.

He grinded his teeth, moving his jaw back and forth, blinking away the water in his eyes. He nodded. "Okay."

"Okay? We'll do long distance—?"

He shook his head. "No. Here's what's going to happen."

Before she could stop him, Archer cupped her cheeks and brought her close.

She sucked in a breath, but she didn't stop him. Didn't hesitate or pull away.

He scanned her face. "You are going to leave, because that's what you think you want."

"It is what I want."

"No, it's not. You told me—" His voice cracked. He cleared it and shook his head. "You think we should take some space? I'm not going to give it to you. I want to be *in* your space. I'm not going to let you hold me at a distance, afraid to take the leap. You're going to leave, and you will be unhappy. Because deep down, you know we are meant to be together. I know you feel the way I do and you won't admit the truth."

She swallowed. "I told you the truth."

He clenched his jaw. "I don't think leaving your mom alone is the real reason. You're not admitting what's *really* going on."

"Which is—"

"You're *scared*, Tea. You're scared to be with me fully because like you said, our future together is not guaranteed. I could get cancer or COVID or get in an accident, and it scares you to put your heart on the line again."

He knew he hit the mark when she didn't respond, her eyes locked on his.

He squeezed, then brushed his thumbs across her jawline. "I know I'm right. So I will wait. I will wait for however long it takes you to realize you're making a mistake. And when you do, you'll come back. You'll stop forcing yourself to be miserable and finally be happy again."

"We could be happy," she whispered, her tone desperate. "Next summer..."

"I'm not living like that anymore, Tea. I want you. *All* of you. And I know that you want the same."

"How can you be so sure?"

"Because even when mates leave their nest, they always return to each other. They always come back *home*."

She closed her eyes. Archer leaned down, his lips practically brushing hers. "You told me you wanted a place to call yours. Let me be that for you, Sweet Tea. I'll take care of you. I'll create that space for you. I'll be your home."

He made a move to kiss her, but then his brother's words stopped him. *Put yourself first.* Letting her go didn't feel like putting himself first, but ultimately he knew he was. He was choosing himself and sticking up for what he wanted. And eventually, she would see that too.

He let her go, took a step back, then turned and left her alone in his cabin. He clipped on the life jacket hanging on his porch, still fully clothed in jeans and a sweatshirt, and walked over to his boat.

He knew he was right about this. But he wouldn't allow himself to watch her leave again. He already did that once, and it destroyed everything he had in him.

Chapter 27

Tea

Once a loon baby hits week twelve, it moves into the fledgling age. Their primary feathers are fully formed, they are able to swim and fish similarly to their parents, and they learn how to protect themselves from predators. This is the stage where the fledgling will take their first flight and will separate from their parents when the mates leave the lake and migrate to the ocean.

TEA STOOD ON THE BEACH, watching Archer's sailboat in the distance. She couldn't stop crying.

His words pinged around in her head.

You're scared to be with me fully because like you said, our future together is not guaranteed.

A slender hand rubbed her back. "You ready, sweetheart?"

She exhaled. "Sure."

She followed her mother to her car, the back packed to the brim with her suitcases and her snake plant. The sun was making its descent, and they needed to get on the road so they could make it to the motel they booked outside Madison before it got too late. She reached for the car handle.

"Wait, I think your grandparents are walking over here."

Tea frowned. "Didn't we already say goodbye?" She *really* didn't want to face Nan's disappointment again.

Her mom squinted at them as they made their way across the lawn. "It looks like she might be holding a present?"

They waited patiently. A soft loon hoot echoed from nearby. She looked at the lake, then realized the sound was coming from the sky.

Three loons were in flight, soaring across the lake. One of them was still relatively brown, the other two in their usual black, white, and grey feathers.

It was the loon family.

Her mouth fell open. "Mom, do you see this?"

Mom glanced back and forth. "See what?"

She pointed to the sky. "The loon baby! Pebble is taking his first flight!"

Mom's eyes widened as she looked up at the sky. "Those are loons?"

She grinned, watching the birds as they circled the lake. Eventually the mates veered off, giving the baby the space to fly and be on his own. The sight of it made her sentimental, sadness squeezing her ribcage. The circle of life, in one short summer.

She was still watching Pebble fly circles around the lake when Nan approached.

She shoved a white box into her hands, tied with a green ribbon. "Take it."

"What is it?"

Nan shook her head. "Do not open it until you drive out of here."

She frowned. "Why?"

"Because Tough Grandma said so."

Her grandmother didn't even hug her, simply turned on her heels and walked off.

Pop shrugged, then wrapped Tea in his arms and gave her a smooch on the cheek. "Love you, angel. Come back soon."

She melted in his embrace. "I'll try."

They climbed into the car. Tea eyed the lake one last time, watching the yellow sail drift among the water, and the loon that flew above it.

"Bye," she whispered.

Mom rolled her car slowly down the dirt road and out of the resort. Tea hadn't seen many of the owners as they left, but she did that on purpose. She wanted to leave quietly.

The box remained on her lap for a few minutes, unopened, as Mom drove along the winding roads leading out of Silver Falls.

"Well, are you going to open it?" she asked.

"I'm a little scared to," Tea responded.

Mom sighed. "Do it. It can't be that bad."

Tea gingerly untied the bow, then tipped the box open. The inside was fluffed with tissue paper, with one item and one note.

The item was a picture frame, one that she'd tried to leave behind. It was the photo of her and Archer, blue teeth, smiling at the camera.

She bit her lip as she picked up the note.

Don't make the same mistake.

She shook her head, shoving both of them back in the box, placing it on the ground, and kicking it in the corner, far away from her reach. It didn't matter what she did. Every decision she was poised to make seemed like the wrong one.

THEY STOPPED at a diner in Madison for dinner. The place looked completely dead, which worked in their favor. They took a booth in the far back corner, away from the counter and the workers, giving them a safe space to eat in peace.

Tea poked at her salad with her fork. She knew she should eat something, but she didn't have an appetite for it. Not after looking at that picture, the image of Archer haunting her. Memories of the boy she used to play with at the lake. Moments with the man she spent wrapped up in this summer, the way he gently cradled her and made her feel safe.

Mom bit her club sandwich, then wiped her hands with a napkin. "Honey, enough sulking. Spill."

She kept playing with her food. "What is there to say?"

"Maybe you can finally tell me what's going on with you and Archer?"

She put down her fork and glanced out the window, the sky dusty as dusk settled in. "He told me he loves me."

When Mom didn't respond, Tea turned to face her. She was leaning back, arms crossed, not looking surprised in the slightest.

She circled her hand, signaling her to continue. "And?"

"And what?"

"Did you say it back?"

She pursed her lips and glanced away again.

"Oh, Tea bear, why not?"

"Because I can't," she whispered.

She could sense Mom leaning in. "Can't, or won't?"

Tea brought her knees close and hugged them. *Screw manners.*

"Do you love him?"

She placed her cheek on her knee, facing Mom again.

Her eyes softened. "Baby girl, why didn't you tell him?"

"Because it wouldn't have mattered. I still would have left."

"Why?"

Tea's forehead pinched as she sat up. "Why? Mom, you drove all the way out here to pick me up."

"Sweetheart, I needed a break from the hospital. And that should *not* be the reason you throw all of this away."

"I'm not throwing it away! You're all alone out there. I couldn't abandon you."

Mom was silent for a beat. "So you decided against staying with him because you were afraid I would be all alone?"

"He doesn't want long distance..."

"I don't mean stay in a relationship, I mean *stay in Minnesota.*" Mom scratched her head. "Why are you pushing him away?"

"Because..." Emotion clogged her throat. She had no words to respond.

"This is so much worse than I thought," Mom grumbled after she didn't respond.

Tea frowned. "Why?"

She let out a frustrated exhale. "Because you're too worried about me to go out there and live your life, sweetheart. You were in Chicago for a few years, and I was perfectly fine by myself."

"Yes, but you always knew I was going to come back. Mom, we *lost* him. I can't leave you too."

Mom tutted. "Can I tell you what I think?"

"Do I have a choice?"

"No, you don't." She folded her hands in her lap. "I think you are using me as an excuse to avoid facing what you're actually afraid of."

"Which is what?"

"Letting yourself take chances." She waved around her, like she had a magic wand. "Letting yourself be in love and try new things. Letting yourself actually face your grief instead of stuffing it away like you have all these years."

It was almost identical to what Archer told her. Deep down, Tea knew they were both right. But it didn't make any of it easier.

She moved her knees to sit crisscross on the bench. "That's not fair. You stuffed it away too."

Mom shook her head. "No I didn't. Remember I went to therapy for a while? And encouraged you to do the same, but you refused?"

Tea pressed her lips into a thin line. "Then why didn't we ever talk about it?"

"Because you didn't *want* to. I tried to bring it up, but it was always too hard. You changed the subject or wanted to do something fun in the city. I gave up after a while and told myself that you needed space to heal. I feel like I failed you as a mom because I saw my kid suffering and didn't do anything to fix it."

"You didn't fail as a mom," she replied softly.

Tea watched her take another bite of her sandwich, chewing thoughtfully. She swallowed. "When we go back, I don't want things to go back to the way they were."

"How so?"

"For starters, you're not living with me."

Tea didn't say anything.

Mom crossed her arms. "I admit, I've liked my independence over the years. It's allowed me to, well, um, have a life of my own."

"What do you mean?"

She cocked her head. "I like having space to myself, to invite people into."

Her eyes widened. "Like, men?"

"*Yes*, men. Did you think I've been celibate all this time?"

Tea's mouth fell open. "You've been *dating*? Since when?"

"Since you left for Chicago. I got on one of those new dating apps. Turns out, there are a lot of lonely people out there in the same situation I'm in."

She was flabbergasted. "Do you think you'll ever remarry?"

Mom shrugged. "Maybe. Did you really think I would remain single my whole life?"

Tea hesitated. "Well, no. I guess I didn't think about it too much."

"And is that perhaps because you didn't want to think about what comes next? To let yourself move on?"

Archer's words came back to her at that moment, about how afraid she was to let someone in. Letting someone in felt like freefalling. You weren't sure what came next. You weren't sure if everything would work out. But...was she really going to live her life standing on the edge, afraid to jump?

"Honey?"

She blinked. "Mmhmm?"

"Do you actually want this job at the bank?"

She hesitated, then shook her head.

"Then why go back? What do you actually want to do?"

Tea thought about it for a moment. "I really liked working for Archer this summer."

"Why? Because you're in love with him and won't admit it?"

She rolled her eyes. "I liked making his business easier for him by taking over the finances and the admin stuff. He was way more relaxed about the whole thing and by the end of the summer, he started really enjoying it." She paused. "Also, Jorge was talking about how his lab is looking for someone to take on their finances. It was hard not to sit through that conversation and think that I could absolutely kill it at that job."

"It sounds like you'd much rather work for small businesses than a large one."

She sighed. "Yes, but I don't have much experience yet. Shouldn't I go do the internship and see what happens?"

"Eh, no, I don't think so." Mom shrugged. "You technically got experience working with Archer this summer. Couldn't that count?"

Tea tapped her fork, thinking it through.

"I think the more important question here is...do you actually want to go back? Or are you only doing it because of me?"

She gazed at her mom but didn't respond.

"I know that look. You know I'm right, but you're too stubborn to admit it. Just like your father." Mom pointed to the car. "You have your entire life packed up in that vehicle. Like I said at the beginning of the summer, you could go *anywhere*." She leaned in. "So...where do you want to go?"

Chapter 28

Archer

"How are you holding up?"

Archer let out a heavy sigh. He'd gotten different itera-tions of that same question the last couple of days, and he never knew what to say. *Awful, thanks? Like a truck ran over me, actually.* He didn't want to get into the details with anyone though, so he answered with a curt "fine" and went along with closing up his cabin and getting ready to leave.

This time it was coming from Rhonda.

He slammed the back of his truck, packed with the few things he brought up there in May. He sucked in a breath to answer her.

"Don't you dare say *fine* because we both know that's bull."

Archer rolled his eyes, annoyed. "How do you think I'm holding up?" he grumbled.

"Not well, I assume." She crossed her arms and leaned against his truck. "Have you heard from her?"

Archer shook his head. It had been thirty-six hours since their awful attempt at a goodbye. He'd thought through what he said to her over and over, how he would wait for until she was ready. It might have been stupid to say, but he didn't regret it at all. He meant it. Tea was *it* for him. If she didn't want it, well, then he was bound to be single forever. That was that.

"It's probably foolish, but I'm hoping she'll come around," he admitted.

Rhonda shrugged. "I don't think it's foolish. I saw the way you looked at her. Sometimes...you just know."

He paused. "Was it like that with you and Steph?"

She nodded. "Yes. It took us a little while to get there, but I knew from the start that she was my person."

Archer looked out at the lake. "That's how I feel."

Rhonda gave him a sad smile. "Come on. I know people are still packing up, but you should make your rounds."

He groaned. "Do I have to?"

"Yes, my boy. You committed to being the manager for a long time. I think it's best you stay in everyone's good graces." Her face hardened. "Although if you want to give Joel a good ol' *fuck you*, I won't object."

Archer smirked. He did as Rhonda suggested and made his rounds, popping outside each cabin and saying goodbye to everyone. No hugs; everyone stood at committed six-foot distances, not wanting to chance anything before going their separate ways. Except for Tea's grandmother, who hugged his chest and told him she loved him. He wrapped an arm around her shoulder and told her the same.

Mom was crying on the porch, like she did every year on the last day at the lake. He bent down to kiss her on the cheek. "It's not going to disappear, Mom."

She slapped his arm and laughed. He always said the same thing to her, and she always responded the same way. Sometimes with an added *"you smart-ass."* He wrapped her up in a hug and said he would call when he got to Minneapolis. He booked a hotel for a week and hoped it would be enough time to find himself a new apartment.

His brow pinched. "Where's Dad?"

Mom frowned. "Not sure."

"Right here!"

Dad jogged up to them from the side of the cabin, his cheeks pink and a dopey smile on his face. "I noticed you forgot a few of your things, so I put them near your truck."

He tilted his head. "No, I'm pretty sure I have everything."

"Trust me, you don't."

Archer followed his father around the cabin to the back lot, Mom close at his heels. When his truck came into sight, he froze at what waited for him.

Three suitcases.

A fucking snake plant.

And the most beautiful woman with wavy red hair.

She grinned, then took off running in his direction. He tore away from his parents and ran to her as well, catching her when she jumped. She wrapped her legs around his chest and nuzzled her face into his neck.

He cried, then he laughed, then he cried again.

She peppered his neck and his cheek with kisses, until she reached his mouth. She kissed him hard, and he kissed her back.

When she pulled away, her face turned serious. "Arch?"

"Yes, Sweet Tea?"

"Take me with you?"

A grin bloomed on his face. "Are you sure?"

She nodded. "I love you, Archer Vincent."

His bottom lip quivered. It was all happening so fast.

He curled his hand around her nape and pulled her mouth close. "I love you too."

She kissed him, then repeated those three words. *I love you. I love you. I love you.* He returned them, surprised by how much he needed to hear those words from her. Surprised at how healing all of this was for him.

"Talk to me," he whispered. "Tell me what changed your mind."

Unlike other times he asked her to open up this summer, she didn't hesitate. She let him. Fully. "You were right," she confessed. "I'm scared out of my mind, Arch. I'm scared to lose you and to experience that kind of pain again. But a life without you..." She shook her head. "I can't fathom it. I would have gone back and lived in New York and been so unhappy in a job that I would probably come to hate, all so I could live close to my mom and likely never see her...and be miserable every minute that I wasn't with you. All because I was afraid to admit that I need you. I need you, Arch. Like a fish needs water or a sail needs wind."

He tucked a hair behind her ear. "I'm so proud of you. Is this hard right now?"

"Yes," she whispered. "But a life without you would be so much harder."

"I completely agree." He let her down gently, then gripped her chin with his thumb and forefinger. "And you're okay with Minneapolis for nine months of the year?"

She nodded. "I think I want to help small businesses with their finances. Maybe I'll reach out to Jorge, maybe see if I could—"

He kissed her on the mouth, not waiting to hear the rest of it. He didn't need to. She chose *him*. She chose *them*.

She broke apart with a laugh. "Wherever you go, I go." She squinted her eyes. "On one condition."

"Shoot."

"No more sticky notes on the wall."

He threw his head back and laughed, his hat falling off his head.

She caught it, then twirled it around and placed it backward on her head. She looked so damn cute, he kissed her silly.

They said a shy goodbye to his parents after they witnessed all of that, as well as the audience of Wild Pines residents who'd accumulated during their spectacle. Archer eyed Rhonda who winked at him from across the lawn before throwing an arm around Steph and heading to their car as well.

He packed up Tea's suitcases in the bed of his truck, placed the snake plant gently in the back seat, then got behind the wheel. He reflexively reached for her hand and squeezed it tightly, because he could. Because she was beside him, and she wasn't going anywhere. Then, for the first time in twenty-six Silver Falls summers, Archer Vincent left the resort without having to say goodbye to the one person who mattered to him most.

Five Years Later

Austin

"Daddy, daddy, daddy!"

Austin threw his head back and groaned. Five minutes. He only wanted five minutes of peace.

Andrew burst into Cabin A. He'd hoped that his son wouldn't think to find him here, but it had taken him all of ten minutes.

Austin rubbed his head, then winced. It was still sunburnt from yesterday's boat excursion. "Yeah, kid?"

"Uncle Archer told me that he needs everyone out on the lawn *right now!*"

"You can tell Uncle Archer he can go—"

Andrew tilted his head.

Austin sighed. *Fuck himself.* He'd stopped swearing around the kids years ago. Swearing was his love language. It felt like the only way he could communicate with his brother. But that was the kind of sacrifice you made when you and your smoking hot wife decided to procreate during a pandemic and make the most adorable (and obnoxious) children in the world.

"Why don't you go find Auntie Tea? I'm sure she can help with whatever your uncle needs."

Andrew pouted and crossed his arms. "Nope. He said you have to go out there. Everyone is waiting for you."

He made a face at his kid. "For me? Why?"

The screen door swung open. Kiera stood there, arms and legs covered in ink, silky black hair tied up in a bun, her eyeliner accentuating her almond-shaped eyes. He did a double take, not understanding why his brother's tattoo artist was *here*, in Silver Falls. On the Fourth of July.

"Dude," Kiera started. "Why the fu—"

Austin pointed at his kid. "Little ears. What the duck are you doing here?"

Andrew laughed. "Dad, you said *duck*."

Austin tilted his head at Kiera. "See what I mean?"

She looked confused. "Do you really not know why I'm here?"

"Don't tell me Archer had you drive all the way up here to do another tattoo? Don't you have a studio to run back in Minny?"

She rolled her eyes. "You better get out there."

Austin glanced around the cabin, annoyed that he couldn't get his five minutes. Archer's cabin was a lot nicer than his parents' place these days. They really had outdone themselves, creating a space that felt cozy and calm, the perfect spot to spend all of their summers in. They called it the nest, which Austin thought was fucking strange, but who was he to judge? Riley had nicknames for the three birthmarks on his back.

He followed them out to the lawn. Everyone was already congregated around the flagpole, like they were waiting for their traditional flag-raising ceremony before the Fourth of July potluck. But they weren't all due to the lawn for another hour or so, and by the looks of everyone's confused faces, it seemed that no one knew why they were being summoned outside.

Rhonda stepped up to the center of the group. "*Silence!*"

The group stilled. Her son Danny whispered something to Chris beside them, the two of them chuckling at something. The pair were one year away from graduating from the University of Michigan. Chris eyed Ashley from across the lawn, but she rolled her eyes and looked away. The two had been avoiding each other all summer. But Austin already knew how that story would end—the two of them would eventually end up together. It's just how things went around here.

Riley stepped up to him and grabbed his butt.

"People are watching, dearest," he mumbled under his breath.

"No they aren't, they're all looking at BILF."

Austin watched as his brother walked to the front with Rhonda. He was dressed up in khakis and a button down, the sleeves rolled up to show off those ridiculous tattoos he had on his arms.

Then the door of Cabin B swung open.

Molly stepped out, then held out her arm.

Tea followed.

Gasps erupted amongst the Wild Pines crew at the sight of her. She was dressed in a strapless sky-blue chiffon dress, her hair long and flowing down her back.

She linked arms with her mom, then the two made a procession over to the group.

"No ducking way," he whispered to Riley.

"Yes...yes ducking way," she replied.

Austin turned to look at his brother, noticing the asshole

had tears streaming down his cheeks. When they reached the center of the group, he wrapped her up in his arms and kissed her cheek, whispering something in her ear. Then he slipped an arm around her waist and faced the crowd.

"Thank you everyone for coming out an hour earlier than usual." He paused and smiled like a goof, which only happened when he was around his woman. "And welcome to our wedding."

Screams and cheers and crying ensued. Once Rhonda finally got a hold of the group, she began the ceremony. Everyone listened to her babble on and on as she told Archer and Tea's story and watched as Kiera tattooed a star on each of their ring fingers. Then they gave some pretty gross speeches about mates and stars aligning or some other garbage that he could barely pay attention to because Penny decided that was the *perfect* time to climb the tree behind him.

Austin helped his daughter down from the tree, then stood still, watching his little brother gaze into the eyes of the woman he was head-over-heels in love with. Even after all of those years of scraping by as Archer tried to launch the Craft Mixology School, or Tea with her freelancing as financial advisor for small businesses like the Minnesota Conservation Lab and the Ten Thousand Lake Loon Committee, they *still* looked at each other that way. It made him stupidly happy to see it.

Rhonda finished up the ceremony, explaining that the couple decided to take *both* names—Vincent as a middle, and Richards as the last. They wanted to keep Gareth's name for years to come. Their decision brought the entire group to tears.

Then Rhonda lifted her hands. *"Kiss and seal the deal!"*

Archer cradled her face. Tea nuzzled his nose. Then he

slipped a hand around her waist, dipped her low, and kissed her on the mouth.

Austin yelled at the top of his lungs. Penny and Andrew ran up to the couple and hugged their legs, and eventually everyone went up to hug them and celebrate. Music blasted from some nearby speaker.

He went up to his brother and slapped him on the back. "Really? You weren't going to tell me?"

Archer grinned. "Don't like surprises?"

He glared. "No. I would have liked to give my brother a proper bachelor party, though."

Archer shrugged. "Didn't have time for it. I proposed last night."

"You *what?*"

Archer laughed. "Yep. In bed. Then I called Kiera and asked her to drive up. Rhonda technically isn't certified, but who cares. We'll go get the official license when we get back to Minneapolis."

Austin shook his head. "You guys are reckless, you know that?"

His brother gazed over at his woman, who was laughing at something Kelly and Wayne said. She was glowing. They both were. Eventually she looked in Archer's direction.

Archer jerked his head, motioning her to *come here.*

When she got close, he wrapped her in his arms. "Austin thinks we're reckless."

Tea smirked at Austin. "You did tell your brother he had five years before you..." She faced Archer. "What did he say? 'Make it my business'?"

Austin racked his brain, trying to remember their conversation on the boat all those years ago. "I'm pretty sure I was talking about him following his dreams," he recalled.

"She was always the dream," Archer replied, his gaze fixed firmly on his wife.

She poked his nose. "I knew it. You think I'm *dreamy*."

Austin rolled his eyes.

Archer cocked a brow at Tea. "Want to be even more reckless?"

"More reckless than getting married in less than twenty-four hours?" she replied.

Archer gave her a devious grin. Then he bent down and grabbed her legs.

"Wait, Arch, *no!*"

He threw his wife over his shoulders, then took off down the dock. She screamed as he jumped, holding her legs tight as the two of them plummeted into the lake.

Also by K. Sinko

Sunday Supper

Please Be Mine

THE SCOOPS SERIES

Safe Harbor

Always Choosing You

The Offer

Notes & Acknowledgments

Wow. I can't believe this book is finished. I have been dreaming up Tea, Archer, and the Wild Pines resort for a long time. *Call Of The Loon* is an ode to my summers in Minnesota, spent with the family I was blessed to inherit through marriage. The landscapes of Northern Minnesota are some of the most stunning I have ever witnessed, and I feel so grateful that I get to spend some of my summers basking in the sunsets, drinking a glass of cold Sauvignon Blanc.

I have to start by thanking my family, the Hickmans. I have been talking about how their little corner of the world would be the perfect setting for a novel, and they embraced my daydreaming over the years. They taught this small town New England girl all the ways of the midwest and a summer by the lake, from hot dish and water skiing to north winds and even the perils of finding out you have swimmer's itch. Thank you for embracing me and making me one of your own.

Another special thank you to the community at Pinewood Resort, and to Nancy Mullin for all of your insights on running the resort and taking care of everyone during the COVID-19 pandemic. All of your stories were vital in making this book a reality.

The little loon facts throughout the book are paraphrased bits of research from a number of conservation labs and preservation committees across America, and I am grateful for their free access to this information. Thank you to the Maine Audubon, the Loon Preservation Committee, the Adirondack Center for Loon Conservation, and the Cornell Lab of Orinthology at Cornell University.

As always, I have to thank my team of people who make my books stronger with each passing day. To my beta readers: Abby Hancock, Marissa Kennedy, and Alexis Wierenga. An extra squeeze for my girl Meagan Williamson, who talked me through all the little details of this book via Marco Polos across the pond. You're the kind of writing buddy authors dream about. So glad the indie author world brought us together. I also can't forget my writing group; Creatives Who Cry. Your encouragement makes this job so much more fun.

Of course, I have to give special shout outs to Britt Tayler for her keen editing eye (and her extensive notes on Minnesota resort culture), and to Jonny Ryley for another *gorgeous* cover.

Lastly, to all of the people who supported me emotionally as I yet again tackle writing a novel. Mom, Dad, Bo... thanks for always caring and supporting me through all of my crazy dreams. And Babe. You already know how thankful I am. I love you.

I knew writing a pandemic book would not be easy, but I think it's necessary. It's a stark reminder of all that we have been through together, all that we have lost...and how much we need love despite the world that tells you to hate. Never stop loving and caring for one another. Be a light in the darkness.

About the Author

K.Sinko is an indie published author with a deep love for love stories. She is the author of *Sunday Supper*, *Please Be Mine,* and the Scoops Series—a trilogy of stand-alone romances featuring the of a fictional ice cream shop. Her debut novel *Safe Harbor* became an Amazon best seller for young adult contemporary romance and is the winner of two Indieverse Awards. *Call Of The Loon* is her fifth novel. Follow her on Instagram and sign up for her newsletter to get the latest book updates.

tinyurl.com/ksinkonewsletter

 instagram.com/authorksinko